SHACKLED TO MY
FATHER'S SINS

a novel

SHACKLED TO MY
FATHER'S SINS

a novel

SARAH MARTIN BYRD

Sequel to *In the Coal Mine Shadows*

AMBASSADOR INTERNATIONAL
GREENVILLE, SOUTH CAROLINA & BELFAST, NORTHERN IRELAND

www.ambassador-international.com

Shackled to My Father's Sins

ISBN: 978-1-64960-308-1
eISBN: 978-1-64960-330-2

All Scripture quotations, unless indicated otherwise, are taken from the King James Version. Public Domain.

Cover Design by Hannah Linder Designs
Interior Typesetting by Dentelle Design

AMBASSADOR INTERNATIONAL
Emerald House
411 University Ridge, Suite B14
Greenville, SC 29601, USA
www.ambassador-international.com

AMBASSADOR BOOKS
The Mount
2 Woodstock Link
Belfast, BT6 8DD, Northern Ireland, UK
www.ambassadormedia.co.uk

The colophon is a trademark of Ambassador

SHACKLED TO MY FATHER'S SINS is dedicated to all my readers. For without you my words would mean nothing. Thank you for being so patient as you've anxiously awaited the release of this novel. As always, I give all the credit for any accomplishment I may make to my Lord. He is the center of everything I write. Thank you to my family who is always cheering me on. You are my inspiration. A special thank you to my publishing company, Ambassador International. Thank you for always believing in me and to my editor at Ambassador, Avrie Roberts, you did an outstanding job editing my madness, thank you so very much.

The next day John seeth Jesus coming unto him, and saith, Behold the Lamb of God, which taketh away the sin of the world.

~ John 1:29

SHACKLED

The Lord giveth,
 The Lord taketh away
Winter steals summer
 The cat catches the bird.

Shackled by nightmares
Demons with no faces
Thieving our minds of peace
Taking possession of our emotions.

Memories are our past
Fading images of yesteryear
A glimpse of a sunset
A preceding thought,
A smell—A touch—A lie.

Where did you go oh my Father
To the sea, across the plains, to the moon
Twinkling as the first star of night
Or down below to infernal Hell?
Hiding, roaming, weeping, searching
Where are you
Why did you go
Sadness, loss, darkness
Will I be shackled to my Father's sins forever?
Or Forgiven?

NOTE FROM THE AUTHOR

The events in the first few chapters of this novel take place before Mame and Clint die in the novel, *In the Coal Mine Shadows*. I thought you might want to spend a little more time with them.

Enjoy,
Sarah

PROLOGUE

KATHERINE CAN'T STOP HERSELF. SHE wills her hand to release the knife, but her mind cannot control her actions. She knows she's asleep . . . Wake up . . . wake up. Just like the night before, and the night before that. She can't open her eyes, not until it is too late. Not before she kills him. But no, that's not Uncle Ben. Who is it?

She looks down at her hand and the knife has disappeared. Strange, now she is holding a child's whistle, the same as last night. The knife has turned into a silly toy.

No . . . no . . . no, don't kill him, she hears herself call out. Why does she care? There was a time many years ago she could have murdered Uncle Ben herself.

Too late, blood. It's everywhere. Squirting up to the ceiling, running down the walls, on her hands, a splatter on her face. Sticky. Katherine rubs her fingers together feeling the warmth of the newly shed blood. She can smell it, too. It reminds her of a rusty nail.

Right before she wakes, Katherine sees his face and knows the truth. Ben is coming.

Soaked with sweat, Katherine sits up in bed. Three nights in a row she has had this terrible dream. Why in the world would she be dreaming about her Uncle Ben? He is safely tucked away in the state prison up in Wheeling.

The sun is just about to lighten up the eastern sky. Time to get up. Grandma Mame and Grandpa Clint will be waking up any minute.

Katherine throws her feet over the edge of the bed and realizes her legs are weak. Not sure if they will hold her up, she sits for a few minutes, hoping the feeling will soon come back in her legs. Stupid dream. Why is she having these horrible nightmares?

Probably because a nightmare is what she's living. Watching her grandma and grandpa waste away is worse than any horror movie she's ever seen or read about. Why do some people have to go through so much pain before they die, and others simply get to drift away in their sleep, no sickness, no disease? Is it our punishment to suffer for our sins and the sins of our fathers?

And as Jesus passed by, he saw a man which was blind from his birth. And his disciples asked him, saying, Master, who did sin, this man, or his parents, that he was born blind? Jesus answered, Neither hath this man sinned, nor his parents: but that the works of God should be made manifest in him.

~ John 9:1-3

CHAPTER 1

Woe unto the wicked! it shall be ill with him: for the rewards of his hands shall be given him.

~ Isaiah 3:11

THE CALL CAME AS THE sun flashed pink in the eastern sky. Olivia Blackwell picked the receiver up, yet dreaded to answer. Good news never came in the middle of the night or this early in the morning.

"Hello?"

"Mrs. Blackwell?"

"Yes, this is she."

"This is Warden Tennison at the West Virginia State Penitentiary. Is your husband home?"

"No, Hank went down to check on a barn of tobacco. Said he might bale up a sack or two before breakfast. Can I help you with anything?"

Olivia knew the call had to be about Ben—why else would the warden disturb them this early? Maybe his execution date had been moved up, or postponed. She wished Hank had not agreed to be listed as Ben's next of kin, but being the oldest uncle, he felt it was his duty, especially with his sister Mame and her husband Clint being so sick.

They couldn't very well handle their murdering son's affairs in the shape they were in.

After all these years Olivia still couldn't believe Ben had murdered his own twin brother. A brother who had the same mother but a different daddy. Could it really be true that twins could have two different fathers?

All the shame will be laid to rest with Ben one day, Olivia thought.

She knew it wasn't Christian of her to wish someone in the grave but she just couldn't help herself. Benjamin Jared Paddington—or Marsh, whoever the father was—had been nothing but trouble ever since he'd come back into their lives when their niece Katherine was about eight years old. What had it been . . . ten, twelve years ago? Katherine was nineteen now so it must have been eleven years.

Olivia stopped herself from thinking about it further and spoke into the phone, "What is it? Maybe I can help you."

"I'm not sure, ma'am. I've got some really bad news. It might be too much for the faint heart of a woman to hear. You better have Mr. Blackwell call me."

"Yes, I'll do that." Olivia hung up the phone.

Muttering under her breath she broke an egg into a bowl. *Faint-hearted? Who does he think he's talking to? He don't know how quick I can wring a chicken's neck and chop off his head, does he?*

The gravy was bubbling when Hank Blackwell came in the back door to the kitchen.

"Good morning, beautiful."

Coming up behind Olivia, Hank hugged her and kissed her on the neck. At sixty-five he was still a handsome man who was healthy enough to work a full day, though most of the hardest work was left to their son, Ike, and grandson, Wesley.

"What are you up to, you old coot?" Swatting him away with the dish towel, Olivia almost forgot about the warden's call.

Chasing each other around the table was normal for the two. Sometimes Olivia thought her husband of over forty years was nothing more than a large child. There were worse things than children growing up and leaving the nest. They'd had a good life, despite the scandal his sister Mame had brought to the family.

"Wait, I almost forgot. The warden up at the penitentiary called about an hour ago and wants you to call him back. Said he had some really bad news. What do you think it could be? The execution isn't for another couple of months."

Hank stopped pursuing his wife and sat down at the kitchen table. He was quiet while Olivia poured him a cup of coffee, adding just the right amount of heavy cream and exactly two teaspoons of sugar, like Hank liked it.

"I better call him. I can't help but dread his news. I still see Ben as that sweet, shy little boy that came to visit when Mama died, before that awful Jack Marsh kidnapped him. It's still hard for me to believe that Marsh was his real daddy and not Clint. Just don't seem natural that a woman could lie with two different men and them father two different babies in the same womb at the same time."

Standing, Hank made his way to the phone that hang on the wall. "Did you write the warden's number down?"

Olivia pulled the scribbled note from her apron pocket, not looking forward to the call her husband was about to make.

Gerald Tennison picked up his phone on the third ring. "Hello."

"Hey, this is Hank Blackwell, Benjamin Paddington's uncle. My wife said you called."

"Mr. Blackwell, I am sorry to inform you that your nephew passed away sometime during the night. He was found dead in the recreation room early this morning."

Hank lost his grip on the phone receiver and it fell, dangling back and forth like a pendulum on an eight-day clock. Did he hear the warden right? Was Ben dead? Why was he so shocked? He knew his nephew's execution was going to be soon anyway.

"What is it, Hank? What's wrong?" Olivia asked.

Hank reached down, picked the receiver back up, and motioned for Olivia to come closer. He put his hand over the receiver and whispered, "Ben's dead."

Olivia moved her lips and silently asked, *How?*

"How?" he asked the warden. "Was it a heart attack? Stroke? He wasn't sick that I know of and he's not that old."

Turning toward Olivia, Hank asked, "How old is Ben? Maybe thirty-nine, forty?"

Olivia wrung her hands nervously, as her mind conjured up memories of the skinny little boy with the dark hair. She quickly pushed Ben's foul deeds to the back of her mind and tried to remember how old he might be now.

"I'm not certain, Hank. I believe he was born in '32."

"Mr. Blackwell, are you still there?"

"Yes, yes I'm here."

"I'm not sure how your nephew got out of his cell last night, but one of the guards found him in the recreation room with his throat cut. I'm afraid he bled to death long before we found him. His body was already cold. There was nothing we could have done to save him."

The image of the little boy, Ben, lying in a puddle of his own blood, mixed with the greasy smell of fatback gravy from the kitchen, made bile rise in Olivia's throat. She swallowed a few times, hoping to keep from vomiting.

"How could this have happened? Who killed him?"

"Oh, I'm sure it was an inmate. Probably more than one working together. Your nephew was a big man; it would have taken more than one fellow to get the best of him, unless they were able to sneak up on him. We'll never know who did it. Your nephew made several enemies while he was here."

Olivia had been listening to both sides of the conversation and had to sit down when she heard the warden talk about Ben lying in his own blood. She felt sick and she could tell by looking at her husband's pale face that he did, too.

"I know this must be a shock for you, but I need to know when you'll be arranging to have the body picked up?"

"Oh, my," Hank said, "I'll have to handle all the arrangements—there's no one else. We'll have to tell Mame and Clint," he said to his wife. "They are both so sick, I'm not sure if they'll be able to survive the news."

This was one time Hank was glad Mame wouldn't be able to understand what was happening around her. Now both of Mame's sons, and baby Daniel, were dead. Hopefully, for her sake, the Alzheimer's disease had erased the boys from her memory. And then there was Clint. How would he feel? Even though Ben was not his real son, he had raised him as such until Jack Marsh took him away when he was eight years old.

"Mr. Blackwell, when can I expect the undertaker? Mr. Blackwell, are you still there?"

Hank's thoughts were scattered over a thousand acres of tobacco fields. For a minute he'd forgotten he had the warden on the line.

"Yes, I'm here. I'll call Sunset Park and make the arrangements. They should be able to pick Ben up this afternoon."

"Very well. My condolences to you and your family."

Hank hung up the phone and lowered his weight into a chair at the kitchen table. He hung his head and ran his fingers through his still thick mane of hair.

"I guess I'll call Carl at Sunset and see if he can make the trip up to Moundsville and get the—the boy. Then I've got to go see Mame and Clint and Katherine. What happened to that sweet little boy we called Ben? And Katherine, I feel certain she will be relieved he is gone."

"Now Hank, that's pretty harsh. I've never known Katherine to be anything but full of love. She has the kindest spirit of anyone I've ever met. She reminds me of Jared, God rest his sweet soul."

Jared, Hank's younger brother, was beaten to death by Jack Marsh many years before just because Jared bumped into him at a saloon and spilled his drink. Yes, Jared had been kind and meek. Katherine did have his ways.

Again, Hank ran his fingers through his hair, pondering life and all the mishaps that had brought them to where they were now. Ben was gone. What a wasted life. If only Jack Marsh had not kidnapped Ben. Surely he would have turned out to be a much better man.

It took Hank an hour to make the arrangements with the funeral home and call his brothers, James, Timothy, Thomas, and Will. They all agreed his body would be laid to rest in the Sunset Memorial Park Cemetery and not on the hill behind the old homeplace in the Blackwell Cemetery.

Doing that would defile the land, in a way. After all, Ben had tried to rape, Katherine, his own niece. He may have been Mame's son, but he didn't deserve the Blackwell—or Paddington—name, and he especially didn't deserve his middle name.

It wasn't Mame who gave Ben Jared's name. It had been Clint who had named him. At the time, Clint knew nothing of Mame's discrepancies, and never dreamed Marsh was Ben's real father.

Hank didn't know how so many bad things could have happened over the past forty years, but he did know that God's ways are not always meant to be understood. Hank knew the Lord could make good out of all circumstances. He'd just have to wait for the Master to show him the good that had ever come out of Ben Marsh. It looked like the rewards of his own hands were given to him: death.

"I'm going to see Mame. Can't put it off any longer," Hank said at last.

"I'll come with you. Let me get my sweater."

Hank and Olivia didn't take time to get the Cadillac out of the garage; they just jumped in their rusty old farm truck and headed to the homeplace . . . to Mame.

CHAPTER 2

And when I passed by thee, and saw thee polluted in thine own blood . . .

—Ezekiel 16:6

1971

WEST VIRGINIA STATE PENITENTIARY

MOUNDSVILLE, WEST VIRGINIA

THE SUGAR SHACK HELD NO hint of sweetness that day, nor had it ever. The scent of sex, disease, and sweat mingled now with the metallic odor of blood—thick and sticky and lots of it.

Soon, as his last breath was wrenched from the lowest chamber of his lungs, the spurting slowed to a trickle as the artery closed off, drained, and emptied. Congealed clots now formed on his neck below the gaping gash where the cold steel blade had severed his carotid artery.

One last rush of precious air pushed forth as his lungs collapsed.

No angels appeared to escort him to heaven, for the demons had already taken possession of his soul. No one was present to shed a tear. Not a living soul cared . . . No one but the man's son, Benny Bauguess.

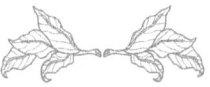

The Gothic structure of the Penitentiary towered several stories high, reaching up toward the heavens as it housed some of the vilest creatures ever born in this world. Murderers, thieves, rapists, some so wicked they couldn't bear to look at themselves in the mirror. Tormented by all the devilish deeds they had carried out, many hung themselves with stolen pieces of rawhide from the blacksmith shop. Or cut their own wrists with homemade knives, staring mindlessly as they watched their life flow from their bodies. No feeling, numb, already dead before the cold set in. Years before the prisoners on death row knew if they didn't take control and end their own life, "Old Sparky" soon would.

Trudy rode shotgun as her son Benny tooled his 1966 Ford pickup up the long drive to the prison that held his daddy captive. He had never seen his father in person, just a glimpse of a mug shot from the news story during Ben Paddington's sentencing.

It had taken them most of two days to drive to Moundsville, West Virginia from the coast of North Carolina.

Twenty-one-year-old Benny Bauguess stopped in front of a sign that read, "Visitor Parking."

"Mama, do you think he'll recognize me? Do you reckon he'll know me?"

"Now how in the name of Adam's house cat do you think he'll know who you are? He ain't never caught a glimpse of you. Don't even know you was hatched."

Trudy Bauguess closed her eyes and let her mind take her back to her youth, and Ben Marsh. She thought she had made the catch of her life when she let Ben join her under the sheets all those years ago. When she mentioned forever, he ran off. The only thing she caught was his seed.

Trudy scooted over and flipped the rearview mirror around to face her. She took out a tube of blazing red lipstick and coated her thick lips.

Would Ben recognize her? Would he be glad to learn he had a son? She smoothed a stray hair back behind her ear. At thirty-six she looked to be ten years older. Cheap whiskey and even cheaper ways had left Trudy a scorned and wrinkled woman who had devoted her life to her son and finding his daddy.

She'd lived recklessly, frequenting bars in almost every town in North Carolina looking for Ben, and all this time he'd presumably been living in West Virginia.

"Come on, Mama, let's go in. Wait till I see my daddy and give him a cussing. Then I'm going to thank him for leading us to the Blackwell fortune. How can you love and hate somebody all at the same time?"

"Danged if I know, son. I've felt that way about your daddy ever since he walked out on me."

Trudy kept stalling, nervous to see Ben after over twenty years of dreaming of him. She flipped the mirror back around and rearranged herself in the passenger seat.

"Just one quick smoke and then I'll be ready."

Fumbling inside her fake leather purse, Trudy pulled out a pack of no filter cigarettes. She tapped one of the cancer sticks into her hand and brought it to rest between her lips. She flipped the cover back on a pack of matches and pulled one free, striking it against the coarse gray flint. The fire torched the end of the cigarette and Trudy drew the heavy smoke deep into her lungs, holding it in for what seemed like minutes instead of seconds. Eyes closed, Trudy was in her own heaven.

She was hardly ever without a cigarette between her fingers, choosing to puff instead of eat. Trudy barely tipped the scales at one hundred pounds.

She was as nervous as she'd ever been. What would it feel like to see Ben again? Was the knot in her stomach because she wanted to see him, or was it just pure hate bubbling up inside her?

Benny watched his mama just like he had a thousand times. To him she was beautiful. His love for her blinded him to the yellow stained fingernails, the dyed black hair, and the circles of sadness under her eyes. When he looked at her all he could see was his mama, the only person who had ever loved him.

"Are you about ready? Visiting hours will be over before we even get in there."

Thumping the cigarette butt out the window, Trudy opened the door of Benny's truck and stepped to the ground. The dirt crunched beneath her open-toed heels. She shivered as the cool mountain breeze clung to her bare skin. It had been sixty degrees at the coast when they'd left two days before. Pulling a light sweater from the truck, she wrapped it tightly around herself.

Benny walked around the truck and tucked his arm through his mama's. "Here we go. I'm finally going to meet my daddy."

Trudy glanced up at the handsome young man that was her son. When she looked at him she was always taken back to the time she spent with Ben. The boy had grown into a replica of the man she had fallen in love—or lust—with all those years ago. Dark hair, ember eyes, and olive skin, he was a fine-looking man.

A guard met them at the front gate barring them from the entrance.

"May I help you?"

Trudy's mouth was so dry she could barely speak. "Yes, we're here to see Ben Marsh—no, I mean Paddington."

"Do you have an appointment?"

The guard grabbed a clipboard that hung on the gate behind him and skimmed the list. "Who did you say you were here to see? Is it Benjamin Jared Paddington?"

Trudy was taken off guard. She'd never heard Ben's full name. The only thing she'd been concerned with was getting a ring on her finger. She could have cared less about his fancy name: Benjamin Jared.

Looking back and forth between the guard and his mama, Benny was anxious to get inside. "That's him, right Mama?"

"Well Mama, is that him? Is that my daddy's name?"

"I'm sure it must be, but really, I don't know."

Trudy was embarrassed that she didn't even know the full name of the man that had fathered her child.

The guard glanced at the clipboard and took a step back. "Excuse me. I have to call upstairs. I'm not sure what the problem is, but Benjamin Paddington's name has been marked off the prisoner visitation list. He's probably in trouble and not allowed visitors. Just give me a minute and I'll find out."

The guard returned shortly with a solemn look on his face. Benny was afraid after all this time he wasn't going to get to meet the sorry, good-for-nothing man who surely was his flesh and blood. Benny wanted to tell him exactly what he thought of him. Leaving his mama like he'd done. Anger raged through him, and at the same time he felt anxious and excited at the thought of finally meeting his daddy.

"Ma'am, sir . . . the warden would like to see you. Follow me."

The clanging of the heavy steel gate ricocheted through the chambers of Trudy's mind as the guard unlocked the chain and slid the door open. Her heart was pounding like a jackhammer. What had Ben done to get marked off the visitor list? Or was he refusing to see anyone? Or maybe he was refusing to see her.

No, he couldn't do that; he didn't even know she was there. Fine, if he didn't want to see her, but there was no way she was leaving until Benny had seen his father. Ben Paddington owed his son that much. Ben had to see them. All the years of searching came crashing in on Trudy until her chest felt weighed down in desperation. She could hear her heart beating in her ears, echoing off the polished tile floor of the hall that led to the warden's office.

"What's going on, Mama?"

"I don't know, Benny, but we're about to find out."

The guard stopped in front of a steel door with a placard on it that read, "Gerald Tennison, Warden, West Virginia State Penitentiary." The guard knocked and a voice on the other side asked who was there.

"Guard Cason, sir. I have the visitors here who want to see Inmate Paddington."

Trudy heard the clicking of at least a half dozen locks before the door opened to a man of great stature, too strong looking to be hidden behind so much steel and all those locks. What could he be afraid of?

"Come in. Cason, would you please wait in the hall for our guests? We shouldn't be long."

"Yes, sir."

"Please, have a seat."

Trudy watched the man as he sluggishly walked around his desk and plopped down heavily in his chair. Warden Tennison let out a loud sigh.

"So, you're here to see Paddington? May I ask how you know him? Are you family?"

Trudy once again found her words were lost in her head and dry on her lips. She willed herself to speak but the words just kept rattling around in her head.

Realizing his mama was tongue-tied, Benny spoke up. "Yes, I'm family. Ben Paddington is my daddy and this is my mama. Now, when can we see him?"

Warden Tennison squirmed in his seat, making the leather pop and crack.

Trudy knew something was wrong, worse than Ben not wanting to see them. Had they already executed him? She couldn't remember the date the newsman had said. Had the prison made a mistake and released him?

"What's going on?" Benny watched as the warden scratched his head and, then popped his knuckles. Why was the man so nervous? There was something strange going on and Benny was going to find out what it was, he was tired of all the chatter.

Benny rose from the chair and leaned in toward the warden and asked, "When can I see my daddy? I'm tired of waiting. I've been searching for him my entire life."

The warden took off his glasses and laid them on his desk. Then he stood up and took his suit jacket off and threw it over the back of his chair before sitting back down.

"What did you say your names were? I don't believe we even got that far. I am Gerald Tennison, warden here at the state prison."

Trudy found her words and spoke. "I am Trudy Bauguess, and this is my son, Benny Bauguess, Ben Paddington's son. Where is Ben? What's wrong?"

"Ma'am, I won't lie to you, this is a corrupt facility. We are ranked by the United States Department of Justice as one of the top ten most violent correctional facilities in the country. With over two thousand inmates, we just don't have the staff to control all the violence that happens within.

"Son, your father was an arrogant man, and very controlling. Not only to the guards but especially to the other inmates. Some of the prisoners have been here most of their adult lives and consider themselves superior to the new convicts. I'm sad to say they run this place, so it didn't take long for Paddington to make serious enemies. Quite frankly, he was not the type of person to want to be bossed around.

"This past year we've broken up so many fights between him and the other inmates we were considering locking him up in solitary confinement for his own safety, but we were too late."

Trudy shook her head and scooted up to the edge of her chair, "What do you mean you were too late?" The knot in her gut was growing larger by the minute. "Benny, what is he saying?"

Benny stood up and paced back and forth on the well-worn wood floor. He didn't answer his mama, he had no answers, so he just continued to pace until the warden spoke.

"Last night one of the guards found Benjamin Paddington in the recreation room with his throat slashed. He bled to death. I'm so very sorry."

Benny stopped pacing, stunned. A cold sweat broke out on his forehead. How could his daddy be dead? They had just found him. Benny would never get to see his own father.

His daddy had jilted him again. Cheated him. Run out on him and his mama one more time.

"Where is he? I want you to take me to him. I need to see Ben Paddington," Benny said.

Trudy gasped when she heard her son say he wanted to see Ben. She had wanted to see him, too, but not now, not dead. A shooting pain ran through her head and it took her a few seconds before she could continue.

"Benny, you can't mean it. Why would you want to see a dead body? He's gone, we can't change that. I sure don't want to look at no corpse. Come on, lets get out of here."

Trudy stood and started toward the door, almost tripping over her own feet.

"Wait, Mama. Don't you understand? I have to set my eyes on him, put him in my memory."

"You can remember him from the television picture, now let's go."

"I'm his next of kin, I have the right to see him."

Warden Tennison spoke up then. "Yes, you do, boy. You have every right. You are his closest kin, other than your grandparents, Benjamin

Paddington's mother and father. I've heard they are both very ill though. I've been in contact with one of your uncles just this morning explaining the circumstances. Your uncle has arranged for your father's body to be picked up this afternoon by the funeral home that will be taking care of the deceased. Are you in agreement with that?"

Benny sat back down, his mind racing.

Grandparents . . . uncle . . . nothing was making sense. If his daddy's mama and papa were still alive then that meant he had a grandma and grandpa. Logic told him that something was wrong here. What the warden was telling him didn't match what his mama had told him all these years.

"Mama, I thought you said my grandpa's name was Jack Marsh, and that he was dead?"

"That's what your daddy told me. That's why we couldn't find him. He told me his last name was Marsh. I didn't know, Benny. Your daddy and I didn't talk much. All I know is he told me his name was Ben Marsh and that he was raised by his daddy, Jack Marsh."

"That makes no sense. The news said he had been convicted a year ago for murdering his twin brother, Walt Paddington. I need some answers, and I'm going to get them. But first I'm going to see my daddy."

Benny stood so quickly his chair tumbled backward, cracking one of the slats on the back. Benny picked the broken chair up and slammed it upright on its legs. What he really wanted to do was throw it up against the wall.

The warden eyed Benny warily after his outburst. "Do you want me to follow through with your uncle's wishes? The funeral home in Beckley should be arriving later today. It's about a four-hour drive, so

I'm sure they are on their way. If you have other plans I can let your uncles know, or you can call them."

Benny thought that was ironic, calling uncles he didn't know he had before a few minutes ago. He didn't even know their names. How many of them were there? And his grandparents too . . . Who were they? Benny didn't know one thing about the lives of his new-found relatives or his dead daddy. Absolutely nothing.

"Let's just stick to my uncle's plan and let the funeral home pick my daddy up." Benny knew he didn't have the means to take care of the expenses of a funeral. He also knew the Blackwell family did, whoever they were.

"Take me to him. It's time I meet this man."

The warden rose. Slumped over with the weight of running a prison, he didn't look quite as tall as he had at first.

"Come with me, son. I'll take you to your father. Ms. Bauguess, would you like to see him, too?"

"Lord have mercy, no. I wouldn't put no corpse's face in my memory for no amount of money. If it's all right with you I'll stay right here. Mind if I smoke?"

"Not at all." Warden Tennison pushed a half full ashtray toward Trudy. "Please bolt the door when we leave—you can never be too careful around here."

Trudy did as she was told, and counted each click as she turned the locks—one, two, three, four, five, six. What was there to be so afraid of? The criminals were behind bars, weren't they? But if that were so, how did one of them kill Ben? Obviously, they have more freedom than she would have thought. She tested the locks one more time; a shiver ran up her spine.

CHAPTER 3

Jesus said, Take ye away the stone. Martha, the sister of him that was
dead, saith unto him, Lord, by this time he stinketh . . .

~ John 11:39

DOWN MANY STEPS, VERY FAR beneath the light of day, Benny
followed the warden. The chill and smell of mold made Benny
tremble and feel sick to his stomach. Here men were once chained
to the walls, tortured, starved, forgotten. Those days had long passed,
but the stench of death hung heavy in the air.

If one looked closely they might see the indentions in the dirt
walls where men tried to dig their chains free from the hard clay.
Or, if one opened their ears and heart, the groans of the suffering
might send them running back up the steps to the light. Agony has
no mercy.

Benny's imagination shifted into overdrive. He could have sworn
he saw someone lurking in the shadows. Was it the inmate who had
murdered his daddy? Was he coming for him now? Or, might it be his
daddy's ghost hovering between here and eternity?

Suddenly, Benny wasn't so sure he needed to see his daddy. He
was spooked and he didn't care who knew it. He stopped, ready to

turn around, to go back to his mama, to safety, to forget he ever had a daddy.

"Mr. Bauguess, are you coming? We're almost there. We have to bring the deceased down here because it's the coolest place in the prison. Once a body dies it quickly starts deteriorating. It doesn't take long before it starts to stink." The warden rattled on, as if he too were trying to convince himself to continue forward. "Come along, son. The holding room is just around this corner."

Benny willed his feet to move. He may be a man at twenty-one years old, but he felt like a little boy right then; a child that was in the middle of a bad dream. He was cold and hot at the same time, like he was burning up from the inside out.

"Here we are. Let me step in and make sure everything is in order. I'll be right back."

The door made a loud squeaking noise as the warden pushed it open. Before Benny could turn his head or close his eyes, he saw the blood and the slit throat of his daddy. The gash ran from ear to ear. It was raw and tattered like it had been cut with a jagged blade or piece of glass. The door closed before he could see anything else.

Too late, Benny felt the bile rise in his throat, and he had to step back into the dark corner of the dungeon to throw up. Closing his eyes to the picture he'd forever have in his mind, he was glad it took the warden a good five minutes to open the door again. It gave him time to pull himself together.

"Come in, son."

His legs felt too weak to carry him. Benny slowly made his way to the slab of metal where his daddy lay. The warden had covered Ben Paddington with a dingy white sheet. It was pulled up under Ben's chin, covering the wound. *Too late.* Benny would never forget that sight. A memory of a daddy should be of games played together, balls tossed, and tight hugs, not cut throats and bloodstains.

Benny stared. The deathly pale skin of Ben Paddington stood out like red mud in the snow. His dark hair was a harsh contrast to the color of his skin. Did they favor each other? It was hard to tell with his face beaten raw, cut and gouged. How tall was he? Benny had so many questions, with no way to get the answers.

Benny lifted the sheet away from the body, letting it fall to the floor. His daddy still wore the pants of an inmate, but was bare-chested. His body was covered with hair, dark and thick like his own.

Benny reached down and took the hand of the stranger he knew to be his father. It was icy cold and his fingers were hard, locked and stiff. The stronghold of death had claimed him. And he stank.

The warden left him alone, standing off to the side with his back turned. Benny stared at death for what seemed like hours, but only minutes had passed. Something about seeing a man's throat severed and laying open was unnerving. Not to mention it looked like someone had tried to pluck his eyes out. What type of person would be able to do such a thing?

Benny turned from the dead body and reached to the floor, picking up the discarded sheet and placing it back over his daddy. This time he covered his face. It was an older version of himself. He'd seen enough. Hopefully he wouldn't end up like his father.

"Do you know who killed him?"

"Not yet. We've narrowed it down to three, but they're sticking together, lying for each other. Truth is, they were probably in it together. We may never know. It really wouldn't do any good if we did. What else can you do to a man who has been on death row for most of his life, waiting, wondering if this would be the day his name would be called and his last meal would be served?"

"There should be more justice than that. You've seen my daddy—nobody deserves to die like that."

Even as he said it, Benny wondered. Did Ben Paddington deserve his fate?

CHAPTER 4

I am a stranger and a sojourner with you: give me a possession of a buryingplace with you, that I may bury my dead out of my sight.

~ Genesis 23:4

MARY KATHERINE PADDINGTON HEARD HER Uncle Hank's truck coming before it rolled into sight. One would think a man of his wealth would be able to afford a new muffler. But that was one of the things she loved about all her uncles. They had worked hard to expand their mother Mary's tobacco empire. Katherine knew they all had money in the bank, but one wouldn't know it to look at them. They'd stayed humble, remembering the days when their daddy had crawled around on his belly in the coal mine not a mile from the homeplace so his children and wife would have full stomachs and a roof over their heads.

Katherine walked past her Grandma Mame and Grandpa Clint on the way to the door. They were so cute sitting beside one another in those old threadbare recliners. Just like Uncle Hank's truck, the chairs were as old as she was. Mame and Clint were both asleep, their fingers intertwined. One of them was snoring.

Katherine spent a lot of time alone. They slept more and more these days. Katherine could tell her grandparents were both fading a little farther away from her every day. Easing out of their earthly bodies, preparing for a voyage of a lifetime to an everlasting home.

One knows what a second feels like. It passes faster than a flash of lightning or clap of thunder. A minute allows one to enjoy sixty seconds of life, and then there are hours and days and weeks, months and years . . . but eternity? How in the world do you measure forever?

Katherine wiped a tear that slid down her cheek. She missed her grandma. The years had already taken her mind and voice, now the reaper was after her body. It was a full-time job getting her to eat enough to survive. Alzheimer's is an invisible predator, a thief in the night, a body snatcher.

Grandpa Clint came back into Grandma Mame's life just in time for her to be able to tell him her secrets. Katherine would never forget that day at the entrance to the mine when they'd found Mame trying to dig out her daddy who had been buried alive in a catastrophic explosion many years before. Or so they thought. Grandma Mame was really trying to get to her son, Walt, who Uncle Ben had hit on the head with a shovel and killed.

Why were all these vivid images coming back to Katherine now? She tried not to ever think of her wicked Uncle Ben who was now locked away tight in a prison further up north near Wheeling. For the life of her, she couldn't understand why he hadn't been executed already.

Sometimes Katherine felt bad about her feelings toward Uncle Ben, wondering if anyone was so unworthy that their life should be taken away from them. Then she remembered her Grandma Mame at the mine telling them how Uncle Ben had slept with her own mother, a mama Katherine had never known. Her daddy and uncle had gotten into a terrible fight and Uncle Ben had hit his brother Walt with a shovel, cracking his skull. If that wasn't bad enough, for years Katherine had to sleep with a knife under her pillow to save herself from Ben's groping hands.

Uncle Hank's knock at the door brought Katherine back from her bad memories. "Hey, Uncle Hank, Aunt Olivia. Come on in. How are you? What gets you two out this early?"

It wasn't unusual for her uncles or their wives to stop by. They'd never told her, but she knew they had a visiting schedule they followed to make sure someone checked on her and her grandparents daily.

It was a lot of responsibility for a nineteen-year-old to take care of a grandma with Alzheimer's and a grandpa with terminal pancreatic cancer. No cure, no hope this side of heaven, for either of them.

In a quiet voice, Katherine welcomed her aunt and uncle into the kitchen away from the sleeping pair.

"How about some coffee? I've got a full pot on the stove."

"That would be nice, dear. It smells heavenly," Olivia said.

Hank looked at his young niece and marveled at her inner strength, yet wondered how long she'd be able to give the kind of care Mame and Clint would soon need. Clint was becoming too weak to help with Mame. Hank could tell he was getting frailer every day. He knew that death would come calling, and soon.

"Yes child, coffee will hit the spot. It looks like Mame and Clint are resting," Hank said.

"They ate very little breakfast and have both been napping ever since," Katherine said.

Katherine knew she should be in college right now, laughing and going to parties with her peers. But she couldn't bring herself to leave her grandma and grandpa.

Uncle Hank and her other uncles had offered to pay for a nurse to be with Mame and Clint around the clock. Katherine declined the offer, remembering Grandma Mame's words well, the woman who had raised her since she was a few months old. *We pay our own way. Katherine. We don't take handouts. We got what we need, always food on the table and a warm bed. You hear me, Katherine? No charity.*

Olivia knew Katherine had weathered a hard life in her few years, but one would never know it. She seldom complained and never asked why, or how come she'd been through such hard times. Katherine just smiled and took care of her grandparents. No thoughts of why, or for how long.

Two cups of steaming hot coffee were set before Hank and Olivia before Hank spoke. "Don't you want a cup, Katherine?"

"No, Uncle Hank. I've been up for several hours and already drank three cups. One more and I'll be bouncing off the walls."

Silence covered the room like a white Christmas snowfall. This wasn't unusual. Living so close to each other and seeing one another often, it didn't take long to catch up. Suddenly, Katherine had an overwhelming sense of dread. Something was wrong. Flashes of the nightmare she'd been having shot through her head.

Speaking softly so the sleeping couple would not be wakened and hear what he was about to say, Hank began, "Katherine, I had a phone call this morning from the warden up at the prison where Ben is."

He paused as he watched the color drain from Katherine's face at the mention of Ben's name.

Katherine's mind blew up with emotion. Her hands became sweaty and she felt like that scared little girl hiding from her uncle in the corner of her bedroom. Was it time? Had the execution been carried out? Katherine had not wanted to know the date. She wanted to rid her life of all memories of her Uncle Ben. Uncle Hank knew that. Why was he here now getting ready to tell her something she didn't want to know?

"No. I don't need to hear anything about Ben. Don't tell me. I don't want to know anything about him. I'm sorry to be rude, but I have to check on Grandma and Grandpa."

"Katherine, wait. You have to listen. Ben is dead."

Katherine closed her eyes and unknowingly let out a sigh of relief. A wave of guilt jolted her back to the present, but not before her hand unclasped, releasing the memory of the knife she once slept with, the same one she had recently been dreaming about. Her childhood nightmare had been delivered to the Devil, did she kill him, or did the man standing over him in her dream murder him? Ben might be gone but Katherine knew he had left scars that she would have to nurse for the rest of her life.

The three sat staring at the walls, silent.

So many questions were popping in and out of Katherine's mind. She couldn't help herself—she needed to know more. "When was he executed? Was he alone when he died? Did anyone from the family ever go see him?" So many questions tumbled through Katherine's mind. Why did she care if he'd been alone? Why did her conscience feel so bothered by the news?

Katherine stood and walked into the sitting room where Grandma Mame and Grandpa Clint both still slept. She looked at them with all the love a person could ever have for someone and a tear slid down her cheek. She had to tell them about Ben. Would they even comprehend what she would say to them?

Hank followed Katherine. He too looked at his sister and Clint wondering if they needed to even know about Ben. He broke the silence in a quiet voice. "No one from the family ever visited Ben that I know of. And yes, he was alone when he died—except for whoever killed him."

"Killed him . . . Do you mean the executioner?"

"No, Katherine. His death was unexpected."

"Unexpected? What do you mean? Wasn't he executed?"

Hank shook his head, hesitating. Katherine wondered why wouldn't he just tell her.

"What was wrong with him? Did he have a disease? A heart attack?"

Katherine imagined Ben's body covered in sores. His eyes set back in his head, ready to close in death. Did he feel sorry for his sins? Did he repent?

Was he in hell?

Guilt rushed over Katherine like the feeling of a child who had just got caught stealing candy. How could she wish such horrible things on anyone . . . even Ben?

Then Katherine remembered Uncle Hank's words. *He was killed.*

She faced her uncle. "Tell me what happened. How could Ben have been killed in prison?"

Hank ran his fingers through his hair and then scratched the stubble on his chin. How much should he tell her, he wondered? Again, he knew the truth had to be the answer.

"Let's go back in the kitchen and I'll tell you. I'd hate for Mame to hear this."

The three stood around the kitchen table. Olivia sat down first, then Hank. Katherine remained standing.

"Ben was murdered. The warden at the prison said they found him with his throat slit, and they don't really know who did it. Could have been one of several other inmates that Ben didn't get along with," Hank said.

"Murdered? How is a person murdered in prison?"

Katherine felt weak and finally sat down. She couldn't help but look at her fingers to see if the blood from her dreams was there.

"All the prison warden knows is that he was found early this morning. He bled to death."

Blood—it was everywhere. Katherine's mind went back in time. Red stained sheets, bloody gown. The feel of the blade in her hand as it pierced Ben's side. Was it her? Had she killed him? No, she knew she hadn't, but she also knew she could have, and would have if she'd had to.

Katherine was ashamed that all she felt was relief. No tears, no sorrow. Her heart was empty. Its chambers held no compassion for her dead uncle. How could she feel anything for the man who had killed her father and tormented her and her Grandma Mame all those years?

Katherine knew Alzheimer's had taken over her grandma's mind, but she couldn't help but believe Ben had simply driven her crazy. No, Katherine felt nothing but relief. The weight of the cold steel of the blade she'd slept with was gone.

Uncle Ben got exactly what he deserved, after he made her and her grandma's lives a living hell for many years.

A noise from the next room jolted Katherine back to the present.

"Katherine, would you bring me a sip of water?" Grandpa Clint asked. "Is someone here? Did I hear voices or was I dreaming?"

Katherine rose on trembling legs, slowly walking to the sink she turned the water on, letting it run for a minute so it would be colder before filling Grandpa Clint's coffee mug. He was getting so weak, it was easier for him to loop his fingers through the handle of the cup to hold onto it than to manage holding a slippery glass.

On Katherine's way to the living room Hank touched her arm, stopping her. "Are you going to tell them?"

"Yes. Grandpa Clint deserves to know. After all, the man who killed his son is now dead himself."

"We should discuss arrangements. The funeral home is on its way to pick up the body."

"I can't think about that right now. I could care less what you do with his body. Throw him in a ditch, for all I care." Turning, Katherine made her way into the living room. She handed her grandpa his water, then pulled a straight-backed chair close to his side. Grandma Mame seemed to still be sleeping, so Katherine decided to share the news with her grandpa and let him decide whether or not to tell Grandma Mame.

Hank and Olivia followed Katherine into the room and sat across from them on the sofa.

"Uncle Hank brought us some news, Grandpa."

Clint looked away from his granddaughter and turned toward Hank.

"You want me to tell him?" Hank asked.

"No, I will. I'll do it."

Katherine leaned closer to her grandpa and took his cold hand in hers. His fingers already felt like a skeleton. Thin flesh stretched over spider-webbed blood vessels and bone. Looking deep into his eyes, she was surprised to see how much more they had yellowed in just one day. His skin was ashen. His eyes set back in his head. Katherine knew she was staring at death.

"What is it, child? What do you need to tell me?"

"The warden called Uncle Hank from the prison where Ben is this morning to tell him that Ben's dead." Katherine sat silent for a few seconds before telling him the rest. "Someone slit his throat last night."

Clint listened as his granddaughter told him the news. He wasn't surprised that she showed no emotion. After all, Ben put her through hell. But, was it Ben's fault he'd turned out so mean spirited?

"Grandpa, are you okay?"

A gush of tears rippled like a tidal wave down Clint Paddington's face. Clint remembered the young, dark-haired boy. The good times when he thought the boy was his own son. Back to the time when he didn't know Ben didn't have the Carter birthmark behind his right ear.

It was still hard to believe that those two boys could have had different fathers. Walt was Clint's son, no doubt. He had the mark, but not Ben. He was the son of Jack Marsh, as evil as the devil had ever crafted.

Clint glanced toward Mame. No matter who Ben's daddy was, Mame would always be his mother. He'd witnessed the delivery himself. Even then Mame had wanted nothing to do with the dark-haired newborn. She'd known who his father was right from the conception, and she had endured a tormented life for her sin.

Lost in the memories, Clint let every emotion he'd ever felt toward Ben flow through the tears. Love. Hate. Envy. Spite. Revenge. Compassion. Then finally, forgiveness.

Katherine's heart broke at the sight of her grandfather sobbing like a small child. She'd spent many hours the past year sitting at his feet listening as he told her every detail of his and Mame's life. She knew the truth even though it was horribly ugly at times. Tattered remnants of lives ruined by deceit and lies were all that remained.

Oh, how she wished she could turn back time and right the wrongs. But no one could do that. Thank goodness Grandpa Clint had been able to forgive Grandma Mame.

Hank had sat quietly but now spoke. "Clint, we have to make some decisions. I told Carl to pick up the body and take it to the funeral home to get ready for burial in the Sunset Memorial Park Cemetery. That is what you want, isn't it?"

Clint looked at his granddaughter. "Katherine, what do you think Mame would want? I really have little say in this. I'm not his father, and he is your uncle."

Katherine's first thought was, *Who cares?* She really didn't care what they did with him. Then, as clear as if she'd spoken it, Grandma Mame's words rung loud and clear in her head. *It wasn't Ben's fault he turned out like he did. I let Jack Marsh raise him. It's my weakness and transgressions that caused all the pain and hardened Ben's once gentle heart.*

Then, as if Mame knew exactly what was going on, she opened her eyes, threw the spread off that had been covering her legs, and scooted her bottom to the edge of the chair, trying to get up before the recliner footrest had been let down.

"Grandma, where are you going? Let me help you."

Mame didn't stop her struggle with the chair. She kept scooting out of the seat until finally she had gotten herself to the edge. Her feet hit the cool floorboards, and her lips moved in a silent gasp. Katherine hooked her arm through her grandma's and helped her stand.

It wasn't unusual for Mame to become agitated, but it hadn't happened lately. At least she hadn't tried to run off like she had those two times they'd found her at the entrance of the deadly mine.

Katherine kept her arm linked with Mame's as they made their way into the bedroom. Mame went straight to the tall dresser that had belonged to her mother, Mary. She pulled the third drawer open and moved a couple of gowns to the side, revealing her cherished box of memories.

How many times through the years had Katherine watched as her grandmother took the box out of this very drawer and sat with it for hours, touching every cherished piece as though she was reliving the times of old? She'd lay the contents on the bed, or she'd walk to the kitchen table and lay everything out there.

Today she took the small cedar box out and brought it lovingly to her chest and just stood, rocking back and forth as if holding a small child against her bosom.

"Grandma, lets get you back to your chair. Here, let me put your box back in the drawer."

When Katherine reached for the box, Mame jerked it away from her. She made her way back through the living room and into the kitchen. She laid the box on the table and sat down in the same chair she always sat in, just like she was remembering her entire life.

Hank and Olivia had followed Mame and Katherine into the kitchen and stood looking over Mame's shoulder. Clint had fallen back to sleep in his chair, unaware of anything going on in the next room.

The three, Katherine, Hank, and Olivia, watched as Mame took each item out of the box. First out was the faded black and white photo of Clint. She held it in her hands, staring at it for the longest time until she laid it on the table. Next, she removed a lavender hair ribbon. Katherine had asked her about it years before but was only told that it was the ribbon she'd been wearing on a very special day at a waterfall.

Then she put the silver quarters on the table, two with 1932 dates on them, the same year Ben and Walt were born. One 1943-D quarter marking the year baby Daniel was born and died. Mame always said it was a special quarter since it was marked with a "D," just like Daniel's name. Another quarter was lifted from the box revealing a 1952 date, the year Katherine was born.

Mame's fingers hurriedly dug through the box. She laid out the 1922 newspaper clipping that listed the men's names that had died in the mine explosion. Her father, Henry Blackwell, was on the list. Then she laid out the tobacco leaf now crumbled and wrapped in a folded piece of parchment paper. Mame never wanted to forget the hardships those tobacco fields had brought her, leading her to make the worst decision of her life. Then came the magnifying glass that had belonged to her Grandpa Thomas. Memories flooded Mame's ailing mind. If the Alzheimer's had not stolen her words, she would have called out to him, *Grandpa are you okay? Can I get you some water?*

Mame would never forget the bloodstained handkerchiefs, the hacking coughs, or the lightning bolt that touched the mountaintop the day Grandpa Thomas was buried up on the hill. There was one thing Mame's disease couldn't rob her of and that was her love of family and her thankfulness for forgiveness.

Suddenly, Mame picked the box up and emptied the rest of the contents on the table. A few other coins fell from the box, a hand printed note and another picture. Mame picked the note up and let her eyes read the words for the thousandth time:

I wuv you Mommy.

Ben

Tears streamed down Mame's face. Her bony fingers stroked the note. Why had she even kept it? Ben couldn't have been more than five the day he'd handed it to her. What had she done? Nothing. Not a kind word, or pat on the head. Mame couldn't remember ever telling Ben she loved him, but deep down she had, and she'd never felt that love any stronger than she did right at this moment, knowing he was dead. Too little love, way too late. She'd heard Katherine tell Clint, and she'd understood. Now she had to do one last thing before her mind slipped away again. Her son must rest for eternity on the hill in the Blackwell Cemetery. For he was half Blackwell no matter who his father was.

Mame knew she was to blame for the way he'd turned out. Every sin he'd committed was her fault. Every wrong Ben had ever done had her name stamped on it: Murder—Mame. Hurting Katherine— Mame. Sleeping with his brother's wife—Mame. Mame knew she was the cause of it all.

Reaching down, Mame fumbled through the items on the table until she found another picture. This one held the images of two little boys. One fair-haired, one dark. There was no mistaking the small boys, Ben and Walt.

Mame stared at the faded photo. Then she looked up and locked eyes with Katherine. She pointed to the light-haired boy. "Yes Grandma, I see. It's my daddy, Walt."

Katherine had not seen her grandma this alert in several weeks. Now she saw the ever-present strength of the once very independent grandma of yesteryear.

Mame then pointed out the window.

"What, Grandma? What do you see? What do you want me to see?" Slowly Mame's icy finger left the window and pointed at Ben in the photo, then out the window again.

Katherine walked over to the window and strained her eyes to see what her grandma might be looking at. There up on the crest of the mountain lay the cemetery.

Back and forth Mame pointed from the image of Ben to the cemetery. "What is she doing?" Hank asked. "What is she trying to tell us?"

"I'm not sure," Katherine said. "Grandma, we know my daddy is up on the hill. Is that what you're trying to tell us? We know you led us to his body in the mine and now he's up on the hill with the rest of the family. We know, Grandma. We know."

Katherine was becoming frustrated with the memories of seeing her daddy's bones that had been exhumed from the mine. Why was Grandma remembering this now? What was she really trying to tell them?

Mame moved her finger again, this time touching the face in the picture that belonged to the dark hair, Ben. Back and forth she pointed from Ben to the window, Ben then the window, again and again Mame pounded her finger from the photo to thin air toward the window and the cemetery that lay beyond it.

"What is it, Mame? What in the world are you trying to make us see?" Hank said, pulling his fingers through his hair, a habit he had when he was agitated.

Mame then took the child's note back in her hand and pointed to the scribbled misspelled word, *wuv*. Then she pointed to Ben, then the window. Time and time again her finger jabbed at the note, then Ben's face, then the cemetery out the window.

Katherine, Hank, and Olivia were all now standing at the window staring up the hill. A storm was brewing on the other side of the mountain. The solemn family gazed at the stones that were shrouded in shadows. There, up the hill lay their ancestors, grandpas, grandmas, sons, uncles, and daddies. Blackwells either by blood or by marriage, they were family.

Thunder rumbled in the distance. Mame rose from the table, legs trembling with the note in her hand. Shuffling her feet, inching her way forward, she stood beside Katherine. Mame took her hand. Then she raised the note so Katherine could read it:

I wuv you Mommy.

Katherine understood. A sorrowful sob escaped her. How could she deny a mother's love? Especially to a mother who had just found out her last living child was now dead. Katherine knew what her grandma wanted, she understood completely.

Grandma Mame was trying to tell them that love covers all things. Love rights all wrongs. Even if Ben's love died as a young boy, it was real back then, and that love was never returned to him.

Katherine couldn't help but wonder if Ben would have turned out a fine man if the circumstances of his childhood had been different. Of course, he would have been different. It's not whose blood that runs through our veins that makes us who we are; it's our upbringing and the things taught to us as children that molds us.

Katherine knew the Scriptures held nothing but truth. *Train up a child in the way he should go and when he is old, he will not depart from it.*

No one spoke. Time stretched from seconds to minutes. Katherine knew her grandma wanted her approval. Grandma Mame remembered the evil her son Ben had committed upon them. She knew the suffering he had brought on Katherine growing up with him, having to sleep with a knife under her pillow.

Thoughts whirled through Katherine's mind. Was it humanly possible to forgive such perversity? Katherine felt Grandma Mame pull away from her. She went back to the table. Sitting down, she pushed the box and its contents away from her. Then she reached to the middle of the table and touched her Bible, the one that always laid there, the one Mame read so often before the sickness took her away.

Mame stared at the Book for a minute, then lifted it and cradled it to herself as if it were a whimpering baby. Slowly she laid it back on the table and opened it, turning the pages toward the back to the book of Ephesians. Flipping to chapter five she moved her lips in silence, reading to herself. Then she looked up at Katherine, willing her to come to her with pleading eyes.

Katherine couldn't stop herself, she moved to the table and sat beside her grandma, watching as her age-spotted hands moved over the Word of God, her finger finally stopped on verses 31-32. Tapping her finger, Katherine knew Grandma Mame intended for her to read the passage. Katherine took the Book in her hands and began to read out loud.

"Let all bitterness, and wrath, and anger, and clamor, and evil speaking, be put away from you, with all malice. And be ye kind one to another, tenderhearted, forgiving one another, even as God for Christ's sake hath forgiven you."

As soon as Katherine stopped reading, Mame once again pointed from the picture of her dark-haired son to the window, then to the word on the note. *Wuv.*

Katherine was weighed down with guilt. Her grandma needed for her to forgive the evildoer. To forget her vile uncle and think of him as the little boy who *"wuv'ed"* his mommy. Grandma Mame's words rung loud and clear in her head, ricocheting off the walls and bouncing back to Katherine's ears, then down even farther to her heart. Was she ready to forgive? Would she ever be?

Katherine could almost hear her grandma's thoughts . . . *It's my fault Ben's like he is. I let that vicious man, Jack Marsh, raise him.*

Again and again, Grandma's words pierced Katherine's heart, breaking down the hardness that had shielded her from Uncle Ben all these years.

Once more, Mame took the Good Book in her hand, flipping to Genesis 23:4. As before she tapped the page, directing Katherine to the Scripture that she wanted her granddaughter to read.

I am a stranger and a sojourner with you: give me a possession of a burying place with you.

Katherine didn't need to read anymore. The words she recited were as if Ben himself was speaking to her, begging to be accepted, pleading for an eternal spot to lay his remains. To be forever laid to rest in the Blackwell Cemetery.

Suddenly, Katherine's heart opened and Ben was that little boy who had been cast out as a stranger, now home pleading for a burial place with his family—because yes, he was family no matter what the circumstances were. How could Katherine deny that little boy, her uncle, Grandma Mame's son?

Wiping her tearstained face with her sweater sleeve, Katherine looked into the eyes of her grandma. Eyes that she knew so well, eyes that were speaking the truth, eyes that were pleading for her to understand. Katherine knew what had to be done. Forgiveness had nudged its way into a small chamber of her heart. There was only one answer.

"Uncle Ben will not be buried at Sunset Memorial Park. He will be laid to rest up on the hill beside my daddy, his brother."

Katherine could now say that without thinking of Ben as her father's killer, but as a sinner who had been forgiven.

Mame laid her hand over her granddaughter's and squeezed. Then she rose, bringing Katherine with her and led her to the window, just in time to see the lightning bolt sear the top out of a white pine high above the cemetery. Ben's fate was sealed. He finally had what he'd always wanted, his mommy's love, a place in her heart and acceptance into the Blackwell family.

CHAPTER 5

I will both lay me down in peace, and sleep . . .

~ Psalm 4:8

THERE WAS NO FUNERAL, NO viewing, no busybody neighbors to snoop around, ogling the crazy old woman and her dying husband.

Out of respect, all five of Katherine's uncles went to the funeral home when Ben's body was ready for viewing. Hank, James, Timothy, Thomas, and William stood beside the casket that had been ordered over the phone, not the cheapest one, but certainly not the best.

Mixed emotions entertained their thoughts. Hank told his brothers about their sister Mame pointing out Scripture about burying places and forgiveness. They had all visited Mame, hoping to see the sane side of her one more time. But no such luck, she'd drifted back to the darkness of the coal mines, to the empty pit where her mind could rest in peace.

Now here they stood on the hill, the Blackwell's final resting place, getting ready to bury their nephew.

Katherine stood back a far distance from the grave, yet close enough to hear the words Uncle Hank spoke.

"And now my brothers and niece, we give back to the earth one of God's children, a little dark-haired boy who strayed from the flock, but was surely pulled back into the fold by the Shepherd. In Ecclesiastes 12:7, it says, *Then shall the dust return to the earth as it was: and the spirit shall return unto God who gave it.* Let us pray."

Katherine couldn't listen to her uncle's prayer. Her mind was back at the house where her grandma and grandpa both lay in bed. Ever since they'd heard about Ben two days before, Clint and Mame had spiraled downward. Eating very little they seemed to have given up. A final blow had been cast upon their spirit.

Katherine knew they were in good hands. Their social worker and nurse was watching over them. Katherine didn't want to go to the burial, but she knew she needed to bury her hate along with Ben there at the grave. She knew it wouldn't be that easy, but for Grandma Mame's sake she'd try. So here she was, at the final resting place of her kin, and her grandparents back home.

The uncles in their dark suits were making their way to her. Katherine watched as the gravedigger behind them threw the first shovel full of dirt into the six-foot-deep hole.

Carl, the funeral director, walked with them back down the hill to Mame's house with Katherine and the uncles. Once inside, he again offered his condolences and stated that he had a small box of Ben's belongings that the prison had sent with him.

"I'll go to the car and get the package. Who shall I give it to?"

Hank spoke for the group. "Our sister, Mame, should have his things."

"Very well, I'll go get the box."

In a matter of minutes, the undertaker was back with the container and sat it on the kitchen table. The items from Mame's box of memories had been picked up and returned to the wooden box but it still sat on the table.

"If I can be of further assistance, please give me a call," Carl politely said, backing his way out of the kitchen and through the door.

The group gathered around the kitchen table staring at the cardboard box. The outside was covered with a picture of a lady wearing a fancy hat. It probably came from someone who had bought a new hat for his or her loved one to be buried in. The picture was black and white but if you closed your eyes and used your imagination you could see the rich colors of the feather clipped to it—purple, emerald, green, and different shades of pink.

Little did the onlookers know that the funeral director had actually picked up Ben's belongings in a brown paper sack, transferring them to this pretty box. He hadn't wanted to deliver a man's only belongings in a paper sack. The Blackwells had been through enough hard times, he'd thought.

"I guess we need to see what's in there," Hank said.

Hank lifted the lid, on top of some clothes laid a brown leather belt. Beneath it was a pair of navy slacks, a striped polo shirt, a designer leather jacket, and pair of shiny wingtip shoes. The clothes were not cheap, but the billfold that was under the clothes showed no sign of Ben's wealth, only a driver's license with the name Ben Marsh on it, and a P. O. box address in North Carolina. The authorities had confiscated all Ben's drug money, his car, and whatever else he had owned of any worth. All they left was what he was wearing when they arrested him.

Hank picked up the box and, turning it over, shook it.

Katherine hoped some sign of Ben's past would tumble forth, something good for them to remember and embrace, a token to leave for Grandma Mame.

The youngest of the brothers, William, picked up each piece of clothing, returning it to the hatbox. The last piece he started to fold was Ben's pants. As William lifted them from the table something fell out of the pocket, hitting the floor with a ping. It landed right in front of William's shoe. He reached down and picked up a metal whistle. He turned it over, examining it, then laid it on the table.

"What do you reckon Ben had a whistle in his pocket for?" William asked.

Hank stepped forward and picked up the child's toy. He stared at it, remembering the day his son Ike had given it to Ben. That was the same day they'd buried their mother, Mary Blackwell. Mame had come home just in time to see their mama before she passed away and she'd brought one of her sons, Ben, with her.

Hank knew it was the same whistle because he'd bought it for his son himself and etched out a "B" on one side, and there it was the same "B" he remembered.

"What is it, Hank? What you got there?" James asked.

"It's Ike's old whistle. The same one I bought for him when he was just a small boy. It was a proud day when he told me he'd given it to Ben so he would feel more a part of the family since he lived so far away. Said he told him as long as he kept that whistle he'd be close to his kin."

Katherine swayed. Was that the whistle from her nightmare? No, she was just being silly. Still, she'd never dreamed Uncle Ben would have kept something so sentimental. In her mind she pictured a young boy playing with his cousins, making friends. She reached for the whistle. Her uncle handed it to her with tears in his eyes. For the first time since learning of Ben's death, the Blackwells were truly mourning their loss. Not the passing of the man, but the innocence of a boy.

Katherine laid the whistle on the table while she lifted the lid off her Grandma Mame's memory box. Gently, she took the whistle and placed it in the box along with all her grandma's good memories, with the ribbon and the "I wuv you" note. She put the lid back on the box and took it into Mame's bedroom, placing it in the third drawer of her dresser so she could find it if she ever wanted it again.

That night Clint Paddington left his cancer-devoured body while lying next to the woman who he had loved with all his heart and at one time hated with all his being. They were living proof that no love is complete until you have experienced both extremes, the ecstasy of love and heart-wrenching pain.

Mame never got out of bed again. She lay motionless like a baby curled into a tight ball, refusing to eat and only sipping a taste of water when her mouth got so dry her lips cracked.

She lasted two weeks after Clint died. She starved herself so she'd be back with Clint quicker. Katherine was with her and knew it to be true. Early in the morning just before sunrise, Katherine woke from resting on the couch. She made her way into her grandma's bedroom and knelt beside her bed silently whispering a prayer. She asked the Lord to heal her, either in life or death. Katherine was not afraid for her grandma's soul, for she knew she'd made things right with her Maker.

The words from the old hymn "It is Well With My Soul" flowed from Katherine's mouth and echoed off the walls of the empty house. They were alone: Katherine, Mame, and the death angel. She was there . . . Katherine could sense her.

Katherine climbed into bed with her grandma and drifted off to sleep. When she woke, her head was lying next to Mame's on the same pillow and their fingers were locked together. Katherine couldn't remember taking her grandma's hand, but she did know one thing, those fingers that were linked to hers were now clinched in death. Prying her own fingers loose from the reaper's grasp, she leaned into her grandma and held her close. She didn't have to close Mame's eyes they were already sealed. Grandma Mame was asleep, at peace, dwelling with the Lord, reunited with Grandpa Clint and her three sons, now they would be together forever.

CHAPTER 6

The Lord preserveth the strangers; he relieveth the fatherless and
widow: but the way of the wicked he turneth upside down.

~ Psalm 146:9

THE DAYS THAT FOLLOWED THE death of Katherine's grandparents were long and empty. Everything had changed. For as long as she could remember, either her grandma had taken care of her or she'd taken care of her grandma. Now she was alone. No mama, daddy, grandpa, or grandma. She was an orphan.

Katherine didn't know what to do with herself. She cleaned, washed clothes, and visited with Stan every day when he dropped by.

Stan, Grandma Mame's social worker and nurse, had come into her life when she had needed help the most. Grandma Mame was losing her mind and Uncle Ben was trying to molest her every chance he got.

Stan had not only been her protector, but also her best friend. She knew she loved him but she wasn't sure if it was for the right reasons. He was eleven years older than she was. At first that hadn't seemed like a lot, but spending so much time with him this past year had shown her that he was ready for things that she wasn't: marriage, babies, commitment.

Katherine knew he wanted more than friendship, but for now he hadn't pushed it. Stan knew that every waking moment she had was devoted to taking care of her grandparents. Nancy, the helper that Stan had lined up to assist Katherine with Clint and Mame's care, had let it slip one day that Stan was paying her to come, not Medicaid. So Katherine had let Nancy go. She'd take the government help that was rightfully theirs, but not charity— not even from Stan.

"Katherine, why don't you come with me? You need to get out of this house. We'll get some lunch and maybe even take it to the stream behind my house. You remember, don't you? The place I took you when we first met?"

Katherine remembered. How could she forget Stan's lips on hers? She'd been scared then, but not anymore.

Stan knew Katherine had been consumed with caring for her grandparents, but now they were gone. It was time she gave their relationship some attention. He had it all planned. He'd court Katherine for a couple of months then he'd ask her to marry him. They'd live happily ever after in his little home. Maybe have a couple of kids, a boy and a girl.

"Come on, Katherine. What do you say we get out of here?"

Katherine glanced around the old farmhouse. The only home she'd ever known. Everything was worn out but still worked. The television was from the sixties, at least ten years old. While her uncles had new color TVs, hers was still black and white. She'd never really noticed things like that before. Grandma Mame had kept her grounded and humble. What would she do now?

All five of her uncles had asked her to come live with them, but that didn't feel right. At nineteen, she was a grown woman, after all.

She'd been an adult for as long as she could remember. Her childhood had ended when she was eight, when her Uncle Ben had come to live with them.

No use dwelling on the past. She had a future to look forward to. Grandma Mame wanted her to go to college. She'd even told her to let her brothers help her when she was gone, to not be stubborn like she had always been. She tried to stop her mind from wondering and pay attention to Stan, but all she could do was think about the future. She'd never had the luxury of only thinking about herself. But now she would be trying on life, just like a brand-new coat—something else she'd never had.

"No, Stan. I don't feel like going out. I need to stay here. I've got a lot of thinking to do."

"But Katherine, you've hardly left the house since your grandmother's graveside service. It's not healthy for you to lock yourself away in this old house."

"I'm not locking myself away from anything. Uncle Hank is coming by this afternoon to pick me up. Grandpa Clint left instructions with him that he was to take me to see his attorney in town. He had a will or something that we have to pick up."

"You still need to eat lunch. Come on, Katherine. We'll just run down to the diner, we won't be gone an hour."

Tired of arguing, Katherine agreed to go with Stan. But she felt uneasy. She didn't like being told what she could or could not do.

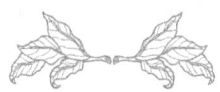

The blinds were closed and the room was dark and stifling hot, fitting the mood of the young man who sat at his mother's side.

On the way from the prison in Moundsville to Beckley near a town called Bluefield, Benny's mama slumped over in the passenger seat. One minute Trudy had been talking to her son, complaining of a headache, the next she was unconscious. Benny pulled off the highway onto the shoulder of the road and tried to wake her, but she didn't respond. All he knew to do was get back on the road and try to find a hospital. Five minutes later, he was never as glad to see a sign in his life. Up ahead was the exit to Bluefield Regional Hospital. The sign said two miles straight ahead.

"Hold on, Mama. I'm going to get you some help. Hold on."

The next several hours were hectic. Tests, scans, needles, breathing machines. Three nurses and two doctors gathering around his mama. Rushing, whispering, faces etched with concern and dread.

Pacing outside the room where they held his mama captive with wires and tubes, Benny waited until one of the doctors exited the room.

"What's wrong with her? What's going on with my mama?"

"Son, is there anyone else with you? Someone you could call to come and keep you company?"

"No, ain't nobody but me and Mama. Never has been."

"Come with me, then. Let's find a quiet place to talk."

The doctor bore a name badge that read "Dr. Harden." He stepped away from the captive room and down the hall until he found an empty cubical.

"What's your name, son?"

"Name's Benny. Benny Bauguess."

"Benny, your mother has a massive brain aneurysm. If it bursts, she will die. All we can do is keep her sedated and hope the pressure will alleviate."

"She'll be all right, won't she? Can't you operate or something?"

"Surgery is out of the question. The aneurysm is deep in her brain. There's no way to operate without doing severe damage to the cerebellum. Was your mother a smoker?"

"Yes, but what's that got to do with anything?"

"Years of excessive smoking weakens the blood vessels in our bodies and when we become upset, or our blood pressure is too high, it strains the vessels and they rupture. Your mother has other smaller aneurysms in other parts of her brain. I'm sorry, Benny. All we can do is keep your mother comfortable."

Benny left the doctor and returned to his mama's room. The news the doctor had delivered was grim. Benny knew his mama was a ticking time bomb.

The area around his mama had cleared except for one nurse. Benny entered the room. Should he get her out of there? Take her to another hospital? He had to do something, but didn't know what, so he pulled a chair up beside the only living soul who truly loved him and took her hand in his.

There he sat except for a quick shower and nourishment for the next twenty-two days. That's when the explosion took away his mama. Her brain flooded with blood and drowned the life right out of her.

His daddy's slit throat, now his mama's brain exploding. What could a man do to deserve so much bad luck? Little did Benny know his cousin Katherine, only an hour away, felt the same way. They had both lost the people they loved most in the world.

CHAPTER 7

For God is not the author of confusion, but of peace . . .

~ 1 Corinthians 14:33

HANK PULLED INTO THE DRIVEWAY of his mama's old homeplace. Clint's car, a 1959 Ford Fairlane, sat in the same spot it had for the past year. Ever since he'd come back into Mame's life. Clint had known the car wasn't much but he'd given it to Katherine, along with all his possessions.

Several months before, Clint had told Hank the details of his estate so Hank could help Katherine plan her future—a destiny Clint knew he would not be able to help her with. He had saved a chunk of money he'd left to his granddaughter. That was one of the things the lawyer would be telling Katherine that afternoon.

As Hank eased out of his truck, Stan's car came into view around the curve. In a minute it pulled in behind Hank and he and Katherine got out.

"Hey, Hank. Katherine says you two have an appointment in town this afternoon. I won't hold you up, I'll be on my way."

Hank watched as Stan planted a kiss on Katherine's cheek. The show of affection unnerved Hank. Stan was way too old for his young niece. Hank could only hope Katherine would be smart and reconsider her relationship with Stan. Yes, he was a good man, but not that special someone for Katherine.

"I'll talk to you later, Katherine," Stan said.

Hank and Katherine watched Stan drive away. Hank wanted to say something, to tell Katherine to take it slow, not to commit, to get an education, to live a little. All she'd ever known was this homeplace, her grandma, grandpa, and himself and his brothers. Hopefully she would make good decisions. She was a very intelligent young lady; she could be anything she wanted to become.

Not able to hold his tongue, Hank had to speak his mind. "Katherine, I hope you will not tie yourself down to Stan right now. You have your entire life ahead of you, you don't need to make any hurried decisions. Give yourself time to think about what is best for you, about what you want out of life."

Katherine was touched by her uncle's words. And she knew he was right. "I'm not rushing into anything. Besides, Stan and I are just friends."

Hank knew better than that. Stan wanted a whole lot more than friendship with Katherine.

"I'll be right back, Uncle Hank. I need to grab my sweater."

The hot Indian summer was quickly turning the evenings cool. It was the end of September. Almost a year and a half had passed since her graduation from high school. So much had happened. So much lost. Opening her dresser drawer to grab a sweater, she willed herself to take her mind off Stan and think about her future and the impending trip into town to meet with a lawyer about Grandma Mame and Grandpa Clint's estate. Estate? An old run-down farmhouse and a twelve-year old car? To some that might not be much, but to

Katherine it was all she'd ever need. She'd never had too much, but she'd always had enough. Owning her own car made her feel rich.

The dirt road that led from the farmhouse to the main road was full of ruts and potholes. The same as it always had been. It was especially rough in Uncle Hank's pickup truck. Katherine turned her head and looked back at the cloud of dust. She could barely see the farm. Her home, Grandma Mame's house. Would it belong to her now?

"Uncle Hank?"

"Yes, child."

"Will I get to stay at the homeplace?"

"Of course you will, if you want to. What makes you ask a thing like that?"

"I don't know. It's just, I feel lost, like I don't belong anywhere anymore. What am I going to do with myself? All I've ever known is these few acres of land. I've got to find a job. Do you think they are hiring at the cotton mill?"

Hank pitied his niece. In ways, she had lived a sheltered life. Never been more than a few miles away from home. Mame didn't like people so there were never any friends around. Mame was so private; she shut herself and her granddaughter away from the world. Unfortunately, Ben had tried to steal her innocence. Thankfully, he had not completely succeeded. There was still a quiet innocence about his niece.

Katherine was very wise in some ways, grown-up more than her nineteen years, but naïve to the ways of the world outside of Beckley.

"You'll find your way, Katherine, just give it time. Don't rush into anything. You'll know what to do when the right thing comes along."

The rest of the short drive into town was in silence. Hank pulled his truck up in front of a sign on main street that read, "Martin Edminston, Attorney at Law."

Together, Hank and Katherine exited the truck. Hank put a quarter in the parking meter and it registered thirty minutes. "If we're in there longer than that I'll come back and add more money," Hank said.

"What's this all about, anyway? I don't understand why I have to see a lawyer."

Hank could sense Katherine was nervous. He knew Mame did the best she could raising Katherine, but it was a shame a beautiful young girl like Katherine was so timid around strangers. Mame had taught her not to trust anyone. On one hand that was a good thing, on the other it could lead to a very lonely life.

"This meeting is just a formality. You're over eighteen so you won't need a guardian. You'll just have to sign some papers to get the homeplace put in your name," Hank said.

Entering the office, Hank told the receptionist their names.

"Good to see you, Mr. Blackwell, and you must be Miss Paddington. Mr. Edminston will be right with you, just let me tell him you are here."

Katherine looked around the office. The walls were covered in paintings. One was a grand old house sitting on a hilltop. The landscape was covered in snow. The only color on the painting was a single red bird sitting on the branch of a magnolia tree. One solitaire little bird, all alone. Just like Katherine. She knew she had her uncles and cousins, but they had families of their own, and a full life running the tobacco business.

Walking over to the opposite wall, Katherine stared at three more pictures, all hosting a title at the bottom of each picture, *Beckley Coal Mine*. The pictures appeared to be enlarged photos, all taken many years ago. The men posing in one of the photos were dressed in early 1900s attire. Was one of those men her great-grandfather Henry? The other two photos were only still shots, one with a coal car heaped with coal, the other of a huge wooden cross not far back from the mine entrance on a high pole.

Katherine hadn't seen her uncle step up beside her, but she sensed a presence. She still jumped when he spoke.

"That's the praying pole. Every mine has one at the entrance. I heard my grandpa and Daddy talk about it often. Not a day went by that they didn't kneel at that cross before they entered the mine, kneeling again as they left, asking for protection when they went in and giving thanks for still being alive when they got out. I guess God wasn't listening the day Daddy was buried by the explosion. My mama wasn't much for praying, but she talked to the Lord a plenty those three days they were trying to rescue the trapped men. I'll never forget, those were some hard times. She drove us young'uns hard, but those times made us better men. And, your Grandma Mame, well I guess Mama pushed her more than any of us.

"You've got the same blood, Katherine; you were born to persevere, to succeed, to prosper. You're part Blackwell and part Paddington, it's in your genes to achieve whatever you set your mind to do."

Katherine needed to hear those words of encouragement. She lacked the confidence to stand on her own two feet, but she would, for she was the granddaughter of Mame Blackwell Paddington.

"Mr. Blackwell, Mr. Edminston will see you and your niece now."

With renewed faith in herself, Katherine led the way into the attorney's office.

"Come in. Please have a seat. Good to see you again, Hank. How's the family?"

Martin Edminston had been handling the Blackwells' affairs for as long as Hank could remember. Martin must have been getting close to eighty years old. But you'd never know it. He was still robust and his mind was as sharp as a straight razor.

"We're all doing fine, Martin. How is Mozelle?" Hank asked.

"She's doing fair. Seems she's moving a lot slower since she broke that hip last winter, but at our age I guess we're lucky to be moving at all."

"Yes, I must say we're all feeling the sting of old age creeping into our bones."

Katherine sat listening to the two friends as they got caught up on each other's lives. Their easy banter calmed her nerves.

Finally, Martin Edminston looked toward Katherine. "This must be your niece?"

"Yes, this is Katherine Paddington, my sister Mame's granddaughter."

"How do you do, young lady? Glad to finally meet you."

Katherine stood and presented her hand for a friendly shake.

"Please sit back down. Your grandfather Clint brought Miss Mame by my office close to a year ago to fill out these papers."

Martin held up a stack of documents then laid them back on his desk.

"Clint Paddington made all the decisions for him and Miss Mame before his health deteriorated. The last time I saw him was about three months ago. I really am sorry about your grandparents. I can attest to one thing, though. They've done right by you. Let's get started. May I call you Katherine?"

"Yes, of course."

"This is the deed to your grandmother's house and the five acres of land that it sits on. Through the years, Miss Mame sold off most of the acreage to pay the taxes and such."

Katherine knew Grandma Mame had sold most of her land, and not only to pay taxes, but also to feed them and buy Katherine new clothes and shoes. Nothing fancy, but Katherine knew she'd always had plenty, more than most because she'd had her grandma's love.

"Just sign your full name right here on this line and the house and land will be all yours," Martin said.

Katherine signed her name with a jittering hand, *Mary Katherine Paddington*, then pushed the document back across the desk.

"Miss Mame had a small savings account. Let me see, there is a balance of $964.32 in that account, and a checking account balance of $291.80. Your name is already on those accounts so all you'll have to do is go by the bank and have your grandmother's name removed."

Katherine's mind was racing a hundred miles a minute. She had to find a job, and quick. There wasn't enough money in both of the accounts combined to run the house for maybe three or four months. She knew because she'd been paying the bills for over two years.

"Miss Mame left this last will and testament stating that you were to have all her possessions. Household items, jewelry, everything that she owned. That pretty much wraps up your grandmother's estate."

Katherine pushed her chair back and started to rise. Hank laid his hand on his niece's arm and motioned for her to sit back down.

"Now it's time to go over your grandfather's will," Martin said.

Grandpa Clint? All Katherine knew he owned was the old Ford he drove, and the three crisp one hundred dollar bills he'd had in his wallet when he passed away. Katherine had added the billfold and the money to Grandma Mame's memory box. Grandpa Clint had tried to give her money this past year, but Katherine, knowing her grandma like she did, knew she wouldn't want her to take it. As long as they had enough to pay the few bills they had and feed themselves, that was all they'd needed.

Now the future might prove otherwise. Katherine's thoughts ran wild. Would she have to sell the rest of the land? Maybe even the homeplace? Would she have to move in with one of her uncles?

No. Katherine would find a way to make it on her own. She would honor her grandma's life long wish to never take charity. She could stand on her own. She would survive, somehow, some way.

"Let's see, we'll start by reading the letter your grandfather left for you. His instructions were that your Uncle Hank read it aloud to you. All you'll need to know about your grandfather's wishes are in there."

Mr. Edminston handed the envelope to Hank. Katherine's uncle took the pages out of the envelope, unveiling three handwritten papers. Hank cleared his throat before he started to read.

My dear, dear Katherine,

These past eighteen months have been so bittersweet. Reconnecting with Mame in the shape she's in has been difficult. But even without words we have shared a bond of love that disease and time cannot take away.

I am content with the fact that only God knows our fate and if your grandmother outlives me, then I know you will continue to care for her as you always have.

Getting to know you Katherine has completed my life. You are a fine and beautiful young lady who has, regardless of her circumstance, become a woman of great strength and virtue. What you have been through with Ben, then having to care for me and Mame, would have broken an ordinary girl, but not you, not Katherine Paddington.

My wish for you is that you will search your heart. What is Mary Katherine's destiny? To become a teacher, nurse, housewife, and mother? Follow the path that will not only make you a living, but a path that will fulfill you, and bring you peace and happiness.

Please don't take this the wrong way, but I don't think Stan is right for you. A dying man has the privilege of telling the truth. The age difference is one thing. It might not seem a big deal now, but the older you get it will. I watch the way he is around you. Too controlling. Don't let him make decisions for you. You're smart, Katherine, use your own head. You can become anything you want to be. Find out who you are before you let someone into your heart.

I know all you've ever known is the homeplace, but I'd like for you to consider stepping outside those walls, away from the coal mines, the tobacco fields, and especially the bad memories. There is a big, beautiful world out there. Don't shut it out.

During the time I was away from your grandmother, I bummed my way through the first couple of years, then I settled down in Elkin, a small textile town about two hours south down highway I-77. Since the new interstate opened a few years ago it's a straight shot from Beckley to Elkin.

I went to work in a mill called Chatham's, named after some rich family there in Elkin. I worked in that place for nearly twenty years. I made a couple of prosperous investments that paid off so I've squirreled away a little money.

I am leaving to you, my only grandchild, the sum of twenty thousand dollars and some odd cents, whatever is in my account. Attorney Edminston will instruct you about the bank holdings and help you transfer it to an account in your name.

Of course, you'll get my old Ford Fairlane. It's not much but I believe it will get you back and forth to wherever you're going for a good long while. Long enough to get on your feet, and buy something newer.

Then there's the farm. Not really a lot of acreage like your uncles have, only twelve, but that should be plenty for you to raise a garden and roam around on. A small frame house with two bedrooms and a bathroom sits on the property. There's a milk barn out back with a shed, I love that old building, it smells like hay and manure, but my favorite thing about the property is the house sits on a rise above the Big Elkin Creek. On a clear summer evening you can sometimes hear a lonely old mountain cat calling for his mate down near the caves on the cliffs above the waterfall. When it rains and the creek swells you can hear the water rushing over the rocks at Carter Falls. Once upon a long time ago the town of Elkin's power came from the hydroelectric power plant at the falls. Not much remains of the plant, just some handmade bricks that once held up the foundation of the powerhouse. The huge rock columns are still there that supported the flume line where the water flowed through, producing Elkin's power. You'll love exploring the falls. It's always been a special place to me, reminding me of long ago, a time with your grandmother at another waterfall.

Katherine, I know you must be overwhelmed, and you very well have a right to be. When your grandmother and I are both gone you'll be alone. Yes, you'll have your uncles, aunts, and cousins, but when the day is done and you lay your head on your pillow, the darkness will surround you.

Don't let nightfall scare you into doing something that is not in your destiny, like marrying the wrong man. Sorry, I'm preaching again.

Lastly, I'd like to leave you my most prized possession, our memories. Remember our talks, walking the dusty dirt road together and just the three of us, you, me, and your grandma sitting on the front porch in the morning sunshine.

Always live for the Light. Don't do anything that will put you in the darkness of sin like your grandma and I did.

Please don't rush into anything. Visit my little farm. I hope you'll find the peace that I found there. If you don't like it, and don't want to live there, then sell it, but please don't keep yourself locked away at the homeplace. Explore, try new things, be all you can be. Please yourself for the first time in your life. Pray to the Lord for His divine guidance. Ask Him to lead you to a future that will be His will for you. My wish is for you to not just be happy, but to be content, to be satisfied, to live life to the fullest. To be at peace.

I hope and pray the words on these pages will console you, encourage you, and give you the courage to make some life changing decisions that only you can, for the future is before you, it's yours to live. Choices are yours to make. Choose wisely.

I love you more than you can imagine. I have cherished every moment we have shared. Now, close to death I am content. I was given the gift of having you in my life, even if it was for a short while, and now I know Mame and I will have each other for all eternity.

Until we meet again.

All my love,
Grandpa Clint

All three sat quietly. Minutes passed. Katherine was in shock. She didn't know what to say or think. Finally, Hank folded the pages of the letter and put them back in the envelope, then handed it to Katherine.

Martin could tell the young lady was close to tears, so he gave her a few more minutes before he ended the silence. "Well, I suppose that's it. Here is the name of the bank where your grandpa's account is. This letter will give the bank permission to transfer the money into your personal account. Do you have any questions?"

Katherine sat, stiff as a pole. What just happened? How could she have not known about Grandpa Clint's house in a town called Elkin? And money? She couldn't even imagine how much money twenty thousand dollars was.

Hank watched his young niece. It wasn't often that good news was delivered, but his heart was blessed by the look on Katherine's face. He knew enough about her situation to know she deserved a break.

Again, the attorney asked, "Do you have any questions?"

Taking a deep breath, Katherine cleared her throat, wiped at a tear that slide off her chin, then squared her gaze at the older gentleman and answered, "No, sir. No questions."

Katherine stood beside her uncle.

She somehow had the good sense to thank Mr. Edminston and ask him if she owed him anything.

"You are very welcome, Katherine. If you need me for anything just let me know, and my charges have already been paid. Your grandfather took care of that at our last meeting," Martin said.

Katherine held out her hand and shook Mr. Edminston's, as did her Uncle Hank, who had been speechless since reading the letter. They turned toward the door.

"Wait. I all most forgot to give you the house key," Martin said.

Opening his desk drawer, he pulled out another envelope. Unsealing it, he took the solitary key out and handed it to Katherine. She stared at the silver object, knowing her future lay in the palm of her hand. In this time of confusion, when her life was in shambles, she was suddenly calm and at perfect peace. This key was her destiny.

CHAPTER 8

Because to every purpose there is time and judgement, therefore the
misery of men is great upon him.

~ Ecclesiastes 8:6

TORMENTED, HE PACES BACK AND forth. Mutterings ramble through his head, blood speckled images flow through his brain.

I've waited long enough. I want what is mine. It's time, all the obstacles have been removed.

The end of my misery is near. It's time for the judgement.

Back and forth, back and forth, minutes turn to hours. Light turns to darkness, day then night. Pacing, back and forth, back and forth.

He's coming.

Stan Matthews looked at the clock hanging on the wall of his office for the hundredth time, 3:45 p.m. Katherine should be home from the attorney's office. He couldn't wait to see her again. Their life together was going to be like a happily ever after fairy tale. Inside his pretty little home by the creek, they'd snuggle on the couch. He'd pull himself away from her long enough to go to work. Then he'd rush back to her. She'd be waiting anxiously at the door for him, arms stretched out to embrace him.

He didn't intend to have children they'd be too much of a distraction for her. Stan wanted Katherine's full attention, all of her. He'd waited patiently for almost two years. Now was the time. The wait would soon be over. He'd give her another week or so to grieve her grandparents' deaths, then he'd propose. Out of respect, they should probably wait a couple of months before the wedding. Maybe at Christmas? It would be so beautiful. Fraser firs decorated with clear sparkling lights. Mistletoe hanging above every threshold, red bows and garland. He knew exactly where to find the mistletoe. Behind his house stood an ancient oak tree. Lots of creatures called its branches home: birds, squirrels, raccoons, ants, locusts . . . and then there was the mistletoe. There were at least half a dozen bunches as large as a peck bucket up toward the top.

Stan would have to get his twelve-gauge shotgun out and fire up into the top of the tree. He'd done it every year since his sisters had been old enough to bring boyfriends home. Now with his sisters away at college living their own lives it was time for Stan to make new memories.

He didn't especially like the sound of a gun being fired. It brought back too many personal remembrances. The noise took his mind back to 'Nam. To the jungles, the heat, the bugs, the smell of death, land mines, gunfire, and grenades. Being a medic, he saw firsthand what a boy's leg, or what was left of it, looked like when the explosive was stepped on. He'd seen dozens of feet blown off, scrap metal sticking out of bone, and M-16 bullet holes that literally ripped the heart out of its target.

Something was wrong in a world where men killed each other, then turned around and tried to save that same person. It messes with a person's head. Kill or save, save or kill? Being a medic in a war zone was living hell.

Stan willed himself back to the present. To his future, his and Katherine's. They'd have the wedding at his house. It was small, but that would mean only a few guests, his sisters, Katherine's uncles and aunts, and maybe a few of his pals from work. He could thank Ben for Katherine not having friends, and especially not boyfriends.

Yes, everything would be perfect. Soon, Katherine would be his, all his. Wouldn't she? A tug inside his belly, the same as when he knew the enemy was near in 'Nam pulled at his gut. Was there really such a thing as gut instinct?

CHAPTER 9

*Sorrow is better than laughter: for by the sadness of the countenance
the heart is made better.*

~ Ecclesiastes 7:3

THE RIDE BACK TO THE homeplace was quiet. Katherine held the key in her hand, flipping it over and over. She thought back through the years with Grandma Mame. So much sorrow in Katherine's life, and she'd had so little time with Grandpa Clint. She hadn't even known he'd owned a farm, and now that secret place was hers.

Excitement rippled through her stomach. She was sad, but knew in her heart that neither her grandma nor grandpa would want to come back to this earthly place, or to their life of heartbreak and sickness that they had lived for so long. She knew they were together forever. Time and circumstances would never part them.

Katherine had attended Sunday School and Bible School with her cousins when she was very young, but hadn't gone back for years. She'd been afraid to leave Grandma Mame. That didn't mean she didn't know the Bible. When she was able, Grandma Mame would set at the kitchen table and read the Word of God out loud. She'd spent hours there. At a very young age Katherine could recite John 3:16 by heart, but more importantly Katherine came to know the meaning of the words, *For God so loved the world, that He gave His only begotten Son, that whosoever believeth in Him should not perish, but have everlasting life.*

Everlasting life? That statement was too profound to understand, but Katherine believed it in her heart. There was no doubt her Grandma Mame and Grandpa Clint were together in heaven. Nothing would ever separate them again. Katherine's worrying was not about her grandparents now, but about her own future. She'd had a lot of information laid on her plate today. She had the means now to attend college. She wasn't sure about much, but she did know she wanted to further her education. To be a nurse, maybe even a doctor? She wasn't sure she was smart enough to do either, but she was going to try. She had to or she'd never know what she was capable of. She owed it to herself and Grandpa Clint who had secured the way for her to prove her self-worth.

He uncle's voice brought Katherine back to the present.

"Katherine, are you okay, you're awful quiet."

"Yes, Uncle Hank, I'm fine. I've just got a lot to figure out. Did you know Grandpa Clint owned a farm?"

"Not until about two months ago. He called me one day and asked if I had time to drive him around. You remember, don't you? I believe it was on a Wednesday?"

"Yes, he was getting so weak I was afraid for him to go anywhere, but he insisted he was fine, and you know how hard-headed he was."

"Oh yes, he was. That day he told me everything about his farm and his money. Made me promise to not tell a single living soul, especially you. We went to Martin Edminston's office and he took down all your grandpa's wishes and wrote his will. You heard it all today. He wanted you to have all he had, and he wanted you to use it to live wisely, to smile, to laugh, and to love. He cared for you and Mame so very much. It's a downright shame they were separated all those years. Yes, it's a shame life gets so twisted out of sorts sometimes."

Silence settled in around them like a blanket of thick fog. Katherine's mind couldn't help but think about her grandpa's letter. She knew he spoke words of wisdom. She knew he wanted her to go to college, to leave the homeplace, to see the world, to succeed. Was she brave enough? Could she make it on her own? Did she want to? She knew that as long as she stayed where she was Stan would be there to help her, just like he'd been doing all most every day for the past two years. Her grandpa's words echoed through her head. *I don't think Stan is the one for you. He's too controlling,* along with a few other remarks. *Take your time, don't commit, go to college. Use your own good mind to make decisions.*

Katherine remembered the first time Stan had kissed her, and then that time on the blanket by the creek. His boldness had scared her and reminded her of her awful Uncle Ben and his unwanted advances.

Now Katherine had become accustomed to Stan's gentle kisses and pecks on the cheek. He was a wonderful man and a cherished friend, but did she love him like a woman should love her future husband? Katherine was so confused.

With the windows rolled down on the pickup, the sound of gravel crunching deep into the road ricocheted through Katherine's head. She looked to the sky, and wondered if she'd ever seen it so blue.

Katherine took a deep breath and a feeling of certainty began to grow inside her. She could become self-reliant. She had really been on her own for years anyway especially before Grandpa Clint came back.

She knew if she could defend herself from Uncle Ben, then taking on the world and whatever this universe threw at her would be a challenge, but a dare she would welcome. Suddenly she knew what she had to do.

"Uncle Hank, do you think you might be able to go with me down to this town in North Carolina called Elkin and help me find Grandpa's farm? I'd like to see it. Then I need to research colleges. I'm not sure what I want to be, but I know I've got to stand on my own, if for no other reason than to see if I can. That and the fact that it was Grandpa Clint's last wish for me."

"Of course I can, Katherine. If you don't mind, I know Olivia would like to go, too. She'll want to add her two cents and get a feel for the place, just like I know you do, too. I don't know what studies you'll decide to learn, but I do know I've watched you tend your grandparents these last months. You've got a gift, child. A special touch and a caring heart. You have the ability to make people feel better even if their body is consumed with disease and pain. You can't teach a person to care, so in my opinion you're already halfway to becoming a first-class nurse."

Uncle Hank was saying exactly what Katherine needed to hear. Her future was being molded. Not cemented, just shaped and formed, a little bit at a time. Katherine knew at nineteen she wasn't the person she was to become. The future had a time all its own. An ever-changing destiny, a coming of age, a time to escape the sadness of the shadows . . . It was time for new beginnings. A time when her spirit would heal, a time when her heart would not feel the emptiness of loss, no more sickness, pain, or struggles. An awakening. A future. This was Katherine's time to embrace life. To become someone she didn't know yet.

CHAPTER 10

For every one that doeth evil hateth the light, neither cometh to the light, lest his deeds should be reproved.

~ John 3:20

TWENTY-SEVEN DAYS HAD PASSED SINCE Benny saw his dead father, and only five days ago the last breath of life escaped his mama's sweet lips. Everything that he'd ever known was gone.

As soon as the cremation service delivered the ashes, Benny drove home to Folly Beach. What now? He held the plastic jar, a pauper's final resting place. Not even an ornamental urn, just a dark plastic container filled with Trudy Bauguess' ashes. How ironic that she was now a small pile of soot, as worthless as the embers she flipped from the death sticks she couldn't live without.

Benny looked around the rented apartment that he and his mama had shared. The only home he could remember. Twenty-one years of neglect was ground into the worn-out carpet. The once white walls were stained yellow from years of nicotine fumes. Layer upon layer of strangling smoke. Benny pictured his mama's insides all jaundiced, just like the walls and ceiling. He'd always hated the smell of smoke. No matter how many times he'd fought with her about her smoking she'd always remind him she had been smoking since she was thirteen and that she was her own boss, and as long as she wanted a puff she'd take it. That which she loved had killed her, and Benny was alone.

He had a couple of distant cousins on his mama's side that lived close by but he never saw them, probably wouldn't even recognize them if they walked through the door.

His Grandpa Bauguess used to come around every few weeks, but that was only to bum a buck or two from his mama so he could buy a bottle of Five Star Wine. He hadn't seen him in three or four years.

Good riddance.

A little less than a month ago Benny thought his life was finally coming together. He'd found his daddy and couldn't wait to tell him what he has practiced saying to him for years. Couldn't wait to let him know what a low-life son of a biscuit eater he was for knocking his mama up, then leaving her high and dry to fend for herself. But he never got the chance, what's the use in telling a dead man he's scum?

What he had to do now was find his Blackwell kin. They owed him, didn't they?

Benny knew what had to be done, but he was confused after that preacher talked to him about all that do-gooding. Why did that chaplain have to come to his mama's room every day while she lay dying? Why did he recite all them pretty sounding prayers? What good had his words done? Dead is dead, with or without prayers. All that heaven and hell malarkey didn't mean squat to Benny. What right did that preacher have asking him if he was going to heaven or hell when he died? How was he supposed to know? All them words about following the Light, and a man he called Jesus, who wasn't nothing but a carpenter just like himself.

That reminded Benny he needed to call Eugene. Benny had been doing carpenter work for Eugene ever since he'd quit school the day he turned sixteen. The rent was due and he'd used almost all the folding money he and his mama had taken with them to find his daddy and get the cremation done. Benny knew he'd have to save up for gas money before he could go back to Beckley to meet the Blackwell clan.

For some reason Benny couldn't get the chaplain's words out of his head, *Evil hateth the Light.* Was his daddy evil like his mama always told him he was? Where was his daddy? A feeling of dread swept over Benny, where would he himself go if he died today? To hell with Daddy or to heaven with his sweet mama . . . or nowhere? Benny couldn't rightly say either place existed.

CHAPTER 11

Take therefore no thought for the morrow: for the morrow shall take
thought for the things of itself. Sufficient unto the day is the evil thereof.

~ Matthew 6:34

KATHERINE SLEPT FITFULLY. HER GRANDFATHER'S letter kept creeping into her dreams. In one day, her life had changed completely. The words in that letter gave her hope. She couldn't help but feel excited about her future. Next week she'd go to this town of Elkin, to her Grandpa Clint's farm.

Katherine knew she'd probably end up selling the property because her life was here at the homeplace, in Beckley with Stan. Wasn't it? Too many uncertainties. Time would open the curtain and reveal the answers. Besides, she knew she wanted to go to college, so that would give her four more years to decide. A quick calculation told her she'd then be twenty-three when she got out of college and Stan would be thirty-four. Thirty-four suddenly seemed really old. Maybe too old.

Waking up in an empty house would take some getting used to. Too quiet. It wasn't that Grandma Mame or Grandpa Clint made much noise; it was just their presence. The silent knowing that family was near.

Katherine stretched, then threw the covers back and swung her feet to the floor. The air had turned cool these past couple of weeks. It would soon be October, then winter. She wasn't looking forward to the long, lonely winter ahead. She glanced out the window toward the woodshed. Her Uncle Thomas kept the building full of good hard maple and oak. Katherine was thankful for her uncles, she just didn't want to be dependent on them for the rest of her life.

Slipping her toes into a fuzzy pair of bedroom shoes, Katherine made her way to the bathroom. She turned the knob on the small electric heater in the wall, knowing the luxury would add a few dollars to her power bill. "Her" power bill, not "their" power bill. Sadness enveloped Katherine. She missed her grandparents so much. Nothing felt complete. Pieces of her life were missing. Gone forever.

Coffee, that's what she needed. The sound of Grandma Mame's aluminum percolator brought a smile to Katherine's face. That little bit of joy chiseled away the sadness in her heart.

Katherine's first remembrance of the coffee pot was when she was about ten years old. The sound of coffee boiling up into the glass globe on top of the lid woke her every morning. Perk . . . perk . . . perk. Then the smell, the rich aroma smelled better than it tasted, but after Grandma Mame doctored her a cup up with a couple of teaspoons of sugar and half a cup of rich cream it wasn't half bad. The years had lessened the need for the sugar but she still wanted a bit of cream and sometimes a spoonful of honey, if she had some on hand.

Saturday. What would she do with herself today? Katherine knew Stan would be stopping by. Usually after lunch he'd show up. Now things were different. Before, mornings were very busy. Breakfast for Mame and Clint. Baths to give. Then it was time to prepare lunch.

What does a body do with oneself with no one but herself to take care of? Katherine felt useless. An hour later she still sat at the kitchen table holding a now cold half cup of coffee.

A strange noise outside the kitchen door roused her from her memories and depression. What was that, a meow? Katherine didn't own a cat, never had. Opening the door, she found a tiny kitten. Somehow it had got caught in between the screen door and the wooden door. Katherine reached down and scooped it up. It was solid white with one blue eye and one green eye. It was so small it fit in the palm of one of Katherine's hands.

"Where did you come from, little bit?"

Just as if the cat understood every word Katherine said, it started a constant meow, meow, meow. If only Katherine could understand cat language. What would this baby creature tell her? Did she climb up under someone's car and then fall out near her door? Or, had someone tossed the poor thing out into the cold? As harsh as that sounded Katherine knew some people were capable of doing just that and worse.

"I'll bet you're hungry. Let's find you some milk."

Holding the kitten in one hand, Katherine made her way to the refrigerator. She took out the half gallon jar of milk she got twice a week from the Collins' farm. She felt sad knowing she wouldn't need that much milk now. No time for such worries, she had a hungry baby to feed.

Katherine poured half a cup into a saucepan and set it on the stove to heat, just a minute to knock the chill off.

"Here you go, little bit."

Pouring the warm milk into a small saucer, Katherine set it on the floor and put the kitten in front of it. The poor little thing acted like it had never drank from a bowl. Probably all it knew was its mother's teat.

Katherine laughed as she watched the kitten climb into the bowl with its two front paws. It would stick its nose in the milk then spit and cough. After several attempts it got the taste and went to town gobbling up the rich cream.

"What am I going to do with you, little miss? First you need a bed."

Katherine went into her room to look for something to make a bed out of. She knelt and looked under her bed. Finding an empty shoe box, she took it into the bathroom. Taking a threadbare towel used for cleaning from the shelf she put it to good use lining the bottom of the box.

Back in the kitchen, the kitten still stood with its front two paws in the milk, or what was left of it. Some had spilled on the floor, some was soaked up in the cat's fur and hopefully some was in the kitten's tummy.

When the bowl was licked clean, Katherine lifted the kitten and hugged it to her heart. The Lord always knows what we need and when we need it. Katherine wouldn't have time to worry about tomorrow, for the day would bring enough worries of its own. Who would ever have thought a tiny kitten would be so much trouble, yet bring so much joy?

By Monday morning, Katherine and Little Bit had settled into a routine. Little Bit was all Katherine could think of when she looked at the cat so she decided that's what she'd name it.

Little Bit kept Katherine busy. She'd gone down by the creek on Saturday afternoon and collected a brown paper bag full of dry sand. Then she found a shallow dish pan to make Little Bit a litter box. She knew Grandma Mame wouldn't approve of keeping an animal in the house but Katherine knew the little creature would never survive outside. The coyotes would snatch her up in no time. So for once Katherine dismissed her grandma's voice in her head and settled in with Little Bit close by, waiting for her uncle to pick her up. She was proud of herself for making her own decision, even if it was a little selfish.

Katherine was ready and waiting for her first trip to Elkin when she heard her Aunt and Uncle coming up the gravel drive. She took her sweater off the hook behind the door, tucked her fake leather billfold under her arm, and went over to the spot in the kitchen floor where Little Bit was sleeping, resting peacefully with her feet tucked up under herself. Katherine had slept better the past couple of nights, too. The bad dreams about death had been replaced with thoughts of a tiny little bit of a white fluffy kitten.

CHAPTER 12

Now mine eyes shall be open, and mine ears attent unto the prayer
that is made in this place. For now have I chosen and sanctified this
house, that my name may be there for ever: and mine eyes and mine
heart shall be there perpetually.

~ 2 Chronicles 7:15-16

THE TWO-AND-A-HALF-HOUR RIDE TO ELKIN, North Carolina
flew by. It was the first time Katherine had ever been out of the state
of West Virginia, or even the county of Raleigh. Katherine watched
the world zoom by out the backseat window of Aunt Olivia's Cadillac.
There was so much to see, mountains, valleys, and then flat land for as
far as the eye could behold. She had never seen so much of the world.
The scenery, plus her Aunt Olivia's endless chatter, made the trip fly
by. Aunt Olivia was well known throughout the community for being
blessed with the gift of gab and today she was living up to her title.

The road ahead stretched for endless miles.

"We're almost there, Katherine. There it is, road number 2042, the
last turn."

Hank turned left off the secondary paved road in a rural
community onto a dirt road. Katherine scooted up to the edge of the
seat so she could see out the side window better. To their right was a

stately two-story house painted lime green. Then they passed a small white frame house and then a brick ranch style. Next was a two-story house painted white with black shutters. The front walkway was lined with huge box wood bushes. They were so big there was hardly enough room for a person to stroll up and down the walk. Next on the right were the wooden remains of what was once a small two-story house with a porch that ran the entire length of the front. Rusty tin roof and rotted boards were all that was left. No telling how many generations had slept there. Now all that was left in the ruins were memories. It appeared that Katherine did not live in the only homeplace there was in the world. She liked the way that thought made her feel.

The next half mile was nothing but woods and pasture land then they topped a hill and there, in the valley sat a small frame house.

"Stop," Katherine said. "That must be it, Grandpa Clint's farmhouse."

Hank halted the Cadillac and took in the surroundings. It was a small, neatly kept house, probably no bigger than eight or nine hundred square feet, with a garden spot that had recently been bushhogged, and the yard was clipped as if someone still lived there. Clint had told Hank he paid a neighbor boy named Tracy to watch out after the place and keep it mowed. Across the road from the house was a farm pond. Cows were taking a dip, water half way up their bellies.

"Well Katherine, what do you think?" Olivia asked.

"I don't know yet. Let's get closer. Are you sure this is it? We need to check the number on the mailbox. The address should say 243. I looked at the paperwork Attorney Edminston gave me this morning.

There was also a plat of the twelve acres. The land borders a creek. Grandpa Clint's letter said there was a waterfall close by, too."

Hank smiled at the excitement in his niece's voice, then drove on down the road, stopping in front of the house. The mailbox was only a few feet in front of them and they could clearly read the hand-painted numbers on the side, 243.

"What a cute little place. You should be able to sell this property in no time," Olivia said.

Katherine's mind raced. Sell it? While the thought had crossed her mind, now she wasn't so sure.

"I want to go inside," Katherine said.

Hank pulled up into the dirt driveway, stopped, and turned off the engine.

Katherine unzipped the change pocket of her wallet and took out the key that Attorney Edminston had given her. She flipped it over and over between her fingers. Why was she so nervous? It was only a house. But it wasn't just any old house; it had belonged to her grandpa. He had lived there for over twenty years. This place was a part of him. The thought of it being full of all his things made her even more anxious.

Hesitating for only a few minutes, she opened the back car door. Easing out of the seat, she stood and slowly walked toward the house. Before going inside, she walked around every square inch of the structure. It had light green siding and a white shingled roof. There was a screened in porch on the back and a woodshed out a ways from the house. The shed was stacked full of split wood. Everything was neat. The house sat high above bottom land and a creek ran below it. Katherine had read on the land plat that the water was called the Big Elkin Creek. A funny thought entered Katherine's head. If that was the Big Elkin Creek, then where was the Little Elkin Creek? The thought made Katherine smile, and it felt good to her. This place felt right. She was ready to go inside where more smiles might be waiting.

Katherine opened the screen door and stepped onto the back porch. The only thing on the porch was a straw broom, a well-used mop and a pair of work boots, presumably her grandpa's. She knelt down and picked one up. They too were well-worn. Katherine sat the boot down and took two steps toward the entrance door. A curtain was pulled together so she couldn't peak inside.

The key was wet from her sweating palm. She took it and rubbed it against her jeans before sticking it in the lock. She turned the key left and heard the interior lock click. The door squeaked as Katherine pushed it all the way open. She stood staring at an outdated kitchen. Much like the one at the homeplace. There was the usual electric stove, refrigerator, two-hole sink and a couple of white metal cabinets hung above the sink and stove. The table may have been homemade. It wasn't fancy but it had character, sturdy and reliable.

Katherine ran her hand over the top. A thin layer of dust rubbed off on her fingers.

"What kind of wood is this, Uncle Hank?"

"It looks to me like cherry. See the red grain? That's the only wood I know of that has that color, except red oak. It looks similar, but I do believe this is cherry."

"Do you think Grandpa Clint made it?"

"I can't rightly say. He told me about this place, but not in detail. Only where it was, and how much land was with it."

That was the first of many questions Katherine would have as she walked through every room. She could tell only a man had lived there.

Everything was simple. No frills, just the basics. Two bedrooms with a bed, dresser, and a wardrobe for hanging clothes. One was empty, while the other held Clint's clothing. What would she do with his things? What would she do with all her grandpa's possessions, which now belonged to her?

The last room was a small bathroom. It had a tub that was a pretty shade of pink. The sink was the same color. The toilet, however, was white, which made Katherine wonder if long ago it too had been pink. It had probably been replaced with the newer white one. A washing machine sat in the corner. Had there been a clothesline outside? She hadn't noticed it if there was.

The living room area was adjacent to the kitchen. It was home to a couch upholstered in a brown and burgundy plaid. Two chairs matched the couch, one rocked, the other didn't. The couch looked so inviting Katherine couldn't help but sit down in it. A television sat in front of her, much newer than the old black and white one at the homeplace. She couldn't help but wonder if it was a color set like she'd watched shows on a few times with her cousins. Grandma Mame always said a television was a luxury and she didn't deserve luxuries, but she'd taken the second hand one her brother Timothy had dropped off one day. Katherine knew Grandma Mame had made the exception for her.

Another foreign piece in the room caught her attention. Pointing, she asked, "What is that, Uncle Hank?"

"That, my dear, is your source of heat. It's an oil circulator."

"Does it burn wood?"

"No, heat is generated by burning fuel oil. I saw the oil tank out back."

Katherine thought she was looking into the future, possibly a colored television, and a heater that didn't require wood?

"If this thing doesn't burn wood, then why is there an entire shed full of wood out back?"

"That's a good question. Let's go back outside and look around."

Hank looked at the woodshed and noticed a chimney jutting through the roof on the back side.

"Look, Katherine. I believe there is where your wood heater might be."

All three made their way to the back of the shed and stopped when they saw a small addition to the back of the woodshed and barn.

"What do you think Grandpa Clint used this for?"

Hank walked to the door and turned the knob. The door squeaked like its bones ached from not being used in a long while. Katherine was at Uncle Hank's heels, on tiptoe peering over his shoulder to get a closer look inside. This was like Christmas, she thought. At every turn there was another surprise. Katherine didn't know much about what Christmas was like for normal people; Grandma Mame thought it too was just a luxury. A time of the year to be showy, and Lord knows Grandma Mame didn't have a speck of high and mighty in her.

"It looks to be a woodworking shop," Hank said.

Katherine knew nothing about building but recognized a couple of different pieces of equipment, electric saws, hand saws, a couple of hammers, screws, and there in the middle of the room was a work table. Scattered throughout the small area were pieces of furniture in different stages of construction, a rocking chair with only one rocker attached, the other one lay beside the chair. Two small tables that were identical except one had been sanded and varnished the other still rough wood. A large piece of furniture monopolized the middle of the floor. It was meant to someday become a china hutch.

The cabinet looked to be almost finished except for the knobs and handles and the empty fronts needed a couple of panes of glass.

"I bet Grandpa did build that kitchen table in the house."

"Yep, it looks like he might have built furniture. Probably his hobby. Look at the detail that was carved into this hutch. He was really talented. Probably did this to keep his heart from missing Mame too much. Idle hands give the brain too much time to think," Olivia said.

Katherine halfway listened to her aunt ramble. All the while taking in the condition of the room she was standing in. Cement floor, unpainted sheetrock on the ceiling and walls, and a pot-bellied wood stove that must have been at least a hundred years old stood on the back wall. It was tiny, but probably gave off enough heat to warm up the fairly large open room.

There was so much Katherine didn't know about her grandpa, and truth be told she was sure some of her Grandma Mame's secrets had gone to the grave with her.

"My goodness, look at this piece. Why, it has a 'M' engraved along the edge."

Upon closer inspection by Olivia, every piece had the "M" embellished somewhere on it in an unconscious spot.

"After seeing these pieces I'll bet you the kitchen table inside has the 'M' on it, too. It's as if Clint dedicated every piece of furniture he made to Mame. It's a crying shame circumstances kept them apart all those years. Who's to say how long it takes for a heart to heal after it gets broken. There's no doubt Mame tore Clint's heart to shreds, but then Clint just ran off and shattered Mame's already fragile mind."

Katherine stood listening as her aunt and uncle reminisced about old times. Most of what she heard she already knew. Grandma Mame revealed a lot of things she probably wouldn't have if not for the disease. Her Uncle Ben could have been her daddy? How sick is that? Thank the Lord for the Carter birthmark, the one Grandpa Clint's mama had, the one Grandpa Clint had, the one her daddy Walt had, and the mark that she had, too. Ben bore no trace of the Carter birthmark.

Katherine reached up and touched the spot where she knew it to be, behind her right ear. Yes, there was no doubt about who her daddy was, because her Uncle Ben didn't have the purple mark, for he had been the son of Jack Marsh. Every time Katherine thought about that twisted tale her stomach rolled in disgust.

How life altering it must have been for her Grandma Mame to have been raped by such a vile man, then give birth to twins with two different fathers. Katherine knew it was true; she'd researched it in the library. *Heteropaternal superfecumdation* is what the scientists called it in the encyclopedia. Twins conceived within two weeks of each other. It was rare but it happened.

Katherine seldom thought about her father, Walt Paddington. A daddy she'd never known. A man struck down by his own brother, Ben.

Since Grandpa Clint had come into her life almost two years ago, Katherine had caught a glimpse of who her father might have been—loving, caring, meek, and humble. When, and if, she ever married she could only hope she'd find a man natured like her grandpa?

Katherine reeled her mind back from the past and to her uncle and aunt's chatter. "Let's go see if the kitchen table has the 'M.' I'll bet it does," Olivia said.

Hank left the woodshop last and pulled the door shut behind him. Olivia and Katherine were two women on a mission. By the time he'd reached the back door of the house his niece and wife were already on their hands and knees looking under the table for the trademark "M."

"I don't see it. Grandpa Clint may not have built this table."

Another few minutes passed with all three sets of eyes scanning the shiny cherry wood. Finally, Hank pulled one of the five chairs out that matched the table and sat down. In the middle of the table sat one solitary quart jar of honey. The top glistened with crystals. Picking up the jar, Hank turned it on its side and found it was mostly sugar.

"You know honey will do that if it sits too long."

"Do what, Uncle Hank?"

"Turn to sugar. See."

Katherine and Olivia stood. Both saw it at the same time. There right smack dab in the middle of the table was the "M" engraved into the rich cherry wood. This time Clint had not put the monogram in a secret place. He put it where his eyes would see it every day. See it, and think of his beautiful wife, Mame.

The other pieces out in the shed could easily be sold, the buyers never knowing about the "M" hidden here or there. Was that Clint's intention? Had Katherine's grandpa built other pieces that were sitting in someone else's home?

"There it is, Aunt Olivia. Right in the center of the table. No matter what happens, where I go or what I do with this place, I will always cherish this table, because it was built with love in remembrance of Grandma Mame by Grandpa Clint."

Katherine ran her fingers over the letter "M." There was so much to think about. Katherine took in every detail of the room. Everything was in its place. Katherine opened the refrigerator door. It too was empty; the interior wiped clean and spotless. Katherine found the same thing in the freezer, except for two aluminum ice trays, the kind that had a pull lever to release the ice cubes. They held no frozen cubes now, empty just like the house.

"Sad to say, but it looks like Clint knew he wouldn't be coming back. That he had made his mind up to spend his last days with Mame. Why, oh why, didn't he do that years ago?" Olivia asked.

She hung her head and a tear fell from her eye and landed on her cheek. She wiped at it with the back of her hand.

"Now Olivia, don't fret or think about all the ifs, ands, and why nots. You know Mame and Clint's history. There is a thin line between love and hate. Who's to say what a man or woman might do if they were in the same situation.

Katherine listened to her aunt and uncle, knowing they knew a whole lot more about her grandparents than she did. She didn't ask questions or inquire into the past; some things were better left hidden. Katherine knew enough to know some secrets and sins were better off kept to ourselves.

A noise on the back porch brought a close to the sad memories that had swallowed their thoughts.

"Hello there, can I come in?"

Not waiting for an answer, the young man stepped over the threshold of the back door.

"You must be Clint's family—or robbers, but you don't look like crooks, so you must be kin. Happy to meet you. I'm Tracy, Tracy Gentry. I live just down the road a couple of miles, across the creek and up the hill. I've been watching out over Clint's place since he's been gone. News of his passing from his attorney tore me up bad. Clint was a good friend to me. He was teaching me all about building furniture and different kinds of wood, and how to cut wood to get the best angle so the pretty grain would show."

The three onlookers watched as the young man hung his head and swiped his hand across his nose, tears close to flowing.

"I've surely missed him this past year. He came by about nine or ten months ago and told me he wouldn't be back. Said he'd found the love of his life again and a granddaughter that he would be spending the rest of every minute he had left with."

Stepping toward Katherine, Tracy stared at her face. "You must be the granddaughter Clint told me about. Let's see, can't honestly say I remember your name, though."

Katherine extended her hand to the stranger, feeling comfortable with his friendly manner. She couldn't help but notice the young man had a slight stutter, or a hesitation in his voice at times, like his brain couldn't keep up with his tongue. It was probably just his nerves.

It was hard to tell his age. Maybe sixteen, or even as old as twenty. Tracy was a big guy, not just in height, but also in girth. Not really fat, just big-boned. She didn't really know this boy, but he seemed to have a big heart to go along with his size. He wore jeans and a white t-shirt and work boots. The part of Tracy that really stood out was his eyes. They were as blue as a robin's breast.

"Katherine. My name is Katherine, and this is my Aunt Olivia and Uncle Hank."

"Real nice to meet you folks."

Pulling his hand from Katherine's, he shook hands with Olivia and Hank.

"What you planning on doing with the place? It's a solid built house. My grandpa built if for a couple that moved here from Florida.

They'd long passed before I was born. All I've ever known is Clint living here. Just needs a touch of paint here and there and the dust brushed off. Maybe a fresh coat of shellac on the floors."

Katherine had never heard a person talk so much, except maybe Aunt Olivia. He barely caught his breath before starting up again. The stutter was becoming less and less noticeable.

"I can show you where the property lines are. Old man Luffman's property joins you on one side and Mr. Walsh's on the other. The back side of the property borders the Big Elkin Creek, with the Gentry place on the other side."

Knowing it was rude, Katherine couldn't help herself and butted in. "Where are the falls? Can I see them from here?" Katherine moved to look out the kitchen window down toward the bottomland.

"You mean Carter Falls? No, you can't see them from here, but you sure can hear them when it's flooding. It's the prettiest place in the country. My grandpa's land borders the head of the falls. I've walked and swam in every inch of them waters."

Tracy moved in a little closer to Katherine and pointed out the window down toward the upper end of the bottom. "See, right down there where the sun is reflecting off the water? There she is running strong."

"Where? I don't see any water," Katherine said.

Hank and Olivia looked at each other, and then back to the young people who were both now leaning over the sink. A smile etched all four faces in the room. Katherine had never had friends, her circumstances never allowed her to have time, or if someone did stop by Ben ran them off.

"Right there. See where the sun is glistening? See the sparkles? That's the river," Tracy said.

"Yes, I see it now. Come look, Aunt Olivia. It's so pretty. I can see a river from my very own kitchen window."

Katherine's reference to the kitchen window belonging to her did not go unnoticed by Hank and Olivia. They smiled at each other as they took in the scenery out the window.

"If that hillside was logged and the bottomland cleared you'd be able to see the river a lot better. I usually bushhog it twice a year for Clint, but he hadn't mentioned for me to do it the past couple of years. Seemed his mind was far away from here. He just told me to keep the yard mowed and trimmed up nice. Least I could do for a man as nice as your grandpa. In case you didn't know he's paid me up through cutting season next year, one less thing for you to have to worry about. Will all three of you be coming here to live?"

"On no, son. I've got a business to run back in Beckley. My wife and I just brought Katherine down to see the place. She only found out a few days ago that her grandfather left the place to her. I don't rightly think she knows what she's going to do with it, do you, Katherine?"

Katherine hesitated before answering. "No, Uncle Hank, I sure don't. I'd like to spend a little more time here and I want to see Carter Falls. Grandpa Clint said in his letter that he wanted me to see it. "

Thinking out loud, Katherine looked at her Uncle Hank, "Carter Falls . . . Grandpa Clint's mother's maiden name was Carter. Do you think it's possible that I could be related to the same Carters to whom the falls were named after?"

"Why, child, I don't rightly know, it'd be interesting to do a little research and try to find out," Hank said.

"Oh, my goodness, so much to think about. I really don't think it would be fair to Grandpa Clint's memory if I just sold this place without knowing how I would feel about living here."

Turning toward Tracy, who for once was silent, Katherine started firing questions at him.

"Are the winters very cold here? Do you get much snow? Where is the closest college and which way to the falls, up river or down?"

"Well, I'll be John Brown, you can talk, and a mile a minute, too."

Katherine was not impressed with the young man's sarcasm. She had many decisions to make and lots of uncertainties to unfold and figure out. She needed time to think before coming to any conclusions, and she also had lots more questions.

"Miss Katherine, you got a lot of questions and I'll shore be happy to answer all of them that I can. Let's see, first of all the winters here in Wilkes County are usually not too harsh. Gets cold enough to freeze the pipes at times, especially if you don't keep them wrapped in insulation. Never known the pipes to freeze here though.

"How about snow?" Katherine asked.

"I was getting to that. Don't rush me."

Katherine ignored his remark but couldn't help but smile. She liked the idea of someone thinking she was feisty. Little did he know just how tough she could be if backed into a corner. Her mind went back a few years to the night she'd had to defend herself against Uncle Ben with the knife she'd kept under her pillow. Yes, she would fight if she had no other choice.

Tracy interrupted Katherine's thoughts.

"I love snow. We never get enough to satisfy me. Maybe four or five inches a couple of times a year."

"What about the falls? Are they close by?"

"The falls are down river. Best way to get to them from here is go down the road, cross the bridge, and up the hill to my grandpa's land. There's a trail down through the pasture that will lead you right to the top where the dam was when the power plant was still operating. There's a lot of history tied to Carter Falls. Maybe I can take y'all down there sometime, show you around and fill you in on some more of the past. Part of the old flume line is still down there. I remember the day the power company blew the dam out. Wasn't but a few years back in 1967. That was the loudest explosion I've ever heard, even louder than when the revenuers blew up a still down in the swamp."

"Sure would like to see them falls, maybe next time we come down the mountain. We could pack a picnic, couldn't we, Olivia?"

"Yes, we could. Fried chicken, potato salad, strawberry shortcake."

"Maybe next summer before the crops start coming in. That is if Katherine decides to keep this place," Hank said.

Katherine listened to the idle talk, not knowing herself what she might do with Grandpa Clint's farm. A lot depended on where she'd go to college.

"Are there any local colleges nearby?" she asked.

"There's two new community colleges pretty close. Wilkes Community College up in Wilkesboro is thirty minutes from here, but then there's Surry Community College in Dobson. That's where I go. Takes me twenty minutes to get there."

Katherine's ears perked up when she heard about the two schools. Community college would be perfect. She couldn't afford one of the prestigious state colleges like West Virginia University.

"Do you know if either school offers a nursing program?"

"Don't know much about the school up in Wilkes, but Surry's got nursing classes. My sister got her LPN license just this past spring. Works down at the Baptist Hospital in Winston-Salem. I'm taking a welding class right now. Something is always breaking on a farm, but what I really want to do is play music. You name it and I can pick it."

Katherine stopped listening when she heard Tracy say there was a community college that offered a nursing program only twenty minutes away. Was that her sign? Too many things were falling into place. Grandpa Clint's farm, his money, a school nearby. Was this little farm house at the foot of the Blue Ridge Mountains to become her new home, her new beginning, her destiny?

All of a sudden, Tracy started singing an old Elvis Presley song. Katherine couldn't help but smile at her new neighbor.

She looked around one more time. The kitchen had come to life with possibilities. A little paint, maybe some new tile on the floor, and curtains. Yes, new curtains would brighten up the room.

Katherine waited until Tracy was done serenading before asking Uncle Hank if they would have time on their way home to stop by the college so she could get more information about their nursing program.

"It's a long way from Beckley to Elkin," Hank said.

"Yes, I know, but it's not that far from Elkin to Dobson."

Hank didn't know what to say, but Olivia did. "Katherine, you can't be serious about moving here. Why, who would take care of you? You're not thinking of marrying Stan and the both of you live here, are you? You'd be all alone with no family to check in on you, and—"

"Hold on," Katherine cut her aunt off mid sentence. "I'm just weighing all my options. Aunt Olivia, you know I've been taking care of myself for years, and no, I am not marrying Stan, not yet anyway. Besides, if I'm in nursing school I'll be too busy to get lonely."

"Well shucks, looks like I got me a new neighbor. I'll look out for you, Miss Katherine. I'm just across the creek," Tracy said.

Not knowing, Katherine looked at her soon to become close friend.

The ride over to Dobson took just less than twenty minutes. Katherine knew she could handle the drive easily.

Pulling the car to a stop, Hank had to admit it looked like a very nice place, not citified, but out in the country.

"I'll be right back. Hopefully there will be someone handy to answer a few questions and give me the information I'm going to need to make my mind up about this new chapter in my life," Katherine said.

While Katherine was inside, Hank and Olivia walked around the campus. It was landscaped beautifully. Though the trees were still young they were quite beautiful with the leaves turning a crimson shade of red.

"What kind of trees are these, Hank?"

"Looks to be Red Maples. Pretty, aren't they?"

"Yes, very. Do you think Katherine is serious about moving here? Do you think she'll be okay?" Concern etched Olivia's face into numerous furrows.

"Odds are, she'll sell Clint's place. She'd be like a fish out of water if she left Beckley. No need to worry about something that's likely never to happen."

"I hope she's not going to be influenced by these new surroundings and her newfound independence. It is a beautiful place. You know she's never completely ever been alone. She's like my own child Hank, I'll worry myself sick if she's not down the road from me."

Hank watched a single tear trickle down his wife's cheek. He bent down and lovingly kissed her on the lips, the taste of salt lingered on his tongue.

By the time Katherine came back to the car, Hank and Olivia were seated back inside waiting for her.

"Sorry it took so long. I actually got to talk to a counselor. She said their nursing program was new and that they would only be taking fifteen students for the winter semester. The counselor said for me to mail her my high school transcript along with all these registration papers and if she likes what she sees, there's a good possibility that I may be accepted."

Hank watched his niece. Excitement rippled through her like an electric current from a hot fence wire. Her face was flushed, cheeks all a glow with adventure. He knew he'd told Olivia not to worry, but he might just have to eat his words. Feeling a knot grow in his stomach, he admitted to himself that he would sorely miss Katherine too if she moved away from the farm.

Katherine knew in her heart that Grandpa Clint's house had been given to her for a reason. Now it was her choice. Would she stay in Beckley, or move to North Carolina? Without thinking twice, she knew her decision was made. A calm stillness came over her.

Then she thought of Stan.

Katherine knew her eyes had been opened. It was her free will to do as she pleased, a career, a new home, and a fresh beginning.

She would forget the dark memories, and Grandma Mame's stories she told at the entrance to the coal mine, and she didn't have to have Stan's blessing. He had been good to her and her grandma, but she knew deep down that she didn't love him like a woman should love a husband, she loved him like a true and cherished friend and that was all.

Katherine's thoughts go back to the small frame house that sits on the ridge above the Big Elkin Creek, and a verse from 2 Chronicles came to mind.

For now have I chosen and sanctified this house, that my name may be there forever: and mine eyes and mine heart shall be there perpetually.

Katherine would forever from this day be a changed person.

CHAPTER 13

For unto us was the gospel preached, as well as unto them: but the
word preached did not profit them, not being mixed with faith in
them that heard it.

~ Hebrews 4:2

BENNY BAUGUESS WAS RESTLESS. HE stood up from the kitchen table for the third time in an hour, closing the Bible for the third time as well.

It had taken some time, but Benny had finally found the Book. He knew his mama had one, and he also knew she had stolen it from one of the hotel rooms she'd cleaned when he was just a boy. He remembered she'd read the Bible for a couple of days after she'd brought it home, then one day she flung it against the wall. It laid on the floor for days, then disappeared.

Benny had never had reason to look for it. That is not until he'd come home with his mama's ashes and the realization that he didn't know if she was now in heaven, or in hell with his daddy. He really didn't know how a person got to one place or the other. What a lost feeling to know your daddy is in hell and your mama could be, too. Or, just floating somewhere in between.

Looking for the Bible, he found it mixed in with a dozen outdated magazines that his mama had stacked in a corner of her bedroom on the floor.

The chaplain at the hospital had told him that the answers to all of life's questions were printed within the pages of this Book. Maybe they were, but he sure as heck couldn't find them. Why was it worrying him so much? Didn't he have better things to do than sit around reading a dusty old book? And, besides that, he didn't understand hardly a word he was reading. The chaplain told him his faith in Jesus Christ would give him understanding, and eternal life.

Benny rubbed the back of his neck and sat back down at the kitchen table. Randomly he flipped the Book open. His eyes fell to 1 John 5:13. *These things have I written unto you that believe on the name of the Son of God; that ye may know that ye have eternal life, and that ye may believe on the name of the Son of God.*

Believe? Eternal life? The chaplain said you only had to believe. He didn't know whether to believe a flesh-and-bone man, but it was written right there in the pages in the Holy Bible.

Believe and know that you may have eternal life.

Benny closed his eyes and pictured his mama's face. Surely she had believed, why else would she have wanted this book so badly that she had stolen it from someone named the Gideons?

Opening his eyes, Benny felt better and more at peace about where his mama was resting for eternity. He wasn't sure about all the things he'd been reading in the Book. So many questions, and the answers were just too hard to understand. Why, the Book even says to love your enemies. How in the name of this Bible's God do you love an enemy?

That brought thoughts of his newfound kinfolk up in West Virginia, the Blackwells. He'd been wrestling with what to do and how to handle meeting them. Reckon he'd just head up that way and claim his part of the Blackwells' good fortune. That had been his plan ever since he'd found out they were his family, but now this Book had his mind all messed up. Should he go, or stay and forget he ever had a daddy or relatives that he'd never seen?

Looking around the kitchen nothing had changed since his mama had sat at this very same table three months ago. The walls were still covered in nicotine residue, the flooring was worn through to the plywood and the drip at the bathroom sink still sounded the same as it did when it started more than a year before.

What was there to stay here for? Yes, he had a job. Eugene had been good to him, but he knew he could find a job doing carpenter work anywhere.

Go or stay? Meet his father's family or forgive? Forget and stay where he was? Could he have it both ways?

That carpenter that he'd been reading about in the Bible would tell him to forgive, but that man called Jesus didn't know how much Benny and his mama had suffered. How could Benny ever forgive a father who had deserted him and his mama? Didn't he deserve his share, his portion of his father's inheritance?

Benny looked around the room. He couldn't see it from where he was sitting but the dripping sink in the bathroom sounded louder than usual, like a steel ball bouncing off the ceramic sink. The noise echoed through Benny's head. Suddenly what had never bothered him before was so loud he covered his ears, trying to drown out the racket. He closed his eyes so he could not see his future. His eyelids did little to cover up the filth and stink of twenty years of living in the past.

He couldn't stay here. He knew his mind was made up. Wherever he went he knew it had to be away from here. He'd tell Eugene in the morning.

Benny opened his eyes and then the Book to 1 Timothy 1:15. *This is a faithful saying, and worthy of all acceptation, that Christ Jesus came into the world to save sinners: of whom I am chief.*

Benny closed the Book and pushed it away. He had read the words but had he really heard them in his heart?

However, the next afternoon when he began to gather his belongings for the trip to West Virginia, the stolen Book was the first thing he packed.

CHAPTER 14

He that hath no rule over his own spirit is like a city
that is broken down, and without walls.

~ Proverbs 25:28

THE PHONE WAS RINGING WHEN Katherine stepped through the door of Grandma Mame's house. She threw her sweater on the wingback chair and picked up the receiver.

"Hello?"

"Katherine, you're finally home. I've been calling for at least two hours. I was beginning to get worried. Where have you been all day?"

"Hey, Stan. You knew I was going to North Carolina today to see Grandpa Clint's farm. You should see it. It is the cutest little farmhouse, and it sits up on a rise that overlooks a river. A neighbor told us there is even a waterfall downstream a short distance. In just one day I've fallen in love with the place.

"We also found out that Grandpa Clint built furniture. He has a shop out back of the woodshed with several pieces that he'd been working on and a beautifully crafted solid cherry kitchen table in the kitchen. He engraved every piece with a 'M.' Uncle Hank and Aunt Olivia and I believe the monogram on his work is in honor of Grandma Mame. Even with all the miles and years separating them, they were constantly in each other's thoughts . . . Sorry, I'm rambling. I'm just so excited about my future."

There was a distinct change in Katherine, her confidence level was rocket high.

On the other end of the line, Stan's heart was pounding so hard he was sure she could hear it through the phone line. It was not lost on him how excited she was about "her" future. He suddenly felt sick, sweat beaded on his forehead. He had to reason with Katherine and get control before Katherine's imagined future led her into trouble. After all, she was only nineteen years old. He had to look out for her. She needed him.

"I'm so happy you had a good day, Katherine. I was afraid seeing your grandfather's house would make you sad. It sounds like it will be easy to sell, especially with access to a river. That's one reason I love my house so much. Remember our first picnic down by the creek and the deer we saw?"

Stan needed to get her mind back to "their" future, not "hers."

Katherine did remember that day and the kiss that scared her half to death. It really wasn't anything that Stan did, it was just the thought of the many times Uncle Ben had tried to corner her and steal a kiss. She may have forgiven him, but she'd never forget what he put her and Grandma Mame through.

"Katherine, you do remember that day, don't you?"

"Of course I do. It was a beautiful day and a magical spot."

Katherine hated to lie, but she didn't want to hurt Stan's feelings. Thoughts of that day often made her flesh crawl.

Stan smiled. Katherine loved the place where they would spend their future together just as much as he did.

Katherine noticed Stan's voice had risen an octave, and he seemed to be telling instead of asking if he could stop by on his way home from work. She wasn't in the mood for company, but again she didn't want to hurt Stan's feelings. "Sure, I'm tired from the ride, but after I freshen up I'll be better company. See you soon."

Katherine jumped when something rubbed up against her leg, but then she realized it was only Little Bit. She reached down and picked her up. Instantly, she started purring. Why was that sound so soothing? Maybe because a kitten only wanted to be fed, petted, and loved. No strings attached, no promises.

Katherine had been saddled with responsibility all her life. She'd done what her heart had led her to do so she had no regrets, but now it was her time to live, to be selfish, to think of herself for the first time in her life. For some odd reason she had a bad feeling about Stan's impending visit. Was it guilt? Stan had been so good to her and Grandma Mame. Did she owe him? She wasn't naive enough to believe that Stan was in love with her. She couldn't ask for anyone to be more respectful and caring. Maybe one day they would have a future together, but for now Katherine had to find out what it would be like to not worry about anyone but herself.

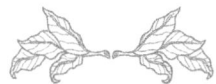

The man locked the door and turned off the lights. It would soon be dark. He tried to stay calm, to not remember the blood, the smell, the cold final blow of death. Things were going to change. Life was about to get better. His future was within his grasp. He deserved it. He had paid the price. It was time for life to issue out some rewards for all his patience and struggles. All he has to do is stay in control. A man without self-control is like a city without walls.

CHAPTER 15

But we are all as an unclean thing, and all our righteousnesses are as filthy rags; and we all do fade as a leaf; and our iniquities, like the wind, have taken us away.

~ Isaiah 64:6

BENNY WAS TIRED. HE AND Eugene had been pulling roofing off a two-story house with a crowbar all day in the hot autumn sun. Maybe since he was so tired he'd be able to sleep tonight. Last night he had nightmares all night. Blood was everywhere, and it had all seemed so real. He could almost feel the sticky wetness between his fingers, just like when he'd touched his daddy's slit throat.

Shaking his head to hopefully clear his mind of such thoughts, he looked around the kitchen, then the two bedrooms and bath. What should he take? He could probably pile most of the furniture in the bed of his truck, but what good was it? The stove and refrigerator belonged to the landlord, people he'd never seen. They lived down in Florida somewhere and left a local realtor in charge of their rental property. The kitchen table now belonged to him. The two padded chairs with the stuffing falling out certainly were no prize possessions beyond a bit of sentimental value from remembering the hours his mama had spent sitting and smoking her cigarettes.

What good was any of it? Benny thought as he skimmed the room, taking in the tattered mismatched couch and chair. *Wouldn't bring a five-dollar bill for the lot of it.* Even if he took the furniture he'd never be able to get the smell of smoke and his mama's memory out of their stuff.

Benny had promised Eugene he'd help him finish the roof before he left for West Virginia. It wouldn't take more than a couple of days. He'd load up all the junk in the house and take it to the dump. What they'd been living with wasn't even fit for one of the homeless people who lived downtown along the boardwalk.

Benny walked into his mama's bedroom. This would be the hardest part, throwing away all her clothes and whatnots. He walked over to her bed. The mattress was so worn out he could see the indention where her body had lain for the past twenty years. He threw the covers back and noticed the large tear at the bottom of the sheet. Her toe had probably snagged a hole and tore it bigger.

Trudy Bauguess had wasted her short life trying to chase a dream. To find the man who had fathered her only child. Benny knew his mama never had much. She never bought new clothes; they always came from the Goodwill store or thrift shop. Benny knew she'd done the best for him that she knew how. From having a baby at sixteen, with little education, working all the odd cleaning jobs or waitressing, somehow she was always able to feed them even if it was leftover scrapes from the restaurants she worked at. Benny knew his mama always gave him the best of whatever they had. Looking at the ripped sheet he knew he'd never had to sleep with a hole in his linens. Even if it was trash to someone else, their filthy rags, someone else's leftovers had always been good enough for Benny and his mama.

The next couple of days were filled with hard work, Benny and Eugene finished the roof and said their goodbyes. "If you ever need a job, come see me. You're the best hand I've ever had. You've got a job with me anytime you want one," Eugene said.

"Thanks, man. I don't know where the wind will blow me, but I know I got to go with it. There ain't nothing for me here since Mama's gone. I know I got rich kin people up north in West Virginia. Guess it can't hurt to look them up."

The two men shook hands and Benny headed back to the rented house, a couple more trips to the dump and the house would be cleaned out. The only items he'd saved was his mama's dime store jewelry and the cigar box she kept it in, his clothes, and the stolen Bible that he threw in a box with his clothes.

Hoping for a new start, he wanted to forget everything about his former life, hopefully little by little his memories would fade, just like the designs on the old furniture he'd taken to the dump. Soon a new adventure would begin. Looking north toward a town called Beckley, he smiled. Would the Blackwells accept him? Did he really want them to, or even care?

CHAPTER 16

But now, O Lord, thou art our father; we are the clay,
and thou our potter; and we all are the work of thy hand.

~ Isaiah 64:8

KATHERINE DREADED THE IMPENDING VISIT from Stan. How was she going to tell him that she would soon be moving over a hundred miles away? She didn't see the need in telling him until she'd gathered all the information and paperwork the college needed and found out if she would be accepted into the nursing program.

Tomorrow she should be able to go to her old high school and get her transcript to mail to the college. She knew she was cutting it close for the winter enrollment but she had to try. If she didn't get accepted she'd try again for the spring semester.

A nurse? Her entire life God had been molding and forming her for this moment. Why else would He have entrusted her with the care of Grandma Mame and Grandpa Clint?

She knew being a nurse would be a very hard profession, a job that would require not only a sharp mind, but also a caring and compassionate heart, and unconditional love for all people.

Katherine could barely contain her joy. For the first time in her nineteen years she knew what it felt like to dream.

A tap at the door brought Katherine back to reality. She hadn't even heard Stan drive up, but there he was. He certainly was a handsome man. Even with the graying at his temples he hardly looked thirty years old.

"Hey, Stan. Come in. How are you?"

Stan stepped through the opened screen door and took Katherine by the shoulders and gave her a sweet peck on the cheek. The kiss was innocent enough, but Katherine knew better.

"I know you must be tired from traveling all day, but I just had to ask if you'd like to have dinner with me on Saturday night? We could go into town and try out that new Italian restaurant. Some of my colleague's have eaten there and say it is delicious. We could make a night of it and go to a movie afterward. I know it's not been that long since your grandparents died, but I believe it's time for us to start living our lives . . . together."

Oh boy, here it comes. Katherine knew it would be only a matter of time before Stan expected more from her than friendship. She could see it in his eyes. An innocent peck on the check soon would not be enough for this man.

Should she give up her dreams and get married, have a couple of kids and make Stan happy? What is God's will for her life? Certainly not to marry and commit to someone she didn't love.

No. First Katherine had to live out the vision for her life. She wouldn't live in the shadow of this coal mine town like her Grandma Mame had. There was a big world out there and Katherine intended to see it, smell it, and experience it!

Katherine heard the words coming from Stan's lips but they held no interest to her. Why, he hadn't even asked about her day and

Grandpa Clint's farm. She prayed she'd be accepted into the nursing program at Surry Community College, then she could get out of this town and away from Stan.

"Katherine, are you okay? If I didn't see you with my own eyes, I'd swear you were a hundred miles away. You look pale, too. Today was just too much for you. I'll help you find a realtor to sell your grandfather's house. You won't even have to go back to that foreign place. You can stay right here, where I can keep an eye on you and look out for your well-being."

Katherine couldn't believe what she was hearing. Who was he to do her thinking for her? Not to mention treating her like a child who couldn't make decisions for herself? She had to put a stop to this now.

"No, Stan. I'll handle Grandpa Clint's estate. I'm not entirely sure what I'm going to do with it yet."

"What do you mean you're not sure what you're going to do with it? Why, a place that far from your home here in Beckley is no good to you. Yes, I'll check into realtors in that area and take care of all the details. No need for you to worry with any of the transactions. The realtor can get an appraisal and have it on the market within a couple of weeks."

Katherine stood with her mouth gaping open. This man in front of her thinks he had her life all figured out, but it wasn't his for the figuring.

Still, Katherine was torn between his wants and her needs. Stan had been her friend and confidant for two years. She didn't want to hurt his feelings. He'd been so good to Grandma Mame when she was first diagnosed with Alzheimer's. She didn't know what to do.

Clearing her throat, Katherine took a step back from Stan, then turned her back completely on him and prayed for the right words to say. "Stan, I won't be talking to any realtor any time soon and you won't either. I appreciate your help and all the ways you've taken care of my grandparents and me. I will forever be indebted to you. But, I have plans, things I want to do with my life. I don't want to rush into anything, especially not sell Grandpa's house. Not yet anyway, and maybe never. I hope you understand."

Every word from Katherine chiseled a piece of Stan's heart away. He felt the sweat bead up on his forehead and he had to remind himself to breathe. He was at a complete loss for words. Never in a million years did he expect Katherine to stand up to him with her own thoughts. Who was this person in front of him? Of course, she was still in shock losing both her grandparents within two weeks of each other. He'd just have to be patient with her and guide her in the way he thought things should go.

"Of course, Katherine, I understand the way you must feel about your grandfather's farm. It does belong to you now and you have every right to do with it as you see fit. If I can help you sell it when the time comes, just let me know. Now, how about dinner and that movie Saturday night?"

Stan's easygoing way was one of the things she loved about him. He had always been patient and respectful with her, why would she think he would be otherwise now?

"Yes, of course, dinner and a movie sound great. I'll be ready by five, and thank you for being so understanding while I feel my way through these decisions I have to make."

"You know I'll always be here for you. I'd move mountains for you with nothing more than a teaspoon if I had to."

Stan turned and carefree as any other day hollered back over his shoulder, "See you on Saturday, sweetie."

Katherine watched Stan pull out of her driveway. This was going to be much harder than she'd thought. Yes, Stan had a gentle, helpful spirit, but he was still a man, and he wouldn't wait forever. Didn't he realize that he had already lived eleven years more than she had? He had an education and a job that he loved. She needed time to accomplish those same things. She'd tell him her plans on Saturday. He'd understand.

Stan smiled and waved to Katherine as she stood in the doorway watching him leave. He knew it would be just a matter of time before he had her molded into the woman he needed her to be. Soon she would be all his, a beautiful wife to love, and someone to love him back. Stan smiled as he dreamed of their future.

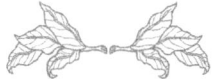

The dream was so real he could smell the dried blood on his fingers. Body parts were everywhere, a leg, a finger, an ear, a ripped open heart, a hand, a slit throat. Would he ever be able to sleep an entire night again without reliving the horror?

CHAPTER 17

*Thou, which hast shewed me great and sore troubles, shalt quicken
me again, and shalt bring me up again from the depths of the earth.*

~ Psalm 71:20

BENNY WAS ON THE ROAD before daylight. His headlights
reflected off buildings, bridges, and road signs that were all familiar
to him. He'd lived his entire life here at Folly Beach. He knew the
best places to go crabbing and where to gig a flounder. He knew the
precise and perfect roll of the tide, the salt smell in the air and the
taste of it on his lips.

Benny felt he'd soon be back; the ocean was bred into him. But
what about the mountains where his relatives live? He had no idea
how much family he had. He was only sure of the one named Hank,
the one the warden said would claim his daddy's body. All he knew
was that they owned the Blackwell Tobacco Company. Beyond that,
he was completely unaware of anything about his dead daddy's family.
His mother had known very little about her boyfriend's family—only
that Benny's grandfather was a man named Jack Marsh, and that he
was dead, too.

Benny didn't have a clue what he was going to do when he got
to Beckley. How do you introduce yourself to a family who doesn't

know you exist? He had a lot of time to think it over. It was more than a four hundred mile trip to Beckley. If he drove it straight through he should get there way before the sun went down.

The first and only time he'd traveled this road heading west was when his mama had been with him. They had been on their way to meet his daddy. And what a reunion it had been. He'd introduced himself all fine and proper to a pale, bloody corpse. Had Benny's daddy been that bad of a person? A killer, drug dealer, and philanderer? Leaving his poor girlfriend to fend for herself, and with a baby on the way?

Benny had to give his daddy some credit—Trudy had never been able to find Ben to tell him he was going to be a daddy. So maybe if he had of known things would have been different. Maybe he would have come back to be a father to his son.

If a man was going to be a womanizer and love them and leave them, Ben Paddington appeared to have been a master at it. Or was he?

But what did Benny really know about his dead daddy, other than what the newscaster said that night all those months ago? His mama had recognized Ben's picture on the television after he'd been arrested. Then his mama had gotten sick so they couldn't travel to see him for a long time. If they'd just have gone sooner, then Ben would have been alive.

Benny couldn't help but wonder what kind of man would kill his own brother, and why? What had happened to turn brother against brother?

Benny rolled these questions over and over in his head. He needed answers. He needed to know where his daddy had come from, and why he'd turned out so seemingly evil. Hadn't he always heard that there are always two sides to every story?

As the miles rolled by the humming of the truck tires soothed Benny's anxious nerves. Each stop he and his mama had made on their previous trip saddened him. He'd loved his dear mama, weaknesses and all. Would he have learned to love his daddy if he'd gotten the chance to know him?

There must be a secret room in a person's heart that makes them overlook the faults in the ones they love. There has to be a section in a person's brain that helps them forget the bad and focus only on the good in their kin.

These thoughts conjured up images of Benny's one and only pet dog, a scrubby mixed bread shepherd of some kind. When he first showed up at Benny and Trudy's house Benny had been mean to him, throwing rocks and kicking the dog. For days, this went on. That sorry, no-good mongrel just wouldn't give up and go away. Every day he kept coming to the back door whining, begging for food. Finally, Trudy gave in and threw him a stale biscuit.

From that day on, Mutt became his best friend. So maybe people are kind of like that dog. He forgot the way Benny was mean to him and loved him in spite of the way he was treated.

Before Benny knew it he had dreamed his way over the Virginia State line. Another few hours and he'd arrive in Beckley. Then what?

Parts of a verse from that stolen Bible of his mama's came into his head, something about having troubles but then rising up from the depths of the earth.

Was Benny's luck about to change? Would his newfound family welcome him like he and his mama had welcomed that old dog named Mutt? Benny would soon find out.

CHAPTER 18

That the aged men be sober, grave, temperate,
sound in faith, in charity, in patience.

~ Titus 2:2

HANK SETTLED INTO THE WORN leather chair in the same office his mother Mary had built all those years ago. His brothers, James, Timothy, Thomas, and William, would soon arrive. Hank lifted a pen from the desk and looked at his swollen knuckles. Arthritis was in every one of his joints and these cool fall mornings weren't helping. The brothers were not young men anymore either. Hank was the oldest at sixty-five, while William, the youngest, had just turned fifty. Where had the years gone?

This would be Hank's last year residing as president of Blackwell Tobacco Company. He would retire and drive Olivia around the country sightseeing. The Blackwell brothers had expanded on the prosperity of their mother. Working hard, staying sober, being sound in their faith, not to mention being very generous to several charities . . . all of which had helped to build their tobacco kingdom.

Today he would tell his brothers and they could decide who would take over the responsibility of running a company that sustained their five families. Would one of the brothers reign or would the tobacco stick be passed to one of Mary's grandsons?

They also needed to discuss Katherine and her future. Since Katherine was only nineteen they felt responsible for her well-being since Mame and Clint had now passed away.

The brothers all arrived within five minutes of each other and took seats in the office surrounding their mother's large mahogany desk.

"What's up, Hank? Not often we get called into a meeting. Sort of makes me feel like I was in school again and getting called to the principal's office." All the brothers had a good laugh but knew something pretty serious was happening by the look on their oldest brother's face.

"What is it, Hank? We got problems?" Without waiting for an answer, James continued. "I checked the price of tobacco this morning and it looks like it's holding its own, even with the Attorney General's warnings that tobacco may be causing cancer. Can you believe we have to have a warning on every pack? And now we can't even advertise our products on television, magazines, or the radio. Before long, just breathing will be outlawed. How's a man to survive with all these rules beating down on him?"

Being next to the oldest, James was usually more vocal than the rest of the brothers.

"No, James. This isn't about tobacco prices or advertising laws. As I've been hinting at for the past couple of years, it's time for me to retire. Before my health gets any worse and this arthritis takes over my entire body, I want to spend more time with Olivia. We've barely left Beckley over a handful of times these past forty-five years. All she talks about is traveling to Alaska and seeing Niagara Falls. So by George, we're going to do it.

"As of December thirty-first the Blackwell Tobacco Company will no longer employ me. I will be a retired man of leisure. So, you four need to decide who the new leader of the company will be."

"Not me," James said. "I'm just holding on until I'm sixty-five. I've just got a couple of years then I'm out of here, too. I'm perfectly satisfied with overseeing the warehouse, just like I've done the past forty years."

Timothy, Thomas, and William all looked at each other like they'd been caught stealing a cookie. Eyes wide and mouths gaping, they didn't say a word.

The brothers knew this day would eventually come, but they were happy with things the way they were. They all had their own responsibilities, and knew their jobs well. Of course, there had been times when they'd had disagreements, but they'd always held each other in the highest respect, remembering the days growing up, wrestling those first few acres of tobacco from the rocky hillside. None of them were strangers to hard work.

"You can count me out, too," Timothy said. "You know I can't be gone from Mozelle any more than I already am. When her multiple sclerosis flares up I have to be with her. Sometimes she can't even hold herself up."

"Well, I guess it's between Thomas and William," Hank said.

"I'll make this easy. I've been thinking about this for a long time," William said. "Unlike you men, I never married, and have lived in the company's housing all these years, so I have saved me a nice little nest egg. Any day now I plan on skipping this place, finding me a nice piece of land on the New River, and building me a sweet little cabin. I've heard the small mouth bass are huge in that river. Might even buy me one of them fancy condo's down at Carolina Beach and fish there, too. So no, my plans are not to spend the rest of my life just saving more money. I'm ready to start spending and enjoying my life. Haven't we all worked enough for one lifetime?"

All eyes turned to Thomas, the only brother who hadn't declined the position.

"That leaves you, brother. What do you say?" Hank asked.

Thomas was silent for a minute; you could tell he was mulling the conversation over in his head.

"You know I'm not a young man either. I'll be fifty-four in a few weeks. Maybe it's time to hand over the leadership to one of our children. I'll have to talk to Nellie and pray about this." Thomas stood to leave.

"Wait, there's one more thing. We need to talk about Katherine. As you know her Grandpa Clint left her a small house down in North Carolina. I think she is seriously considering moving there and going to nursing school at a local community college. Do you think that is a good idea? She's only nineteen years old."

"I don't see how we can stop her. She's old enough to make her own decisions, and besides, with everything that girl has been through her insides are probably as old as our outsides look. Nothing we can do but let her go, and pray for the best," James said.

All five nodded in agreement.

"Suppose there's not a thing in this world we can do about it. It might be good for her to get out of these mountains, and I believe she'll make a fine nurse. Look how she took care of Sis and Clint. She's got the gift of caring. We need to let her go with our blessing," William said.

"I can go down and check on her more often when I retire," Hank said.

"I will stop by and see her in between trips from my cabin by the river and my condo at the ocean," William said with a huge smile.

A knock turned their attention to the door.

"Who could that be? I thought everyone had gone home for the day," Timothy said.

James, who was closest to the door, rose to answer the knock.

CHAPTER 19

For I was an hungred, and ye gave me meat: I was thirsty,
and ye gave me drink: I was a stranger, and ye took me in . . .

~ Matthew 25:35

IT HADN'T BEEN HARD FOR Benny to find the location of the
Blackwell Tobacco Warehouse. The service station attendant had
been very informative. The man not only told Benny how to get to
the warehouse, he also told him how nice the entire family was, and
that they didn't act all biggity just because they were rich by West
Virginia standards. The attendant even speculated on whether or not
the Blackwell brothers' sister, Mame, had been sick with Alzheimer's
or if she was indeed just a crazy old woman who had cut herself off
from society. And, the granddaughter called Katherine who had
turned hermit herself, giving up her life as a teenager to take care of
the old woman and her sick husband.

Benny left the service station wondering if all his kinfolk were
head crazy. And, it sounded like this crazy woman, who would have
been his grandmother, was now dead. Benny now sat in his pickup
truck outside a huge building with a sign over the door that read,
"Office." It was eleven past five in the afternoon and he'd watched

vehicle after vehicle leave for the day. There must have been fifty or more that pulled out.

What was he doing here anyway? Why would these people want to know him? Or, believe that he was any kin to them? He had uncles—the service station man said there were five of them. Were they all behind that door? Should he tell them who he was or just feel them out, maybe apply for a job?

Even as Benny opened the truck door and stepped out, he didn't know what he was going to do or say.

Since the sign said "Office" he didn't know whether to walk right in or knock. Taking a deep breath, he chose to knock.

The sound of footsteps coming toward the door sounded like the waves washing up on shore at home during the onset of a hurricane. Benny felt overwhelmed. Is that what this was going to feel like? What would he say? What was the worst that could happen? Surely the hurricane waters wouldn't engulf him, it was only water and these bodies behind that door were only men.

The door opened to a reveal a man in his late fifties, maybe early sixties, a nice-looking guy for his age. He didn't look like a wealthy business owner with his dirty flannel shirt and worn jeans.

"Can I help you, son?" James asked.

Another deep breath, and Benny just did what he knew to do . . . tell the truth.

"Yes, sir. I'm looking for the Blackwell family."

"Well you've found them. Part of us, anyway. I'm James"—motioning toward each of his brothers, he introduced them—"and these are my brothers, Hank, Timothy, Thomas, and William. Now, what can we do for you?"

Before Benny could answer, Hank stood up and walked toward the young boy. "Do I know you, son? You look so familiar. Have you worked here before? I know I've seen you somewhere before today."

"No, sir. I'm sure we've never met. I'm from down in Folly Beach. Never been here in Beckley except passing through a few months ago on my way to Moundsville to the state penitentiary to see my daddy."

Time stood as still as a copperhead just before it strikes.

"Moundsville? What did you say you were doing up at the penitentiary?" All kinds of thoughts swept through Hank's mind. Somehow, he knew this boy was connected to his dead nephew. After a pause, he said, "Ben?"

"No, name's Benny, Benny Bauguess. But my mama told me Ben Marsh or Paddington was my daddy. I couldn't rightly guarantee if I was his or not by the way he looked dead, but I know my mama didn't lie about it, so it's a fact that Ben was my father."

The brothers looked shocked. Benny knew they were being cautious about who he really was and what he wanted. *Do they think I look like their nephew?* Their silence was etching on Benny's nerves. What were they thinking? Could they see any resemblance in him and the little dark-haired boy his daddy had once been?

The brothers were quiet remembering Ben as the little boy who'd come to visit when their mama Mary was dying, this young man definitely had Ben Paddington's genes, with his dark hair and olive skin like his grandfather, Jack Marsh.

Not being able to stand the silence any longer, Benny asked, "I was wondering if you could tell me about my daddy. You see, I'd never seen him until I saw his mug shot on television when he was arrested. My mama recognized him from over twenty years ago when he'd had his way with her when she was only fifteen then run off." Nervous, Benny rambled on, "What kind of man was my daddy? What did he do for a living? Was he ever married? Do I have brothers and sisters?" Benny didn't give the uncles a chance to answer, but kept talking.

"My mama died a couple of months ago, so now I'm pretty much on my own. A man gets to pondering when he's by himself. You want to know things like what kind of man had sired him, and why he was in prison. I just need to know some things . . . I need to know."

The brothers watched as this stranger in Ben's skin that claimed to be their great-nephew wiped at a single tear as it slid down his cheek then dropped from his chin. Was it all an act? Were they looking at a con artist? Only time would reveal this man's true character.

The brothers looked from one to the other, speechless. Then they all turned to Hank, who had always taken charge. Hank knew they looked to him for guidance, but for the life of him no revelation came to him. Should he trust this boy or turn him away? Hank searched his heart and knew the answer.

"Benny. It was Benny, right?"

"Yes, sir, Benny. Benny Bauguess."

"So, you just arrived in town, right?"

"Just pulled in from Folly Beach when I knocked on the door. Been driving since before daylight this morning."

"Do you have anywhere to stay? A plan for the night?"

"No, sir, probably just pull over and sleep in my truck."

Silence took over the room like a man under conviction of sin.

Finally, Hank spoke, "We've got an empty company house just a half mile down the road. Why don't you settle there for the night and we'll figure all this out in the morning? The shack ain't much, just a bed, bathroom, and small kitchen, but it's clean, and it's got to be better than that truck seat. We can talk more tomorrow after we've all had time to absorb this news."

Hank avoided eye contact with his brothers, he knew they must think him crazy to invite a stranger into their midst, but he couldn't help himself. When he looked at the boy he couldn't help but see young Ben blowing on the whistle that his cousin had given him.

Hank turned, his eyes still looking at the floor, and headed to open a side drawer in his desk. He took a key from it and walked toward Benny.

"Here, take this. You can stay in the company house until we've figured all this out and we've answered all your questions. Be prepared, son, it might take a while and you might not want to hear some of the truths. Some things may be better left unsaid. But we'll tell you all you want to know, fair enough?"

Benny couldn't believe they were going to give him a place to stay. All he could think to do was mimic his uncle. "Fair enough."

Hank gave Benny directions to the house and without saying another word, Benny turned and left.

"What in the world just happened? Do you really believe that young man is Ben's son?" James asked.

"Well, we may never know the truth, but from the looks of him I'd bet my part of the farm he is who he says he is," Hank said.

"What do you think he wants? Will he be satisfied with only answered questions?" William asked.

"We'll soon find out, brothers. We'll soon find out. Let's go home. We've all had enough surprises for one day," Hank said.

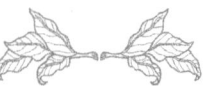

The time is near. A day of reckoning. His time . . . The world will finally revolve his way and everything will go as planned. No more assuming, only the truth.

CHAPTER 20

But the Lord sent out a great wind into the sea, and there was a
mighty tempest in the sea, so that the ship was like to be broken.

~ Jonah 1:4

BENNY SAT IN HIS TRUCK a few minutes before cranking it. What
just happened? Cry? Benny couldn't believe he'd started to cry in
front of them. Must have been his nerves. He'd not shed a tear, except
for when his mama was sick and dying, and then when he'd been a
small child and his mama switched him with a green willow branch
for saying a cuss word. A grown man tearing up like that, Benny felt
ashamed of himself. He bet those men were laughing their insides out
at him. Well, they wouldn't be laughing when he got through with
them. No, sir. Benny made a decision in that moment, that not only did
he deserve some of the Blackwell wealth, he now knew he wanted it.

Turning the key, the Ford engine cranked up. Benny shifted to
reverse and gently eased out on the road. Just a short distance down
from the Blackwell Warehouse sat a small farm house. There were
three numbers over the doorframe that matched the address Hank
had given him.

Benny opened the door and jumped from the seat of his truck.
He stood looking at the small cottage. From the look of the outside

this place in front of him was even smaller than the one he'd grown up in. The weatherboard had been painted a pale yellow that had faded over time. The tin roof was corroded with a bit of rust here and there. There was no front porch, just an oversized flat rock for a doorstep. The yard around the house was small with a poplar tree towering on the west side of the house casting a shadow over Benny's new residence. Except for the grass needing mowing, it wasn't a bad place. It was sort of cute in a way.

Benny reached in the back of the truck bed and grabbed the satchel that held all his belongings. He'd never had much, but what more could a man want? Two or three changes of clothes, a couple pair of socks, and boots.

Benny settled in at the small house. It proved to be very comfortable. Furnished with a couple of chairs around a kitchen table. A couch, a chair that reclined when you pulled a lever on the side, a black and white television set that picked up three channels, and a fireplace. Benny had no idea where he'd be when winter hit, but he doubted he'd be around here to light a fire.

There was one bedroom and a bathroom with a toilet, shower stall, and pedestal sink. A shelf over the toilet held half a dozen white towels and washcloths. There was even a new bar of soap lying by the sink.

The bedroom was barely big enough to cuss a cat in but it housed a double bed with fresh sheets folded and lying at the bottom of a stain free mattress. That was certainly a first for Benny. The springs under the mattress squeaked loudly when he sat down on the edge. At the bottom of the bed was a chest, a perfect place to house his belongings, and somewhere to sit when he shed his boots.

Benny rose and went into the kitchen. There on the counter sat a short miniature refrigerator, and a two-burner hot plate. There was a cabinet under the makeshift stove and a one-hole aluminum sink with a cabinet over it. Benny opened the door over the sink and found two shelves. The lower one held a coffee cup, two plates, a couple of bowls and some silverware. On the top were a small saucepan and a cast iron frying pan.

When Benny opened the cabinet door beneath the hot plate, he found several canned food items. Three cans of different kinds of beans, home canned corn, pickles, and two mason jars, one said blackberry jam, on top of the other said peach preserves.

Benny thought about opening a can of beans but wasn't sure if he should or not. He'd make a trip into town for a few groceries tomorrow. Turning, he opened the door to the refrigerator and found it completely empty. Yes, he'd have to get a few things to hold him over until it was time to move on.

By the time Benny put the sheets on the bed, darkness had fallen. He'd found a hand-stitched quilt and two pillows in the chest so he spread it out over the bed and punched the pillows a couple of times before throwing them back on the bed.

After a hot shower Benny's stomach was growling, so he opened up a can of pork 'n beans and ate them cold, straight out of the can. He'd replace the food item tomorrow when he went to the store.

With his belly semi-full he turned off the television that was mostly a screen of snow flakes, then checked the front door to make sure it was locked. There was just something unnerving about being in a strange house in a different part of the country. Right at that moment Benny missed the smell of salt in the air and the stinging scent of his mama's cigarette. *I'm going to get what is rightfully ours, Mama. I know that's what you'd want.*

The bed was actually better than his old one back home and it had been a very long day, so Benny was asleep before he could even count sheep. But the good night's sleep was short-lived. Benny dreamed. Tossing this way and that upon the crests of huge waves, the tempest of the sea threw him from bough to stern. Relentless, the sea pitched and churned and upon the tips of every wave was the blood red slit of his daddy's throat. Would he ever stop dreaming of these horrible images?

Before daylight, Benny rose and dressed in the same clothes he'd wore the day before. Starving, he left the little house to find some breakfast. What would the day bring? Should he go to the uncles and demand his father's inheritance? Or, bide his time and see what happened?

He passed the tobacco warehouse, then another farmhouse on the right at least twice the size of the one he'd spent the night in. Little did he know that was where cousin Katherine lived. Would they meet? Become friends, or enemies, like her and Benny's daddy?

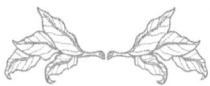

Katherine heard the loud muffler of a truck as it passed her house. Looking at the clock it was barely five o'clock. Who could that be this early in the morning? She was used to the sound of her uncles', aunts', and cousins' cars and trucks, and the company house down the road was empty, so who could it have been?

Katherine drifted back to sleep. She too was restless, dreaming the nightmare that had not plagued her since Grandma Mame died.

But this morning her fears seemed very real as Uncle Ben chased her around the house.

The sound of purring woke Katherine. Her kitty, Little Bit, was nestled up close to her ear. It was Saturday. Dread welled up inside her. Was it the awful dreams she'd had about Ben chasing her or was it because Stan was going to pick her up at five? Should she tell him her plans of moving before the movie or wait until he brought her home?

She hated the thought of hurting Stan. He'd been so good to her this past year. A sweeter soul she'd probably never find. Maybe one day they could be more than friends, but for now Katherine knew she had to do some things for herself. She had a deep burning desire, a calling to become a nurse. Even though her high school years were tainted by rumors that her Uncle Ben had started about her, she'd learned to be tough when faced with snide remarks about her being "easy," or snickering about her living with her crazy grandmother. Then when word got around that she had stabbed her own uncle, what few so-called friends she'd had disappeared.

Katherine eased out of bed trying not to disturb Little Bit. The kitten was growing every day but still looked tiny, just a wad of fuzzy white hair lying on the ivory cotton sheets.

The early fall day was all aglow with sunlight. Katherine knew if she wasn't careful, she was going to become lazy, sleeping until after the sun came up. That would have been unheard of while she was taking care of her grandparents. There was always something to do. Cleaning, laundry, cooking . . . now only for herself.

She needed to get busy. Katherine couldn't spend day after day sleeping late. She had to accomplish something. Much more than mopping the floor, she had to get back to school and make something of herself.

Before Katherine knew it, it was three in the afternoon, she had done two loads of laundry, ironed her favorite blouse, along with several other small chores. It would soon be time to get ready for her outing with Stan. What was she so worried about? It wasn't like she was going to tell him she never wanted to see him again. She just had some things to do before she could make a commitment to anyone. He'd understand. He may not like it but Stan would be fine with whatever she needed to do. He was the most thoughtful person she had ever known.

At 4:45, Katherine heard the car tires crunch on the gravel driveway out front. Stan had arrived. Katherine met him at the door; a shoulder bag looped over one arm and a sweater over the other. It was always cold in those movie theaters.

Katherine had the front door closed before Stan had time to help her with it. He was always so polite, opening doors for her, holding her arm as they walked. You'd think she was a tottering old woman not sure of her steps any longer.

"Katherine, here let me help you."

"It's okay, Stan, I think I can make it down two steps by myself."

"Of course you can—I didn't mean you couldn't—it's just something I do. I like to take care of people."

"I know you do, and you do a very good job of it."

Dropping the subject, Katherine walked past Stan, heading to the passenger side of Stan's car. It was a beautiful autumn afternoon, not too warm. There was a crisp bite in the air, and it refreshed Katherine as she breathed it in.

Of course Stan stepped in front of Katherine so he could open the door for her. Katherine had never understood the reasoning for thinking a girl could not open her own door.

"Thank you, Stan, but really, you don't have to open every door for me."

"Of course I do. That's what a gentleman does for his lady."

His lady? Katherine spun the two words around in her head. Her news was going to be a lot harder to share with Stan than she had imagined.

"Where would you like to eat? Are you in the mood for steak, chicken, Italian, or plain old pizza?" Stan asked.

"I really don't care. That new Italian restaurant you were telling me about is right on the way to the movie theater, why don't we try that? Some pasta sounds good to me," she said.

"Well, here we go, Italian it is."

Katherine couldn't help but feel guilty. Stan was always so good to her. Never denying her anything. She couldn't let these tender emotions over rule what she knew had to be said. After the movie she'd tell him her news. She had to.

THE NIGHT WAS OVER BEFORE Katherine knew it. Supper had been delicious and the new western, *The Hired Hand*, had been quite entertaining. At 9:45, the movie was over and they were on their way back to Katherine's house.

"Stan, do you have time to come in for a cup of coffee or hot chocolate? I've got something I need to talk to you about."

Stan's heart leaped in his chest. Things could not be going any better. He reached his left hand down in the side pocket of his door pouch and touched the wrapping of the small box. His plan was unfolding perfectly.

"Of course, I'd love to have a nice cup of hot chocolate. Do you have marshmallows?"

Katherine couldn't help but smile. In some ways Stan seemed to be a young boy. Was eleven years' difference in their age really that big of a deal?

Benny finally found a diner that was just turning their lights on when he pulled in. The door was unlocked and the sign was flipped to open.

The middle-aged waitress hollered at him as she walked behind the counter. "Be with you in a few . . . got to get the coffee going. You want a cup?"

"Yes, ma'am. Take your time."

Benny was in no hurry. The only plans he had was to go back to the warehouse and talk to his uncles. But before that he'd talk to as many of the locals as he could. People loved to gossip. Sometimes you can learn more from a stranger than you could your own kin.

It took about five minutes before the waitress showed up with a steaming cup of black coffee.

"Here you go, mister. You'll have to settle for me this morning, Hatchet's late again. That man just can't get up in the mornings. Stays up all night playing music and partying. If you don't want nothing fancy, I can stir up a scrambled egg and fry some bacon."

"Sounds good to me. If you'll throw in a couple slices of toast or a biscuit, I'd be obliged."

"Toast I can do, biscuits I cannot. You'll have to wait on our cook, Hatchet, if you want a biscuit. My old man used to complain so much about my biscuits. One of the last things I ever told him was he'd never see me sifting flour ever again, and he didn't."

"Toast will be fine. Do you mind me asking why you call the cook Hatchet?"

"No, don't mind at all. He served twenty years in the state pen for nearly chopping off his wife's leg when he found her in bed with another man. Can you believe that? The things people do. He'd probably have hacked them both to shreds, but he slipped on his old ladies bra and fell on the blade. Cut his belly wide open. He'll show you the scar if you ask him to. Judge gave him twenty years for attempted murder.

"He came home about five years ago, and everybody has called him Hatchet since. The wife and boyfriend moved way off up to Wheeling. If I was her, I'd be scared he'd come find me and finish the job. You ready for that grub?"

"Yes, ma'am. I sure am. By the way, name's Benny. Benny Bauguess."

"Well, it's right nice to meet you, Benny. I'm Lois. Are you just passing through?"

"Maybe. Don't know yet. Going to be visiting with my cousins for a while. Might be here a day, or maybe two or three."

"Who are your cousins?"

"The Blackwells. You know them?"

"Why Lord have mercy, yes. Everybody knows about them, and their tobacco company. Them's some good boys. Every one of them comes by at least once a week. Sometimes they'll bring their wives, sometimes not. My sister Nancy helped care for Mame when she first started losing her mind. That granddaughter of hers, Katherine, let her go when she found out her friend Stan Matthews was paying for her to help.

"Katherine Paddington—now there's a proud one, and strong, too. Had to fend off her uncle Ben and take care of her Grandma Mame, and then her Grandpa Clint. She helped them all till their dying day. That young'un never has had a life of her own. Hope she don't turn out like her Grandma and live like a hermit."

Benny sat listening, yes, he was sure Lois was probably telling him things his uncles never would. All in good time he'd know all about his kin, all in good time.

"Lordy, help my time. I've got to get busy. That Hatchet, where is he? Be right back with your breakfast and top off that coffee."

"One more thing, Lois. This girl named Katherine, does she live around here?"

"Oh yeah, down at Miss Mame's house. It was her mama Mary's place way back when before she died. It's the farmhouse on the left right before you get to the warehouse."

Lois didn't wait for more questions. The door slammed and three more customers walked in. Benny knew Lois wouldn't have time for any more news sharing today, but there was always tomorrow.

Benny remembered the house Lois was talking about. Not a mile from where he was staying. What had Lois meant about Katherine having to fend off her uncle Ben, his daddy? And Lois had confirmed that he'd never meet his Grandma Mame, for she was just like his mama, dead.

CHAPTER 21

I will stand upon my watch, and set me upon the tower, and will watch to see what he will say unto me, and what I shall answer when I am reproved.

~ Habakkuk 2:1

KATHERINE PUT THE KEY IN the front door lock and turned it. Even with her Uncle Ben dead she still locked her doors. A habit she had formed as a young girl to keep Uncle Ben out of her bedroom.

"I'll put the milk on the stove. Make yourself comfortable."

Stan watched Katherine lay her sweater over the back of the couch and go into the kitchen. He put his hand in his jacket pocket and felt the box that promised his and Katherine's future. He'd slipped the box in his pocket before getting out of the car. He was so excited. Would a few months' engagement be enough? He hoped Katherine would want a late fall wedding or at least a Christmas wedding. He couldn't wait to tell his sisters Annie and Rebecca. They could help Katherine make all the plans. The wedding would be perfect.

"Here we go. Hot chocolate with marshmallows on top."

Katherine handed Stan the cup, then sat down beside him. Silence folded around them like a winter blanket of snow. Half their drinks was gone before Stan spoke.

"Katherine, I have something very important to ask you."

"And I have something to tell you."

Stan sat his mug down on the coffee table, never acknowledging Katherine's words. He rose, put his hand in his jacket pocket, then slipped off the couch and onto the floor and bowed down before her on one knee.

What was Stan doing? Did he drop something? Katherine's heart began to race, making her head swim. No, this couldn't be happening. It was too soon. She wasn't ready for this. Her mind screamed NO!

"My dear Katherine. I know you must realize how I feel about you. I have loved you from almost the first moment I laid eyes on you. I love your caring nature, strength, courage, spirit, and beauty. You will make me the happiest man in the world if you would honor me by becoming my wife."

Stan took the box out and opened the lid to reveal a solitaire diamond with black onyx orbs two on each side of the diamond.

"Will you be my wife? Will you, Katherine?"

Katherine sat as still as a groundhog being held in the sights of a twelve gauge shotgun. How could this be happening? Why now? It was going to be harder than ever to tell him she would be moving to North Carolina to attend school. Maybe one day she would be ready for this but not now, she was sure of that.

Katherine took a deep breath, reached out and closed the lid on the ring box.

"Stan the ring is beautiful, and I am honored that you would want me to become your wife, but I'm just not ready for that kind of commitment."

Silence echoed off the walls. All of a sudden Little Bit's purring sounded louder than a chain saw. Stan rose, putting the ring back in his pocket. He stared at Katherine as if she'd just shot him in the heart. His brokenness was obvious.

"Stan, I'm sorry. Let me explain. Come sit."

The last thing Katherine wanted to do was hurt Stan, but she had to be her own person before she could be someone else's forever.

"Please Stan, sit. We need to talk."

Stan choose to sit in the chair facing Katherine. She could barely stand seeing the torment on his face. Should she reconsider, tell him yes, she'd be his wife? What then? Continue to live her life for someone else and forget all her own dreams? The contents of her Grandpa Clint's letter echoed in her head, *I don't think Stan is the right one for you* . . . No, she couldn't do it, she wouldn't.

"The time for us to be together may someday come. I can't accept your ring right now, but one day I may, that is if you still want me. Now I have some things I have to do with my life and for myself. I'm moving to North Carolina to live in Grandpa Clint's house and go to nursing school at Surry Community College. With the money he left me, and if I get a part-time job I can do this all on my own. I have to. I want to. Do you understand? I am so very sorry to disappoint you. The timing could not be worse.

"Stan, I owe you so much. You have been so good to me, and to Grandma Mame and Grandpa Clint. I do love you, but I'm not sure what kind of love I feel for you. I can't be someone's future until I pursue my own. I might fail and come dragging my tail between my legs back here to Beckley, but at least I will have tried. I'll never be happy until I give myself this chance. Do you understand?"

Stan sat, rigid as a totem pole. The cat continued to purr; the clock struck 10:30, but time seemed to have stood still.

"Stan? Please talk to me."

Stan cleared his throat, eased up to the edge of the chair and faced Katherine eye to eye. "Katherine, in less than a year I will be thirty years old. I should have realized a long time ago that I was too old for you. I can't wait forever. What if I want children? A few more years and I'll be old enough to be their grandfather instead of their father?"

Children, how could she think about that now when there were so many other things she needed to do. She didn't think Stan realized just how young she was and how much more life he'd lived than her. She had to get him to understand. She had to stand on her own two feet to prove to herself that she could live on her own before she committed to a relationship . . . and children.

"You're not that old. There's plenty of time for children, but I do understand if you want to see other people, and if you meet someone else, I'll completely understand. Who knows what will happen in the two years it will take me to get my degree?"

Stan listened to Katherine, realizing she couldn't love him like he did her. But he didn't really care, in time she'd learn to love him, he was sure of it. Why, she was practically telling him he should go and find someone else. What could he do to change her mind?

"Katherine, do you realize how far away you'll be from your home and your family? If you needed us it would be hours before one of us could get to you. You can't be serious about living by yourself. A young lady like you could never make it on her own. No, Katherine, you can't go to North Carolina."

Katherine could not believe her ears. Was Stan really telling her what she could and could not do? Obviously, he didn't really know her, or what she had lived through in her short nineteen years. Why she'd even stabbed her Uncle Ben to defend herself. Oh yes, she could take care of herself and live alone, and she would.

"Stan, I'm sorry you feel that way, but I can take care of myself, and I am moving to North Carolina. I've made up my mind. If I get into the fall program I'll be gone in a couple of weeks. If I have to wait until the winter semester I'll leave right after Christmas. Your friendship means the world to me. Please understand."

Stan had to put his hands into his pockets so Katherine wouldn't see them shaking. Just like in 'Nam when he knew the enemy was close, his entire body would start to jerk. What could he do? He'd never felt so helpless.

"Katherine, I am just so afraid for you. All I want to do is take care of you for the rest of your life, but it sounds like your mind is made up. Far be it from me to hold you back from your dreams."

Stan knew words were not going to change Katherine's mind. All he could hope for was that she would fail and soon come back to him. He rose from the chair, stepped around the table, took Katherine by the arms, and pulled her up from the couch. Leaning forward he gently kissed her on the forehead.

"I think you are making a huge mistake but I'll always be here for you. I'm only a phone call away."

Not waiting for a response from Katherine, he turned and walked out the door and out of Katherine's life.

Katherine couldn't stop the tears from running down her face. Was she making the biggest mistake of her life? Should she run and stop him? She took a step toward the door, then another. Softly she called his name, "Stan, Stan. Come back."

Stan never heard Katherine; he was already backing out of the driveway. She was glad because deep down she really didn't want him to come back. She knew her love for him was as a sister to a brother. Katherine knew there must be a deeper love between a man and woman to keep them together for a lifetime.

Stan's harsh words only increased Katherine's will to succeed. She wiped the tears from her cheeks and watched as Stan's taillights faded into the night. She closed the door and turned the button to lock it. Katherine couldn't help but feel relief. She checked the door lock a second time, took a deep breath, and began to ponder her future.

CHAPTER 22

Brethren, I count not myself to have apprehended: but this one thing
I do, forgetting those things which are behind, and reaching forth
unto those things which are before . . .

~ Philippians 3:13

SUNDAY MORNING, BENNY WOKE UP a little later than he had
the previous day. He dressed and made his way out to his truck just as
the first rays of sunlight marked the eastern sky. He knew where he
was headed, back to the café he'd eaten at the day before. Hopefully
the crowd would be thin this morning and Lois would be there and
have time to tell him more about his kin.

The parking lot at Flip's Pancake House had at least a dozen
vehicles parked in it. Well, even if Lois was too busy to talk, he could
get something to eat. That can of sardines and pack of crackers he'd
had last night for supper hadn't done much for a hungry stomach, a
loud growl proved him right.

As soon as Benny walked through the door he spotted them, his
great-uncles, all five of them. They were all dressed up in Sunday
meeting clothes and engrossed in conversation.

Benny didn't know whether to go over to them or shy away
in a booth in the back by himself. All day yesterday he had rode

around. He'd gotten the uncles' addresses out of the phone book so he'd visited each house from a distance. It seemed they all lived on the inherited farmland of their mother, Mary. Their houses were all within a couple of miles of each other. They were modest homes, all five brick ranch style with neatly kept yards. If these men were as rich as Benny was led to believe, then they certainly didn't flaunt it.

Benny had also found the address of Mame Paddington, his so-called grandmother. The grandma that Lois told him had died a few months back. That would also be where his cousin lived. The one who had some kind of bad dealings with his daddy, Ben. This afternoon he might just pay Cousin Katie a visit. *That was her name, wasn't it?* Benny thought to himself.

Benny had hesitated too long, one of the uncles spotted him and was motioning for him to come over. Benny couldn't tell them apart, or know which name went with which face except for the oldest one that had done all the talking on Friday. It was Hank who beckoned him to their table.

"Benny, come on over here and grab a seat. We were just talking about you. Let me introduce my brothers to you again. I'll go down the line by age. I'm Hank. This is James, Timothy, Thomas, and William. Our brother Jared and sister Mame are no longer with us, passed away. Jared died when he was no more than a boy, and we lost Mame less than six months ago."

Then to everyone's surprise, William spoke up. "Mame was your grandmother. She was always so good to me. A mother when my own mama, Mary, didn't have time to be. I remember when mother was dying and Mame brought your father Ben to visit. He couldn't have been more than eight or nine years old. He was a quiet boy, not much to say, but I remember he sure had a good time playing with our kids.

"Hank, wasn't it your boy that gave Ben that whistle? We have Ben's things, just a set of clothes and shoes, and the whistle. It was in his pants pocket. Kept it all these years. Hank, you still got Ben's stuff?"

The brothers were surprised that William was accepting Benny as Ben's son. There was really no way to know for sure but he did favor Ben in more ways than one. Even though he'd never met his daddy, Benny's gestures were similar to Ben's, the way he held himself and the tilt of his head, not to mention the dark hair and complexion.

"No, we left that box of his personal items at Mame's house. Remember, Katherine showed the whistle to Mame and then Mame went to the bedroom and brought out her memory box. I believe there was even a note in there that your daddy had written your grandma. That whistle is in Mame's keepsake box, too. I'm sure Katherine wouldn't mind giving it to you, that is if you want it?"

Benny was still standing. It was so strange to hear people talking about his daddy, a real person who wrote notes to his mama, and carried a boy's whistle in his pocket. It melted his heart to know he was not entirely the evil man he'd been led to believe he was.

"Pull up a seat, son, and order you some breakfast. Then come on to church with us. For years it's been a habit of ours to have breakfast together on Sunday morning. That's really the only time we have to catch up on family matters, and the only time we don't talk about work and the price of dried tobacco," Hank said.

Benny reached behind him and took a chair from another table and placed it between Timothy and Thomas. A waitress came to take their order, but it wasn't Lois, she must be off on Sundays.

"How are you faring at the company house? Got everything you need?" Hank asked.

"Yes, sir, right comfortable little spot. When can I get my daddy's things? I'd really like to know all about him too if you don't mind telling me."

The brothers fell silent. Their food came and they said grace, then gave in to eating instead of talking. Knowing they couldn't put off answering the boy forever, Timothy finally addressed his newfound nephew.

"Benny, before you came in we were trying to decide whether or not to accept you as Ben's son. I suppose William clarified that by calling Mame your grandmother. So be it. Now you have a choice. You can remember your father as a young boy playing with a whistle and his cousins like we've chosen to do, or you can dig up all the skeletons of a man who spent his last days in the state pen.

"Ben's daddy, your grandfather, was a cruel man named Jack Marsh. He killed our brother Jared. He attempted to kill Mame, leaving her in the woods for dead. You already know Ben killed his own brother Walt all those years ago. You saw that on the news. So, have you heard enough? I hope so, because sometimes our sins are better off left buried with the past. That's my advice to you boy, leave the dead buried."

Timothy was a man of few words but when he spoke he was to the point, and again his point had hit the mark.

Benny lowed his head, trying not to picture his very own daddy killing anyone, especially not his brother. And, to hear the things his grandfather did, maybe he didn't want to hear anymore.

Benny knew what his uncle said was probably good, solid advice but he wasn't sure he could leave well enough alone. He wanted to look to the future but he felt a great pull to follow his roots back to the past.

"I must agree with Timothy. You are young, what are you about twenty, twenty-one?" Thomas asked.

"I'll be twenty-one in January."

"Well, you've got your whole life in front of you. I don't know where you came from, or who your mama was, but I do know that even though you got your daddy's and grandpa's bloodline, you don't have to have their sorry, good-for-nothing ways. The choice to live in the light instead of the darkness is yours. Now come on, let's go to church. The wives will be waiting on the porch for us. You coming, Benny?" Thomas asked.

All the brothers thought Thomas had missed his calling by not being a preacher; he always wrapped a sermon around everything he said.

"I might meet you there. Ain't ever been to church though. I don't have any of them fancy Sunday clothes like you're wearing. I guess I'll have to pass on the Sunday preaching. I can get my religion the same as always by reading my mama's stolen Bible."

Thomas and the rest of the brothers didn't ask questions. Some things you're just better off not knowing.

"Well, if you change your mind come on down to the church. It's just a mile down the road. Preaching starts at 10:45," Hank said.

James took the bill and headed to the register. The brothers took turns paying the tab so it was James's turn.

Benny followed James to the counter and told the man taking money to count his out of the Blackwells' tab.

"No way, Benny. Breakfast is on me this time."

"I can pay for my own breakfast; you're already doing enough by giving me a place to stay. I ain't no charity case. I can work and make my own way."

James could only take Benny at his word, and time would eventually reveal the true character of Benny Bauguess, and the kind of man he is.

Benny sat in his truck for a long time, letting the past hour run through his mind. His great-uncles seemed to be fine, church-going men, and they were accepting him into their lives on just his word. He'd not expected them to be so hospitable.

Did he fit in here? Would he eventually see these uncles as real family? Not the kind of kin that he and his mama had known, but family?

Benny had always been a loner. He and his mama had lived a simple life just the two of them. They'd gone to work, then came home to their small apartment, did their chores, cooked supper, went to bed, and got up and did it all over again. When Benny did go out it was usually down to the pier to fish or take his flat bottom wooden boat out in the calmer intercostal waterway to fish under the bridges. His mama went with him one time, but she couldn't swim so she was terrified the entire time and swore she'd never get on another boat, and she hadn't.

Right then, Benny had to swallow down tears. An overwhelming need to see his mama took over every emotion in his body. Just a whiff of cigarette smoke to know she was near, anything to help him not feel so alone.

Was it time to reach forth to the future? To forget those things which were behind?

Benny took a cleansing breath and wiped his eyes. What kind of wuss was he, sitting here crying like a newborn baby? The future was his and there was no better place to start than to visit his cousin, and the house where his grandmother had lived. He'd start by asking for his daddy's belongings. What was the girl's name? Kathy? Katie? He'd soon find out.

CHAPTER 23

Behold, I give unto you power to tread on serpents and scorpions, and over all the power of the enemy: and nothing shall by any means hurt you.

~ Luke 10:19

OLD HABITS ARE HARD TO break. That's why Katherine was up and dressed just before seven on a Sunday morning. She was used to it because she had always had to get up early to take care of Grandma Mame and Grandpa Clint.

She woke even earlier than usual this morning. She couldn't get Stan off her mind and the night before, and she'd had that awful dream again. Had she done the right thing? She had visions of the hurt look on Stan's face all night. Then in her dreams he had walked through a door and disappeared. Just vanished out of sight, like a blanket of fog. One minute it covered the land from earth to sky, next second it lifted and was gone.

Little Bit rubbed against Katherine's leg. That small kitten had been a gift from God. It is amazing how much comfort you can get from a kitten. She reached down and picked up the little ball of fur, hugging it to her gently. Was this cat all she had left? Her uncles were right down the road but they all had their own lives with children and grandchildren to love and care for. Katherine had no one now that Stan was gone?

Katherine heard a few vehicles pass. Most likely her uncles going to Flip's for breakfast just like they did every Sunday morning. She considered getting dressed up and going to church with them but that wasn't a habit she'd had the luxury of doing. She couldn't leave her grandparents, and now, well, she just didn't want to go. She'd rather stay home and sit quietly with Little Bit in her lap reading Grandma Mame's Bible. She couldn't help but think of her grandma. She'd never had friends; she lived inside her head with her own demons. Would Katherine turn out just like her grandmother, a recluse, living in the shadows of the past?

No. As soon as she was accepted into the nursing program she would move to Elkin, to Grandpa Clint's house above the river. Deep down she knew there had to be more to life, a better future than her past had been. The past was just that, the past. She had survived and now she'd either float or drown.

Another vehicle passed, but this time it stopped and backed up. Katherine held Little Bit while looking out the screen door. Someone was just turning around. No, they were coming up the drive. A black Ford pickup, and who was that driving it, and what did they want?

Remembering her childhood, Katherine went into Grandma Mame mode. She ducked her head down and made sure the door was locked, then she crept to the back door and shut and latched it. Katherine wasn't scared, she was just cautious. She was fully aware of what kind of people roamed this land. Some were no better than the serpents and scorpions that hung around the woodshed and creek bed, just like her Uncle Ben.

Peeking out the kitchen window she saw that the truck was almost to the house. She couldn't tell who was driving but she knew it was a stranger because she'd never seen that truck before. It couldn't be one of her cousins come to show off his new hotrod pickup because she knew they'd all be in church.

The truck stopped but the engine kept running. What was that person doing? Several seconds passed before the stranger finally shut off the engine and opened the door. Katherine could now see a pair of legs with cowboy boots unfold from the truck. The man could just as well be faceless because Katherine couldn't see anything but the top of a cowboy hat because the man had his head lowered.

When he got to the front porch, she couldn't see him anymore, but she could hear him knocking. Katherine's heart pounded in her chest. Who was this person and what did he want? No one except family ever came to see her.

"Hello, is anyone home? Hello, are you there, Katie?"

A cold sweat broke out on Katherine's upper lip. Katie? No one had ever called her Katie except her Uncle Ben. This boy must be at the wrong house, if she could only get a look at him. Should she go to the door and tell him he's at the wrong place? *No*, Grandma Mame would say, *trust no one*.

So Katherine stayed silent while she was crouched down in the kitchen floor. Time stood still. The man continued to knock and call out to this person named Katie. Katherine was about to give in and go to the door when he finally gave up and headed back to his pickup. Just before he opened his truck door and got inside, he took his hat off and ran his fingers through his unruly black hair. Uncle Ben's hair.

The next thing Katherine knew she had slumped over in the kitchen floor. She sat for a minute to regain her composure. Had she passed out? What happened? She wasn't sick, and she surely hadn't fallen asleep. Then she heard it, a vehicle had just started its motor and she could tell it was moving up the driveway toward the road. The man's words came back to her swiftly, like a kick in the gut. No doubt this man was her Uncle Ben, but how? He was dead, and he would have been much older than this young man looked.

Katherine was afraid to move. Little Bit strolled over to her and climbed up in her lap. She was frozen in time, back to the years right here in this exact house, to the first time she ever saw her Uncle Ben. Her Grandma Mame had sat right down in the same kitchen floor she was sitting in now and cried when she heard her son Ben was back in their lives. From then on there was nothing but fear and uncertainty.

Surely she had misread the visitor. Feeling silly, Katherine tried to stand up. She was surprised at how weak her legs were.

Was she just under too much stress? Her encounter with Stan last night, her worries over getting into college and moving over a hundred miles away, was a lot to handle at one time. Was she rushing things? Maybe she should just spend the winter here in Beckley and try to enroll in the spring at Surry Community College.

The thought of staying here, in this house doing nothing all winter almost smothered the life out of Katherine. She didn't need to put off living her life any longer. If she stayed it would be harder on Stan, too. Yes, a clean break, that's what she needed.

Laughing at herself for sitting on the floor, she lifted Little Bit from her lap and stood on trembling legs. It was just a coincidence that the stranger at her door resembled Uncle Ben. Maybe she would go to church with her uncles and their families after all. She could use the experience driving and she had to start making herself get out in the world. Katherine knew she was way too much like her

Grandma Mame, she couldn't hide out in this house for the rest of her life.

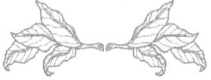

The service had already started when Katherine arrived at Flat Bottom Church of the Brethren. She slipped through the door and luckily there was an empty seat on the next to last bench.

There was a trio singing a familiar hymn that she had heard on the radio many times, *How Great Thou Art*. One man played the guitar while another sung lead, then the others joined in on the chorus and harmonized.

While listening she let her eyes roam. Some of the faces were familiar from seeing them while shopping for groceries and running errands, but most were strangers, just like the man who came knocking at her door that morning. She soon spotted the uncles and their families. The church was small so the Blackwells took up all of the first three benches.

How could it be that she was nineteen years old and hadn't been in this church for at least ten years? When she was much younger and before Grandma Mame got so sick one of her uncles would stop by and pick her up for Sunday School, and of course she went to Bible School in the summer, but by the time she turned ten Grandma Mame really wasn't sick or even that old but she clung to Katherine. Not telling her she couldn't go to church, just encouraging her to stay home with her and they'd read the Bible together. So that's what they did. They'd read the entire Bible through twice.

It was as though Grandma Mame was afraid her granddaughter would leave one day and not come back. Maybe the Alzheimer's had already started to attack her brain. Katherine really didn't mind being a shut-in with her grandma, she enjoyed the solitude and quiet times with Grandma Mame. By the time Katherine was twelve years old she had already told her uncles not to stop anymore to pick her up because her grandma needed her at home.

Was there ever a time when Katherine had not felt responsible? Would she be able to put the needs of others like Stan behind her and move forward and think of herself first? She knew she'd never be satisfied if she didn't try.

Continuing to look around she realized that the sanctuary was very small. As a child it had seemed much bigger. There was probably enough seating for maybe a couple of hundred people and today it was over three-fourths full. The size of the church may have shrunk but the stained-glass windows were just as lovely and alive as her memory recollected. The Bible scenes were all familiar, a group of small children sitting at Jesus's feet, the woman at the well kneeling in front of Jesus as he touches her face, a sinner forgiven and saved by grace. Others she recognized, but her favorite was the one of Jesus ascending into the clouds to heaven.

Katherine remembered well the summer she was nine years old. Her Bible School teacher told them the story of Jesus coming into the world as a baby, then growing up to become the greatest teacher of all time as he roamed through the countryside proclaiming the love of God, His heavenly Father. The teacher told the class that at the young age of thirty-three Jesus went to the cross, taking each and every one of our sins with Him. He suffered and died for all who would call upon the name of the Lord and believe that He is the Son of the living God.

The most miraculous part was that Jesus didn't stay in that tomb. On the third day after His crucifixion, He arose and again walked the earth, revealing Himself to His disciples and others. He told His followers that soon He would have to ascend to His Father in Heaven, but this time for all who believed, He would be leaving a comforter, the Holy Spirit. This Spirit would lead and guide His children and one day they would be able to join Him in Heaven.

Katherine had believed the words of her teacher and later spoke with her Uncle Thomas about what she'd heard. Uncle Thomas had prayed with her and she knew without a doubt that she was saved, that her sins were covered by the blood of Jesus. Gone, never to be remembered again. She'd never forget the cold mountain waters down at the Pettyjohn baptizing hole as they flowed over her, washing her sins far away down the creek.

All her uncles were present to witness the moment when Katherine was dunked beneath the waters. Grandma Mame came, too, but she stood back from the crowd who had come to witness the four young people being baptized. Katherine knew the boys from church and school. There was Mark, who was tall and lanky with a sun-bleached cowlick in the front of his hair. Then there was Ricky, who was always getting into trouble, mouthing off at the teachers. Maybe the creek would wash away the bad words that rolled off his tongue so often. Then there was Buddy. He was a quiet, humble boy, a little taller and slimmer than Mark. Katherine always felt safe around Buddy. She could tell he had a gentle spirit.

Instead of listening to the preacher, Katherine had been daydreaming for so long he had finished his sermon and was getting ready to pray. Right as the final amen was said Katherine stood and slipped out the back door, but not fast enough. James's grandson Kermit spotted her as she made her way to the car.

"Katherine! Hey, wait up. What are you doing here? I've never seen you at church."

Katherine stopped and turned toward her young cousin. How old would he be now? Maybe twelve, thirteen?

"No, Kermit, you haven't seen me here because I was always busy caring for Grandma Mame and Grandpa Clint."

"Oh yeah. Grandpa James told me you were a saint. Is that right? Are you a saint? I ain't never met a real live saint before."

Katherine couldn't help but smile, etching deep creases in her cheeks. "No, Kermit, I'm far from being a saint. Not even close. I'm just a below average common girl."

By this time some of the other family members had gathered around Katherine. They hugged her and told her how happy they were that she was there. Katherine couldn't help but feel a bit smothered by all the attention and was happy when Uncle Hank took her by the arm and led her away from the crowd.

"Katherine, I don't know what I was thinking. I suppose I wasn't or I would have paid you a visit late Friday and told you the news."

"What is it, Uncle Hank? What news?"

James and Thomas had joined them and soon after Timothy and William came to stand with them, too.

Katherine couldn't help but feel a little anxious. What kind of news could be so important that all her uncles had to deliver it?

Thomas spoke up first, addressing his brothers. "I can't believe we didn't think to tell Katherine the news as soon as we found out."

"Well, we're not for certain that it's the God-honest truth yet," William said.

"True or not, Katherine needs to know what's going on." Hank shuffled his feet and cleared his throat. "Katherine, me and the brothers had a visit from a young man on Friday afternoon at the warehouse. The boy said he was a relative of ours."

Katherine felt confused. As she looked out at the rest of the family, aunts and cousins, she realized that she wasn't very close to any of them. Uncle Hank and Aunt Olivia were probably closer than any, so what was the big deal if another relative showed up?

When Uncle Hank took her hand, she flinched, drawing it back to herself. That was so unlike him, what in the world could be so serious that he would have to hold her hand to tell her?

"Katherine, the young man who came to see us says he is Ben's son. Says his name is Benny Bauguess."

It took a minute for Uncle Hank's words to sink into her brain. Ben's son? Uncle Ben never married that she or Grandma Mame knew of. Certainly, they would have known if Ben had any offspring.

"How can that be? Wouldn't Ben have told some of us if he had a son? Wouldn't Grandma Mame have known?"

This time James spoke. "The boy said Ben didn't know about him. He told us that Ben had his way with his mama when she was only fifteen and then ran off. She never saw him again until she recognized his mug shot on the television during Ben's sentencing for the murder of your daddy."

None of this made any sense and Katherine thought the uncles were creating a mountain out of a molehill, then a flash from the morning entered her mind. A young man in a cowboy hat, with dark hair, Uncle Ben's hair. That was Ben's son at her door.

Suddenly, Katherine felt weak. The cool autumn day did nothing to cure the rise in her temperature. Sweat beaded her brow and upper lip. Why was she upset? It wasn't Uncle Ben back from the grave, it was just a young man who happened to look a lot like her Uncle Ben.

Taking a deep breath, Katherine took a step back away from the uncles.

"I knew we should have told her sooner, I thought about it yesterday but never made it to her house," Thomas said.

The uncles were huddled together, mumbling amongst themselves just as if Katherine wasn't there.

"I saw him." Katherine had to repeat herself before she got their attention.

"I said, I saw him."

All five brothers turned to her. "You saw who?"

"I saw the man who is Ben's son. He came to my door this morning. I didn't answer it, but as he was leaving, he took off his hat and for a minute I thought it was Uncle Ben."

"Why did he come to your door?" Thomas asked.

"I told you I didn't answer his knock. You know Grandma Mame taught me never to trust a stranger."

Remembering their sister Mame, the uncles couldn't help but grin. She was a strange one. Life had thrown her some hard blows, but she'd taken each and every one of them and stood on her own two feet, raising a granddaughter, and doing a fine job of it, too. The brothers' admiration for their sister ran deep.

"I know why the boy went to the homeplace. Remember we told him that Ben's things were there. He probably came to claim his daddy's belongings. We should have told him to get with one of us and we'd take him to get Ben's things. Katherine, I'm sorry. We all are. We should never have put you in a position to have to deal with Ben's son. If you'll gather up the box with Ben's clothes, I'll take it to Benny. Before I forget to tell you, we are letting him stay in the company house just down the road from your place," Hank said.

Never in a million years would Katherine have thought her simple act of going to church would have turned out like this. She needed to get some facts straight in her head.

"So, you're telling me that this young man who calls himself Benny never met his daddy? Didn't know the first thing about him until he saw him on the news?"

"All he knows is what his mama told him. He said Ben was with his mama for a few weeks down at Folly Beach in South Carolina twenty years ago. When Ben realized the girl, Benny's mama, wanted to get married, Ben ran off. She never saw him again. After seeing Ben on the news, the boy and his mama made a trip up to Moundsville to the State Penitentiary to see him, but they were too late. All the boy got to see was a stone-cold corpse with a beat-up face and slit throat. On their way home to South Carolina, Benny's mama suffered a massive stroke and died a couple of weeks later," Hank said.

How very sad, Katherine thought, that the man named Benny had lost his daddy before he ever got to meet him, and then his mama. Katherine couldn't help but feel sympathy, and a bit anxious.

"How long will he be staying in the company house? I can get the box with Ben's things for you to give him as soon as I get home, and then he can be on his way."

Katherine knew she shouldn't judge the boy just because he probably was Ben Marsh's son, but she couldn't help herself. When the boy's face flashed through her mind, she couldn't help but shiver.

Katherine had heard enough, she needed to get home.

"If one of you will stop by the homeplace, I'll give you the box," Katherine said.

"Yes, Olivia and I will get it. Then we'll take it directly to him. They'll be no other reason for him to bother you," Hank said.

As soon as Katherine arrived home she bent down and gathered Little Bit up and hugged her tight. Grandma Mame may have been right, maybe she shouldn't ever leave the house unless it was absolutely necessary. No, she couldn't, and wouldn't live that way. She had to stop living in the past. She had to leave this safe haven and make her way in the world, and not depend on her uncles for support. She couldn't hide out in this house for the rest of her life, or be tied down with Stan. The thought smothered her.

Katherine set the kitty down and went straight to Grandma Mame's closet in her bedroom. The hat box of earthy possessions sat on the floor. By the time she took it to the front door, Uncle Hank was stepping up on the porch.

"Here's the box, and good riddance. The last of the memories goes with this. No more thoughts of the past. Only the future. Take it, please."

As the last part of Uncle Ben left her hands, a weight lifted from Katherine's shoulders, but then the dark hair of the young man invaded her thoughts and an even bigger weight than Uncle Ben jackhammered its way into her chest, weighing her down even more than before.

As soon as Uncle Hank headed toward the highway and down the road toward the company house, Katherine knew this should be the end of the boy named Benny, but deep down she could feel her world tilting just a bit off center. Katherine had planned her course, but was it really up to her? What would her future reveal?

CHAPTER 24

And Cain talked with Abel his brother: and it came to pass, when they

were in the field, that Cain rose up against Abel his brother, and slew him.

~ Genesis 4:8

BENNY LEFT HIS GRANDMOTHER'S HOUSE with an uneasy feeling. He could sense the girl's presence. His cousin was either in the house or close by. Couldn't blame her for not answering the door. He was a stranger. An older model Ford Fairlane sat in the drive, but the girl could have ridden to church with one of her uncles. He didn't think so, though. He felt like he was in an old horror movie. He couldn't shake the feeling that eyes were following him while he was standing on the porch.

Not knowing what to do with himself, Benny decided to drive around for a while and then come back and see if anyone would answer the door later. He really did want his daddy's belongings. That was all he had of the man who had sired him.

As Benny navigated the curvy mountain terrain, he enjoyed the different colors of the leaves. The cool autumn nights would soon suck the life completely out of the leaves and they would fall to the ground, but for now they were beautiful. Benny wasn't used to the mountains and the change of seasons. Coming from the coast, there was mostly evergreen trees, pines, palms, and magnolias. Here he was enjoying the yellowing poplars, the burgundy oaks, and his favorite, the red maples.

A hunger pain told him it must be close to lunchtime and church would be letting out soon. He'd go back to the company house and eat a bite from the supplies he had bought yesterday, then he'd head back over to his grandmother's place.

While Benny sat eating a cold can of tuna, he heard a steady stream of traffic pass by. The family must be heading home from church.

The thought of him having family stirred up feelings he'd never had. He felt resentment toward them, but couldn't justify it. They knew nothing about his existence so they couldn't be blamed for not trying to find him. All the fault fell on his daddy, and with him gone he had no one to take out his anger on.

Just as Benny took the last bite of tuna, he heard a vehicle slowing down as it approached the driveway to the company house. He threw the empty can in the trash and then the fork in the sink.

When Benny got to the front door, he saw Hank stepping out of a black Cadillac. The car wasn't new but it still put off an air of wealth. Benny's gut spasmed. Would he be satisfied to leave without what surely should be his daddy's inheritance?

Benny opened the door and stepped out on the front stoop.

"Hey Benny, glad I caught you at home. I have something for you."

Benny watched his uncle step around to the back door of the car and open it. He reached inside and took out a tall, round box. He figured it was a hat box since a picture of a lady with a hat was on the side. What was his daddy doing with a woman's hat box?

Now standing face to face, Hank offered Benny the box.

"What is this?" Benny asked.

"Son, these are your daddy's belongings. I stopped down at my sister Mame's house and picked it up for you. My niece said you might have been there this morning looking for Ben's stuff. Thought I'd save you the trouble of going back for it. No need now to go back to the homeplace."

As Benny listened to Hank, he realized that the girl must have been inside this morning when he'd visited. He knew his senses hadn't failed him.

"Yes, I went to the house. The one you said belonged to my dead grandma, but no one came to the door."

"That's right, my niece was taught to be cautious. She wouldn't have opened the door to a stranger."

The more Benny heard, the more he wanted to know.

"What did you say your niece's name was? I'd like to stop by and introduce myself to my cousin. I'd like to meet all my relatives. Did you tell the girl about me so I won't scare her when I stop back by?"

Hank avoided Benny's questions. The less he knew about Katherine and all the Blackwells, the better.

"I thought you'd be on your way back to South Carolina now that you have what you came for."

Two could play at this game Benny thought. He offered no answer to Hank's question.

"So, your niece, how old is she? Does she live in the house alone or does she have a husband and kids?"

Hank was beginning to feel uncomfortable with all Benny's questions. He needed to tell him as little as possible, but still get him gone and away from Katherine.

"My niece will soon be twenty years old. She lives alone since Mame and Clint passed, but we all stop by and check on her regularly. The house now belongs to Katherine. My sister left it and a few acres of land to her. Her Grandpa Clint left her another small farm down in a little town called Elkin in North Carolina. She'll probably be moving there soon to attend college to become a nurse." Hank knew he'd just said too much, but he couldn't take the words back.

"So, let me get this straight. Your niece—Katie?—she inherited two farms? One from her Grandma Mame, who would be my real grandma, right? Then she inherited another farm from her Grandpa Clint, who isn't my real grandpa? How did that happen?"

Hank looked out at Olivia sitting in the car and knew she was anxious to get home and get lunch on the table. "Let's not get into that right now, Olivia needs to get home to serve lunch. You're welcome to come and eat with us. I think we're having a pork roast. Olivia is a fine cook. You can tell that by looking at me."

"No thanks. I just ate, but I would like to get together with you soon. I need to know about my daddy's life, and how he ended up an inmate in the state penitentiary."

Hank knew he couldn't deny the boy the truth, especially since he was asking for it.

"Why don't you stop by the house around four this afternoon and I'll tell you all you want to know, and probably more than you'll want to hear. I'll be up from my nap by the time you arrive," Hank said, chuckling.

"I'll be there."

"My home is on down the road past the warehouse. House number 872 is on the mailbox."

Hank turned and walked back toward Olivia's car, not knowing Benny already knew where all his uncles lived.

Benny went back inside the small house. For a while he paced back and forth. He hadn't noticed before how worn the linoleum was. The path from the front door to the entrance of the kitchen was a couple of shades lighter than the route less traveled.

Benny couldn't help but think about what Hank had just told him. This cousin of his had inherited not only one farm, but two. The small house was nothing fancy, but it was a million times better than the place he and his mama had called home.

Why should this cousin get all of Grandma Mame's good fortune and he get nothing? There was a lot of questions to be answered, and he needed to think of a way to get his part. Before, Benny wasn't sure, but now he knew he deserved his cut of the Blackwell fortune. Benny Bauguess was as much of a grandson to Mame Blackwell Paddington as this Cousin Katie was.

Benny hadn't even realized it but he was still holding the box that Hank had given him. He took it into the kitchen and set it on the table. For a least fifteen minutes he circled the table glaring at the closed box. His daddy's clothes, these items had touched his skin, they had known him when he was alive, while warm blood still pumped through his veins. All Benny knew of his daddy's touch was the cold bitter hand of death.

Finally, Benny took the lid off the box and sat down in front of it, staring at the leather belt that lay on top. He couldn't help himself. He undid his own belt buckle and pulled the belt through the loops on his pants, letting it fall to the floor, then he put his hand into the box and took out Ben Marsh's belt. He rolled it over and ran his fingers back and forth across the smooth leather. The belt had been tanned a rich brown, it was fairly new, but Benny could tell where his daddy had kept it fastened around himself.

Slowly, Benny fed the belt through the loops in his jeans. Benny had to tighten the belt one notch tighter than his daddy had so he knew his father was about thirty-four inches around. How ironic for that to be the most personal thing a boy would ever know about his own daddy.

The belt wasn't the only item Benny tried on, the fancy designer jacket that he pulled from the box fit him a bit loosely but it would do. He unfolded the striped shirt and navy pants and brought them up to his face taking in the aroma of his daddy. Benny caught a hint of Old Spice aftershave and cigar smoke. Such little things a kid should know about his father, things Benny never got the chance to experience.

Benny neatly folded the items and laid them on the table. Next, he took the shoes and saw right away they were a size 10, the same size he wore. Benny knew that even though the size was right be would never wear the shoes. Shiny, dress platform shoes were not his style. He was a boot man all the way to the core, but he'd keep them anyway. He'd keep all these things because that's all that was left of his daddy.

The last item in the box was a worn leather billfold. A quick search revealed a North Carolina driver's license. Benny sat and stared at the man's picture on the license for a long time, he would have been thirty-nine years old according to his birth date on the license. That was the third time he'd seen his daddy. The first time on the news, the second at the state prison, and now in this picture.

The photo portrayed a nice-looking man with dark hair that could have used a trim. Benny was sure he would resemble this man even more in twenty years when he would be closer to his age in the picture.

There was nothing else in the billfold, just the license with a post office box number in North Carolina. Benny remembered the news had said the feds had confiscated all Ben's possessions because he was a drug dealer and murderer.

Benny still couldn't believe he could be the son of a man who would kill his own brother. There had to be more to the story. Looking at his watch, he realized by the time he got down to Hank's house it would be close to four o'clock.

Benny put each item back in the box, except for the belt. He'd leave that on, always.

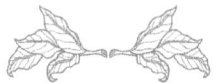

For the next two hours, Hank answered question after question from the boy who most likely was Ben's boy, and his own nephew.

"How can this man named Clint be my cousin's grandpa and not mine? My daddy was her daddy's twin, right?"

"As we told you before in the cafe, there are some things that you might not want to know. Life's not all been smooth for the Blackwells."

"I want to know everything. Tell me, why did my daddy kill his own twin brother?"

"Hold on boy, one question at a time. First, Clint was not your grandfather, or so the medical experts say. Your Grandma Mame was in love with Clint Paddington, she got pregnant and then soon after that she was raped. It seems that your Grandpa Jack Marsh's seed took hold, too, so that's how you and Katherine can have the same grandma, but not the same grandpa."

"How is that even possible? I just don't believe that."

"I'm afraid it can happen."

"Now you want to know how it's possible to have two different daddy babies in the womb at one time, well there's a name for it in the medical books, it's rare, but it can happen. It's called hetero-paternal superfecundation."

Benny leaned forward and put his elbows on his knees, taking in every word. He was young but not that naïve. He'd have to have a little more proof than Hank's word to believe that was possible.

"I just don't believe that can happen. You just made that up to mess with my mind."

"If you don't believe that, then there's the Carter birthmark. A purple blemish behind the ear. Can't remember which ear. Clint Paddington's mama and grandma had the mark and probably many generations before them. Clint had the mark, and so does Katherine, but your daddy didn't have the purple spot."

Benny lifted his hand and felt first behind his left ear, then behind his right. On an impulse Benny stood up and took the few steps to stand in front of Hank.

"Do I have the mark? Maybe them medical experts don't know what they're talking about and the birthmark skipped a generation."

"I'll look, but I can assure you, you look just like your daddy when he was your age."

Hank stood up. "Take your hat off and let's have a look-see."

Hank pushed Benny's hair back away from the spot behind each ear and even parted the hair in places just so he wouldn't miss it in case all this two-daddy stuff was garbage. Hank, too, found it all hard to believe.

Deep down Benny wanted his uncle to find the mark, because in the pit of his stomach he really didn't want to have a daddy who had killed his brother and sold drugs.

"I don't see any mark, Benny. Skin's as clear as a baby's bottom. Ben Paddington was your daddy and Jack Marsh was your grandpa."

Benny really didn't know what to say, so he just turned and sat back down. Then got right back up and walked over to a mirror that hang on the wall. Turning sideways Benny folded his ear down and pushed his hair to the side. Maybe Hank had missed it. In his mind Benny willed the mark to appear.

Hank watched as Benny struggled with all the information he'd shared with him. Maybe he'd had enough. "Are you sure you want to know why Ben killed Walt, his own brother?"

Benny turned away from the mirror and smoothed his hair down. His mind wandered, trying to block out the bad stories. Did he really need to know the details of the killing? Several minutes passed before Benny spoke. "Yes, sir, I'm sure."

"Well, here you go. The man who raped my sister Mame—not once, but twice—was a lowlife thug named Jack Marsh. He was obsessed with Mame. He didn't know his attack had fathered a son, not until Ben was eight years old. When Jack learned about the boy, he molested Mame again and kidnapped your daddy. Ben was raised by one of the meanest men it the country.

"Is he still alive?"

"Ben told Mame he'd died years back. I believe some type of cancer got him."

Benny couldn't help but feel the loss of yet another family member. Even if he was a mean soul, he had been his grandfather.

Hank sat silent, watching Benny, letting the boy digest the story about his daddy and grandpa. He could see the pain as it glazed over his eyes. Hank couldn't imagine what might be going through the boy's head. He couldn't help but feel sorry for him.

Finally, Benny spoke. "Why did my daddy kill his twin brother? I've just got to know. No one could be that mean without a reason."

"I can only tell you what little I know. My sister Mame was a very private person. Most of what I know came from Katherine. She heard her grandma confess her sins to Clint at the entrance to the mine where Mame and Ben took Walt's dead body."

"What? My grandma was a part of killing her own son?"

"Now, just hold on. Let me try to explain. When Jack Marsh kidnapped Ben when he was eight, he told Ben that Mame, his mama, didn't want him and she had paid him to take Ben away. As the years passed, Ben realized it must be true because no one had come to rescue him from Jack. When Jack died, Ben set out to find his family, a mama that didn't want him and a brother that she had wanted instead. Hate and resentment toward Ben's twin brother had been building for years.

"The day Ben came home to Beckley was Walt's wedding day. Walt married a beautiful young lady named Emily. Seeing his brother so happy only added fuel to his fiery anger. A few days after the wedding, Ben went to Walt's house after he'd left for work and raped, or seduced, Walt's young bride. There are conflicting stories about what really happened."

Benny's head was spinning. What kind of a family did he come from? A bunch of liars and rapists? The picture of his own mama Trudy and the life that they'd lived didn't look so depraved anymore. Hank could tell the boy was sickened from what he'd heard.

"Have you had enough? Do you want me to stop, because there is a lot more, if you can stomach it."

Benny didn't respond for a few minutes. Thoughts of what kind of bad blood was running through him made Benny feel sick, but he had to know the rest; why brother had killed brother.

"I want to know everything, I have to. Go on, tell me why my daddy killed his brother."

"Are you sure?"

Yes, Benny was sure, and no, he wasn't. He couldn't help but wonder if he might have been better off to have stayed at Folly Beach and left this crazy family and the past behind him. Then he realized his daddy came from a different blood line, Jack Marsh. Still, all this evil he'd been told was blowing Benny's mind, and he couldn't help deny that that same blood ran through him from both sides of the family. What kind of a monster would he turn out to be?

"Go ahead, tell me the rest. I need to know."

"After Ben slept with Walt's new wife, he left Beckley before anyone else besides Emily knew he was there. The problem was Ben couldn't get Walt's beautiful young wife out of his mind. Within a year, Ben was headed back to Beckley. He went to his mama's house to confront her about selling him to Jack Marsh when he was just a young boy.

"When Ben entered the homeplace he found Mame sitting in a rocking chair with Katherine, who was only a few months old at the time. He confronted Mame and she tried to make him believe that Jack Marsh had kidnapped him, she had not sold him and that Clint had searched for him for so many years that it had finally drove him to drink, and they lost everything.

"The Paddingtons were a very wealthy family. Clint's daddy bought the first load of tobacco that my mama Mary took to market in Beckley. Through the years they became friends, but that friendship ended when your Grandpa Jack beat my younger brother, Jared, to death in a barroom fight. Mama never was the same after Jared died. He was the most like our own daddy, Henry, who died in a coal mine accident. It was like Mama lost her husband twice."

"Wait just a minute, you mean Jack Marsh killed your brother?"

"I'm afraid that's the truth, son. I told you the lives of your daddy and grandpa were just about the most evil story I've ever heard. They were full of the devil."

Benny stood up and paced back and forth on the braided rug that covered a large area of the sitting room. He hung his head, embarrassed by the things he'd heard about his kin, a daddy and grandpa that he really didn't know, but was ashamed of.

"You heard enough?"

Had Benny found out enough about the lives of his ancestors? Yes, but he couldn't let his uncle stop without knowing the rest.

"Don't quit now. I have to know why Ben killed his brother."

"This might take a while to explain. You see, the day Ben came back to confront his mama, Mame was taking care of baby Katherine because Walt had taken his wife Emily to the doctor. She was expecting another baby and was having a hard time carrying this one to term. When Ben looked at Katherine it didn't occur to him that he could be her father. Emily had confessed her transgressions with Ben to Mame so my sister already knew what had happened between Emily and Ben, but Walt didn't have a clue.

"What Ben didn't know was that Walt and Emily had come back to the homeplace and had heard Ben as he'd told Mame about the day he'd had his way with Walt's wife. When Emily realized Walt now knew what she had done she passed out, and a pool of blood surrounded her. Emily miscarried the baby and bled to death right there in front of them all.

"Later that evening, Ben and Walt fought and Ben hit Walt on the head with a shovel. Cracked his skull wide open. When Mame saw what had happened she was hysterical, but Ben guilted her into helping him load Walt up in the truck of his car and take him to the deserted mine shaft and bury him underneath the cold black coal dust."

"You mean Mame helped Ben get rid of the body?"

"Yes, but she didn't rightly have a choice. Ben convinced her it was her fault he and Walt had fought because she had let Jack Marsh raise him, that she had never loved him, but had always doted on Walt. Why? Because Mame knew Walt was Clint Paddington's son, and that Ben was Jack Marsh's boy."

"How do you know all of this? Looks like Mame would have taken information like this to the grave with her—I sure would have."

"Your Grandma Mame had Alzheimer's, but near the end before she completely lost her mind and voice, she went to the entrance of the mine where her daddy had died, and where she and Ben had hidden Walt's body. We found her there one day trying to dig her way into the mine. We all thought she was trying to find our daddy's bones, but she was really trying to get to Walt.

"Months later, after Clint had come home, we found her again at the mine entrance. This time she confessed that Jack Marsh had fathered your daddy and that Ben had killed Walt and that she wasn't sure or not if she herself had killed baby Daniel who came along after Jack Marsh had raped her the second time."

"I think I've heard enough. Daddy a killer, Grandma an accomplice and a baby killer?"

Benny felt sick to his stomach, but he knew there was one more person he needed to know about, and that was cousin Katherine.

"One more question. Where does Katie fit into all this mess?"

"Your cousin's name is Katherine, and she's been a part of all this from the beginning. When Katherine's mama Emily died, and then when your daddy killed her daddy, that left Katherine an orphan. Of course, Mame took her grandchild in and raised her.

"Mame had lost almost everything, her husband Clint, three sons, two to death, the other to the devil. Katherine was all she had left. Ben had run off after he killed his brother and didn't show back up until Katherine was eight or nine years old. He became obsessed with her because she looked so much like her mama Emily, the one woman he could never scald from his memory.

'Sometimes when he would come home to Mame's house drunk he would call Katherine Emily. He terrorized that child until the day he was finally arrested for the murder of Walt, and for trafficking drugs. More than once he tried to molest her, she even had to cut him with a knife one time to defend herself. The child has had a hard life. Mame was not an easy person to live with either. She carried so much guilt until it finally drove her crazy."

"So, that's why Katherine inherited Mame and Clint's houses? Because Mame raised her?"

"Well yes, that's part of it, but Katherine is Mame and Clint's only grandchild, and she cared for them around the clock until the day they died."

Benny could feel the hair on the back of his neck crawl. Only grandchild? No, he was as much a part of Mame Paddington as Cousin Katherine was. He had to stand up for himself.

"No, you're wrong. Whether you want to believe it or not, I know I am just as much of a grandkid to this Mame woman as Katherine is. My mama would not have lied to me about who my daddy was."

Hank could sense the boy was heading in a direction that could only lead to trouble. Hank himself was confused. Did the boy deserve an inheritance? How could he? Katherine had spent her entire life taking care of her grandma. The boy may be blood kin, but his heart was not tied to any of them, Blackwells or Paddingtons.

Needing to get control of the situation, Hank asked Benny about the contents of the box he'd dropped off earlier. "Sorry there wasn't anything of more value in the box. That whistle is probably the best thing in there. I remember it being made of sterling silver."

"What whistle? There wasn't any whistle in the box. Just some clothes, shoes, jacket, and an empty billfold. Oh, and this belt."

Benny stood up as if modeling his new accessory to Hank.

"There was a whistle in the box. Maybe you just didn't see it."

"I'm sure there was no whistle. What good is a silly whistle anyway?'

"That whistle is maybe the best part of your daddy, that and the note he gave his mama when he was just a boy that said, *I wuv you mommy.*"

"How can a whistle and note mean anything?"

"When my mama Mary died, Mame came back to the homeplace and she brought Ben with her. He was eight years old, before he was kidnapped by Jack Marsh. My boy Ike gave him the whistle. Told him as long as he kept the whistle, he'd always be close to his kin. The whistle fell out of Ben's pants pocket when we got them from the undertaker, so it looks to me like Ben kept it with him to remember he did have a family, maybe even a family who cared about him. I believe that showed the good in him, and especially the note he'd written to Mame. I'm afraid your daddy changed under the roof of Jack Marsh. He evolved from a sweet, innocent boy to a man who had fashioned himself after the man who had sired him."

"So, you're telling me that my daddy should have had a different life? That he had deserved a better life? That he was culled by a mother who didn't want him and taken in by a terrible father who did?"

"It's complicated, boy. There's no way to go back and fix any of this. The best thing for you to do is go back down to the coast to your home and live your life. Forget all this."

Good ol' Uncle Hank was nicely telling him to leave. Who did he think he was to boss him around? Benny Bauguess doesn't have to answer to anyone.

Benny wanted what was rightfully his.

"I want the whistle and the note. Where are they?"

Hank noticed the change in Benny's attitude, and he didn't like it. Could son be like father, even if they knew nothing of each other?

"Does Katherine have the rest of my daddy's stuff? I'm going to go get it."

"No. I'll stop by tomorrow and ask her if she knows where the whistle and note are. You don't need to bother Katherine; she's been through enough."

"She's been through enough? Really? What about me? I've been searching all my life for my daddy. Then when I find him his throat is cut, and now I'll never get to hear his side of any of these tales you've been feeding me."

Benny rose from the chair, "I've got to get out of here. I need to think. I want that whistle and note, and everything else that should rightly be mine."

Hank sat quietly as he watched the boy storm out the front door. He had an uneasy feeling about what Benny might do. It was getting late, but he'd better call Katherine and warn her not to go to her door if Benny comes by there to get the whistle and note.

CHAPTER 25

A good man leaveth an inheritance to his children's children:
and the wealth of the sinner is laid up for the just.

~ Proverbs 13:22

KATHERINE LOOKED AT THE CLOCK when she heard the phone ring, it was 6:35. Who could that be? Most likely one of her uncles, or maybe Stan?

She had not heard from him since their confrontation last night. Did she really expect to? She had made it clear to Stan that she was moving to North Carolina. No, after last night she didn't expect to hear from him for a long time, maybe never. This only made her feel sad, not really for herself, but for Stan. She knew he really cared for her.

The ringing phone brought her back from her thoughts.

"Hello?"

"Katherine. How are you?"

"Fine, Uncle Hank, how are you? Is everything all right? You sound a little bothered."

"I've been talking to that boy, Benny, for the past couple of hours, so I guess I am a little flustered. I gave the boy Ben's box of things, but the whistle wasn't with the clothes. I also told Benny about the note. He wants both of them."

"They're in Grandma Mame's memory box. I put them in there before Grandma passed, the day we were sitting at the kitchen table discussing where Ben would be buried."

"Yes, child, I figured something like that had happened. I told the boy I'd pick up the items from you in the morning and get them to him. Maybe he'll be on his way back home to Folly Beach after he's got what he wants. I got an uneasy feeling about him. Make sure your doors are locked up tight and don't let anyone in."

To make Katherine feel more at ease, he added, "I don't think there is any harm in the boy, but you never know. He is Ben's son, or so he says."

Hank realized as soon as those words came out of his mouth they would not ease Katherine's mind.

"I'm sorry, Katherine. Why don't you come down to the house and spend the night with me and Olivia? She'd be tickled to death to have you to fuss over."

Katherine had never run away to her uncles and stayed, and she didn't intend to now. Every night since she was an infant she had slept in this house; she wasn't going anywhere now. That thought took her to North Carolina. Could she really leave her home here in Beckley?

"Katherine, you all right? Come on down now, we'll eat some leftover chicken from lunch."

"Uncle Hank, thank you but I'll be fine here. You're just being paranoid. I don't run away, and besides, how many grand- and great-grandbabies do you have now for Aunt Olivia to spoil. I don't think she needs me to dote on at all. She's got plenty of babies to pamper."

Katherine smiled, running the names of her cousins over in her head.

"You're always welcome."

"I know, Uncle Hank, but I'll be fine. I'm going right now to check my doors, then I'll get the whistle and note from the memory box and lay them on the kitchen table so you'll have them first thing in the morning when you stop by."

"I'll get Ben's things on my way to work in the morning about seven. Will you be up?"

"Oh yes, I'll be up by then."

"Okay, if you're sure you won't come stay with us, I guess I'll see you in the morning."

"Sounds good. Good night, Uncle Hank."

Katherine hung up the phone and made her way into Grandma Mame's bedroom. She knew exactly which drawer the memory box was in. She opened the third drawer and took the box out. She sat down on the bed and opened the lid. The whistle and note lay right on top. She took the items and closed the lid. She didn't want to go down memory lane tonight, Katherine only wanted what the future had in store for her.

Placing the box back in the dresser drawer she took the whistle and note into the kitchen. She couldn't help herself and opened the note and read the words one more time. *I wuv you mommy.* For the life of her she could not see her Uncle Ben as a small innocent boy. She folded the note and laid it beside the whistle. Benny was welcome to the items. Good riddance to the whistle, the note, and all memories of Ben Marsh.

Katherine decided a nice hot bath was exactly what she needed, then maybe a bowl of popcorn before she turned in. She might even turn on the ancient black and white television and watch one of the three channels it picked up. Sunday night was Bonanza night. For as long as Katherine could remember, Grandma Mame had let herself enjoy one thing and that had been the pleasure of that single television show.

Later that night Katherine woke up still on the couch with a half-eaten bowl of popcorn about to topple onto the floor and the television set dark, with the National Anthem playing. She felt groggy and lightheaded as she made her way into the kitchen. The clock on the electric stove read 12:05.

Katherine sat the popcorn on the table. After checking the door locks one more time, she was off to bed. She didn't bother setting her wind-up alarm clock, she was always awake by five or six o'clock.

The sound of someone pounding on the door woke Katherine. She looked at the clock. 6:45. Goodness, she'd never slept this late. Flipping her legs off the bed, she grabbed her bathrobe and slipped it on. Out the living room window, she could see Uncle Hank's old work truck.

Making her way to the door, Katherine felt like she'd been asleep for days and her mouth was dry and tasted sour. Of course, she had stayed up too late last night and fallen asleep on the couch before brushing her teeth.

Katherine unlocked the door. "Uncle Hank, come in. Sorry I wasn't up. I can't believe I slept this late. I must be getting lazy."

"My goodness, child, I don't blame you for sleeping in. You don't have your grandparents now to worry over. You should pamper yourself every now and then. Where are Ben's things? I'll get them and run before it gets any later. The brothers will be wondering where I'm at."

"Of course. The whistle and note are right in here on the kitchen table."

Hank followed Katherine into the kitchen and almost ran into her because she had stopped so suddenly.

"They're not here. I know I laid the whistle and the note right here on the table." Katherine patted the spot where she had put Ben's things. "I took the items from Grandma Mame's box as soon as I hung up from talking to you last night. I laid them right here."

Katherine lifted the popcorn bowl that was half full last night. Now it only held a few un-popped kernels.

"What's going on here? I know this bowl was half full last night when I went to bed."

Hank watched Katherine and saw the confusion on her face.

"You must have dreamed all this, child."

"No. I didn't dream a thing last night. I know I put the whistle and note on the table right after I talked to you last night."—*Was the whistle and note still there when I left the half-eaten bowl of popcorn?*— "I'm sorry, Uncle Hank, I don't know what's wrong with me."

Katherine still felt like her head was packed full of cotton. She reached way down inside her brain and tried to remember. Could it all have been a dream? Was she sleepwalking?

"I'm sure I didn't dream all this last night. Let's go look in the memory box and see if the whistle and note are still there."

Katherine rushed into Grandma Mame's bedroom. She opened the same drawer she'd opened last evening and took out the same box she'd taken out the night before. The whistle and note should have been laying on top, but they were not. Katherine fingered through the items and finally flipped the box over and emptied it all out on the bed.

Picking up each item, she quickly realized there was no note and certainly not a whistle. "What could I have done with them?"

Katherine headed back to the kitchen and once again checked the table, she even picked up the empty popcorn bowl and looked inside. Then she took a couple of steps and looked inside the trash can. Nothing in there except an empty soda bottle and a butter wrapper from the melted butter she'd drizzled over her popcorn last night. Katherine looked everywhere for the whistle and note, but found nothing.

Hank watched his niece open every drawer and cabinet door in the house searching for the missing items.

"Katherine, I've got to get to the warehouse. It's almost 7:30. I'm sure the whistle will turn up. Just give me a call when you find it and I'll run back and get it."

"I don't know what in the world I could have possibly done with those things. I'll keep looking and call when I find them."

"Okay, dear. You'll remember where you put them. You've just been under a tremendous amount of stress lately. You'll be okay, just calm down and it will come to you."

Katherine didn't answer her uncle, she just stood and watched him leave.

When Katherine felt something against her ankle, she jumped. It was only Little Bit.

"Hey there, sweet kitty. How are you this morning?"

Glancing at Little Bit's food bowl she saw it was empty. "Oh my, you're hungry."

Katherine opened the back door and stepped into the porch where she kept the cat food. She didn't notice that the door was unlocked.

He put the whistle to his lips and softly blew. With each puff of breath, the whistle sounded louder and louder until the noise blasted through his head like a tire exploding. He spat it out on the floor. What good was a damned old whistle anyway? He wanted more. He wanted what was his.

Katherine searched all day for the whistle and note. Her uncle had called at noon to ask her about the lost items.

"No, Uncle Hank, I can't find the whistle or the note. I've turned this house upside down and they're not here."

Hank had been thinking all day about what could have happened to the items.

"I've got a theory, Katherine. Didn't I hear you complaining about having a mouse problem? Maybe it is more of a rat problem. A rat could have been lured in by the popcorn and it could have eaten the note and swallowed the whistle or carried it off to its nest."

"Oh, my Lord. If that's true it must have been a wolf-rat. Surely not . . . is there even that kind of rat in this area?"

"Sure there is, and it makes perfect sense, doesn't it? Rat eats the popcorn and note, then steals the whistle. I've seen television cartoons that happened just like that."

"I suppose it's possible, but this isn't a silly television program. If that's what happened then that whistle could be anywhere. It's really the only explanation."

"I'm going to call Charlie and have him come over to your house and give it a look over to see where the vermin might be coming in, and set some traps. He might even find the whistle in the rat's nest."

"Oh no, you can't set traps. Little Bit might get caught in one of them, and no poison either. She might eat some of that, too."

"I'll tell Charlie to be very careful when he sets those traps. You've really got to do something. If you've got a rat that big getting into your house then he may just drag you off next time."

Katherine couldn't help but laugh as a vision of herself being dragged away by a gigantic rat ran through her mind.

"Thank you, Uncle Hank. What will you tell Benny when he comes after his daddy's things?"

Luckily Hank had not heard from Benny. "I'll just tell him the truth. He may not like it but it can't be helped. Maybe the whistle will turn up yet. I'll talk to you later, Katherine, and I'll send Charlie over this afternoon to set those traps."

"Okay, thank you."

For the rest of the afternoon Hank expected Benny to show up. He never heard a word from him. On Hank's way home he went by the company house where Benny was staying. There was no sign of Benny's truck, and after glancing in the front window and seeing no sign of him, he then knocked loudly on the door. When he felt confident the house was empty, he took the spare key he'd brought with him and opened the door.

A quick walk through of each room showed no sign of a visitor. The only thing that proved someone had been there was a key lying on the kitchen table, the same key Hank had given Benny. Hank picked it up and flipped it between his fingers. How strange that yesterday the boy acted like he wanted to cause trouble and today he was gone. Hank figured the boy had taken his advice and went back home to Folly Beach.

CHAPTER 26

Thou shalt rise up before the hoary head, and honour the face of the old man, and fear thy God: I am the Lord.

~ Leviticus 19:32

TIME, PRECIOUS TIME. HE KNEW he had to be patient, and he knew he could. He'd done it many times before. All good things must be waited on. He closed his eyes and the plan formulated in his mind. He would get what was his.

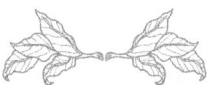

Katherine heard the vehicle coming up the drive and saw Charlie get out of one of her uncle's company trucks.

Katherine opened the door and stepped out on the front porch. "Hey Charlie, how are you?"

For as long as Katherine has had a memory, Charlie Height has been in it. He was always there when she and her grandma needed anything. A finer man could not be found anywhere.

"Good afternoon, Miss Katherine, I'm doing as well as can be expected for a man my age, thank you for asking. I hear you got a problem with some mice."

"Not mice—rats. Big enough to eat half a bowl of popcorn and carry off a child's whistle."

"Lands sake, I ain't never seen a rat that big. You sure got a powerful imagination, Miss Katherine."

Katherine watched Charlie reach into the back of the truck and lift out a half dozen steel traps.

"I heard it must be a big one, so I come prepared. I'll just put a couple in the crawl space, and a few around the outside of the house and in the barn. I got a trick to baiting them. I roll me up a chunk of white bread and dip it down in molasses. Mice can't resist the sweet taste of it. It's a guaranteed catch every time. Now don't let that little old kitten out of the house while these here traps are set."

"Don't you worry, Charlie. I'll keep Little Bit inside where she will be safe."

"Don't know how safe she'll be inside either with a rat big enough to eat a whistle running around under your feet."

The thought of a rat being in her house didn't make Katherine too happy. Funny, she had found very few mouse droppings inside.

By the end of the week Charlie had caught three rats and a half dozen large mice. However, he didn't find their nests and no whistle.

Uncle Hank had not heard anything from Benny, so life was delivering a bit of normalcy, that was, until Katherine went to the mailbox on Friday.

Inside the mailbox was a large brown envelope with a return address to Surry Community College. She was so excited she almost didn't see the electric bill and a couple of pieces of junk mail.

Katherine raced up the driveway and flung open the screen door. Katherine could almost hear Grandma Mame telling her not to let the screen door slam, but she let it anyway. She had more important things to think about.

The envelope in her hand felt electric, like it had a life source of its own. Maybe it did, for inside it held Katherine's future. She took a knife and opened it. Turning the envelope upside down, three pages fell out. The first was a letter and the second and third were forms to be filled out.

Katherine knew she held all of her tomorrows right there in her hands. Even if she didn't get to start until the winter semester, she would at least know she had a spot.

Holding her breath, she started reading the letter.

Ms. Paddington,

We are pleased to inform you that we have an opening for you in our Registered Nurse Program starting Monday, September 20, 1971.

We are sorry for the short notice, but we had a cancellation for our fall program, and you were next in line.

We will need the enclosed forms filled out and your tuition payment of seventy-three dollars in our possession by Wednesday, September 15, 1971.

If you are unable to attend at this time please call our registration office as soon as possible.

Sincerely,

Trish Alexander

Director of Nursing

Surry Community College

Dobson, NC 27017

336-386-8121

Katherine lowered herself into the nearest kitchen chair and read the letter again, slower this time so as not to miss anything. She had been accepted. Now what? Today was Friday, September 10. In less than two weeks she would be living in North Carolina and going to nursing school. Excitement cruised through her; she had never felt this alive.

She didn't even consider not accepting. Yes, she was a little scared, and there was so much to do to get ready for her move, but she was ready to start a new life. No more school where rumors of stabbing her uncle followed her up and down the halls. Not to mention being made fun of constantly for living with a touched-in-the-head grandma. People could be so very cruel. Grandma Mame was not crazy, she was just different. She just didn't trust people, and who could blame her for that?

Katherine had held up well under all the gossip and whispers but she was looking forward to a new start and a fresh beginning.

The first person she called was her Uncle Hank, who seemed excited for her, yet concerned. Then she found Tracy's number, her soon-to-be neighbor, and told him she would be arriving on Wednesday and would he mind bushhogging the pasture and the bottom land?

Tracy was so excited to hear Katherine would soon be coming to live at Clint's house he could barely get his words out, so Katherine just helped by finishing his sentences. When she finally got off the phone with Tracy, she had an overwhelming urge to call Stan. She missed her friend. She'd see how she felt later when it was time for Stan to be home from work.

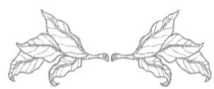

By Tuesday, Katherine had packed up everything she could possibly need to start her new journey: toiletries, clothes, a few keepsakes, Grandma Mame's Bible, and the memory box.

Aunt Olivia had invited her to supper along with the other uncles and their families to say goodbye. With close to thirty people to feed, everyone agreed it would be a potluck supper. They'd spread all the food outside on pieces of plywood that had been laid on sawbucks. With the makeshift tables they had plenty of room.

Just before five o'clock, Katherine took the keys to the Fairlane off the hook on the wall beside the back door and headed out to Uncle Hank's house.

Her Uncle William had showed up bright and early that Monday morning to take her car down to the service station for Greg to change the oil, check all the fluids, and get a new set of tires.

The uncles were uneasy enough about their niece driving so far by herself. The very least they could do was make sure her car was in good repair.

Uncle William even brought a map back with him of North Carolina, Virginia, and West Virginia. He sat down with her at the kitchen table and highlighted the route she was to take. Highway 77-North to exit 85 toward Elkin, then onto CC Camp Road to Highway 21-North to Brookfall Dairy Road, to rural route road number 2044, then onto rural route number 2043, then home. It seemed so very strange for Katherine to call Grandpa Clint's house her home.

Katherine looked around the old homeplace. Memories of her life rippled through her and passed slowly like the sands of time measuring a three-minute boiled egg.

She'd checked everything off her to-do list, down to the last thing when she'd called the post office to have her mail forwarded. She'd leave the power on because she was sure she'd be back once in a while on weekends. She would, however, have to get Charlie to winterize the pipes before it got too cold. She knew she'd be extremely busy going to school, and of course she'd need to find a job, so she wouldn't be back often.

Suddenly, Katherine felt a bit overwhelmed. Could she really strike out on her own? She had only been out of Raleigh County the one time with Uncle Hank and Aunt Olivia when they'd took her to Grandpa Clint's farm in North Carolina. She was more than a bit nervous about driving on the interstate, but she knew she could do it. She'd just take her time, and enjoy the scenery. The leaves on some of the trees were already turning yellow and red. Katherine had lived through scarier times in her life than this.

With that thought, her mind drifted to Stan. It had been over a week since she'd seen him and turned down his proposal. She had tried to call him three times, but each time there was no answer. It was probably for the best. No use in a second goodbye. Hopefully her absence would help Stan get over her sooner.

Little Bit's meow made her realize she'd have to rig up a temporary litter box in the back floorboard. Maybe a shoe box would work since the box from the house was too big to fit.

Katherine was so thankful that someone had deserted Little Bit. The kitten had been a lot of company these past few months, and she knew Little Bit would be even more company in North Carolina where she knew practically no one. Katherine picked the small cat up and nuzzled her up under her chin.

"Tomorrow we start a new life. I hope you'll like your new home. I hope I do, too."

Katherine sat Little Bit down and headed out the door with a chicken pie in tow. It would be a good reunion with all her family. Even though all their faces were familiar she felt distant from them.

Grandma Mame had been so withdrawn and isolated from the world that her cousins had been afraid to come and visit. More than once Mame had hollered at the unknown face behind the knock to, "Go away."

Katherine knew Grandma Mame didn't mean to run everyone off, she was really only punishing herself. Grandma Mame thought she didn't deserve friends or casual company. She tolerated her brothers, Clint, and Katherine, and that was about it.

Enough dwelling in the past. Katherine was off to Uncle Hank's to bid farewell to family, and to the memories she would hopefully forget.

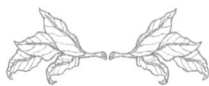

He was thankful news spread fast in a small community. Katherine would leave tomorrow. How long before she would come crawling back?

He knew it was just a matter of time before Katherine was back home. He'd just be patient until the time was right.

CHAPTER 27

But they that wait upon the Lord shall renew their strength;
they shall mount up with wings as eagles; they shall run,
and not be weary; and they shall walk, and not faint.

~ Isaiah 40:31

THE OUTDOOR GATHERING AT HER uncle's had been very pleasant, but Katherine had felt out of place with her extended family. Her Grandma Mame had taught her well the ways of a recluse. She did have to admit she had teared up when her uncles gathered around her with their heartfelt goodbyes and said a prayer over her.

Now morning, Katherine looked around the modest home of her childhood and couldn't hold back the tears. Nineteen years of memories all came back in an instant. The good times with Grandma Mame, the last months with her and Grandpa Clint. She was so thankful she'd been able to care for them right up till the end. It saddened her so much to think lies and deceit had kept them apart for so many years.

As Katherine swiped at the tears, she made herself a vow that if she ever really fell in love, there would be nothing but honesty. Pulling herself together, she bent down and picked up Little Bit. Walking to the front door, she turned back and glanced at her bedroom door.

Retracing her steps she pulled the door closed, shutting the ghost of Uncle Ben inside.

Finally, behind the wheel of Grandpa Clint's Fairlane, she eased down the driveway, not once looking back.

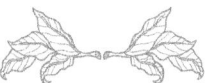

Lying in a ditch close to the barn, he watched her steer the Ford out the drive and away from the homeplace. He watched her load her belongings into the trunk and back seat, then herself and the mangy cat. Looked like she would be away for a long while. Patience, that's all he needed, patience. Reaching inside his jacket pocket he felt the paper with the stupid note. Who really cares if their mommy loves them or not?

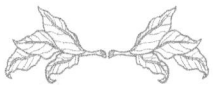

Katherine gripped the steering wheel tight with both hands as yet another semi-truck raced past her. She was only an hour into her drive to Elkin, but her nerves were clinched tight. She needed a break. So many thoughts raced through her mind. Should she turn around and go back to the homeplace? Was she being foolish to think she could live so independently?

The next exit was a good choice. There was a Phillips 66 gas station and an open area with a picnic table. Katherine pulled up next to the gas pumps and topped off the tank. Inside she paid for the gas and a sixteen-ounce RC Cola. Then she went to the restroom.

Back in the car, she moved it out of the way, parking next to the picnic table. Katherine walked around to the back door. She opened it and lifted Little Bit from the clothesbasket she'd made her a bed in. Gently she placed her in the sand-filled shoe box so she could do her business. Then she poured water into a small bowl for her to drink. With Little Bit taken care of, Katherine took a few minutes to stretch and walk off the stress.

Soon, her head was clear and she was once again her confident self. It was almost 10:30. She didn't have to rush. She had plenty of time to go by Surry Community College to drop off her enrollment papers and first semester's check. She calculated the time and estimated her arrival at the college around noon. Then another twenty minutes on to Elkin, and home.

Katherine stopped two more times before arriving at Dobson, North Carolina. She pulled into a parking space close to the administrative office. Thankful it was a cool autumn day, Katherine knew Little Bit would be fine waiting in the car. The shade of the tree she parked under would also help keep the inside of the car from overheating.

Lifting the envelope from the seat beside her, she took her purse, the one that Aunt Olivia had given her and headed toward the entrance. Just before stepping inside, she inhaled a deep breath and said a short prayer.

Lord, You already know I don't have a clue what I'm doing. I can only ask for Your help and continued guidance. Please help me to be smart enough to fulfill my dream of becoming a nurse, and a servant to Your people. Amen.

Oh yeah, one more thing. Thank You for the strength Grandma Mame taught me to have, and the legacy here in North Carolina that my Grandpa Clint gave me. Amen again.

Inside, a lady behind a sterile looking metal desk took the papers inside the envelope out and looked them over.

"Everything seems to be in order. I have your name on the list to start the Registered Nurse program this Monday morning. You should be here by 8 a.m., and go to room number 177. Here is a map of our campus, that will help. So, you're from West Virginia? Is your family in the coal mining business?"

Katherine would soon find out that when people hear you are from West Virginia they automatically assume you are a coal miner.

"No, ma'am, not anymore. My family raises, buys, and sells other people's tobacco for a living."

"Tobacco in West Virginia? That doesn't sound possible."

"Well, that's not what my Great-Grandmother Mary believed, but it was what her neighbors thought when she set the first plant over forty years ago in that rocky soil."

"I guess we learn something new every day. Where are you living since your family is in West Virginia?"

"I have a little house not far from here in Elkin."

"Yes, yes. I live in Elkin, in a small community called Pleasant Hill."

"That's funny, the community I'll be living in is Pleasant Ridge."

"Well, isn't that pleasant?"

Katherine couldn't help but laugh at the lady's pun. Katherine liked this woman, but knew if her Grandma Mame was here she'd say the woman was just plain ol' nosey.

Katherine turned to leave, but she couldn't leave before thanking the lady for her help. The sign on her desk had said her name was Magdalene Wall.

"Thank you, Ms. Wall. I guess I'll see you Monday morning."

"Sure, stop by and let me know how you're doing. And please call me Magdalene, or Matt. Ms. Wall is my mother-in-law."

Katherine left feeling like she'd just made her first friend.

The drive through the two-lane roads to Elkin was a far cry from the busy interstate. Katherine enjoyed the gentle rolling hills and the view of the Blue Ridge Mountains in her rearview mirror. Hard to believe a couple of hours ago she'd crossed over those mountains. She was in no hurry to do it again. That mountain called Fancy Gap was terrifying. Katherine kept her eyes straight ahead on the road, knowing that if she looked over the guard rail to the drop below, she would panic.

Before she knew it, she was turning onto road 2043. The sights looked familiar, and soon she was pulling up in "her" driveway. Before she could open the car door, Tracy was running from the side door where he'd been sitting on the porch step waiting on her.

"Miss Katherine, Miss Katherine. You're here, you're really here. I've been waiting for a long time. I cut your grass and bushhogged the pastures like you asked. Is it okay? How did I do?"

Listening to Tracy, Katherine remembered the speech problem Tracy had and how simple he saw things. This was a major life change for her and all he could think about was whether or not she liked the way he mowed the grass. Life with Tracy for a neighbor was going to be very interesting and entertaining.

Katherine didn't speak until she got out of the car and stretched. "The lawn looks beautiful, and look at all those flowers."

"They're called black-eyed Susans. I don't rightly know who planted them but they come back every year and bloom till the frost bites them."

Katherine stood for several minutes taking in her new home and the surroundings. It wasn't a showy place, but that suited her just fine, for she was far from a fancy person.

"Miss Katherine, can I help you bring your stuff in? I hope you don't mind, but I let myself in with the key Clint gave me and knocked down the cobwebs, dusted the furniture, and swept out the floors. I started to wash your sheets but Mama never did teach me how to wash clothes, and the one time I tried to put clean sheets on my bed they stayed twisted up underneath me all night. Mama fixed them for me the next morning. She never asked me to do that again. Reckon she knew I was a hopeless bed maker."

Katherine couldn't help but feel a little threatened at the thought of Tracy having a key to her house. Should she ask him for it? Besides, he really was a stranger. Then she thought of Grandpa Clint. He had trusted Tracy, so why shouldn't she? She had to get the mistrust that her Grandma Mame had passed down to her out of her head. All the world wasn't bad.

"Thank you for everything. Please tell me what I owe you?"

"No, no, Miss Katherine, your grandpa paid me a plenty in advance to look out after you and your place."

Before she could reply, she heard the familiar sound of Little Bit meowing.

"Oh my, Little Bit, I've got to tend to her. I hope she likes her new home."

"You have a cat?"

"Well, she's more of a kitten than a cat."

Katherine reached inside the car and took out the basket that held Little Bit. Tracy was like a young child who had just been given his first pet.

"Can I hold her? She's so pretty and white. Look, she has one blue eye and one green eye."

Katherine didn't go into detail about white cats and that some are blind in one eye while others are deaf.

Tracy took the kitten in his arms and cradled it like a baby. Immediately he started to sing another Elvis tune and Little Bit started to purr. Just that quick, a friendship had formed.

Tracy wasn't of much assistance helping Katherine carry all her things inside. He was too busy with the cat. It really wasn't a big job. Katherine owned very little in worldly goods.

When her stomach rumbled, she realized that the first thing she needed to do was to find a grocery store.

"Tracy, where does your mother do her grocery shopping?"

"She mostly shops at Lowes Foods, but sometimes she goes to the Winn-Dixie when their meat is on sale."

"Are the stores close by?"

"Yep, just right over on North Bridge Street. Just turn right when you get back to Highway 21, and the stores and restaurants are down the road. We even have a new Hardee's."

"Great. I'm going to make a list and head that way. You can play with Little Bit while I'm getting my thoughts together concerning what I need."

"Okay, Mama said she was going to make you a pie, but I'm not sure what day."

Katherine smiled at Tracy and the simple way he had with words.

The list done, Katherine didn't want to be rude, but it was almost three o'clock and she hadn't had lunch.

"Tracy, I'm leaving now. You're welcome to come anytime to play with the kitten. And please tell me when I need to start paying you for the work you do around here. I'm sure I wouldn't be able to keep this place up without your help."

Katherine's words made Tracy blush. His ears turned as red as a sour cherry. He stood up, leaving Little Bit lying on the floor.

"I reckon I'll be heading home now, so you can go about your business."

Tracy walked to the porch door and opened it. "I'll see you soon, Miss Katherine. Call me if you need anything. Bye, Little Bit."

Just like that, Tracy was gone. He might be a simple talker, but he had a lot of common sense.

The grocery store was easy to find, and Katherine surprised herself by not only buying necessities like bread, milk, and butter, but also a pack of cookies that were called chocolate fudge. She never treated herself after Grandma Mame got so sick and wouldn't eat. Of course, she'd make homemade sweets like sugar cookies and rhubarb pie, but she couldn't enjoy them when her grandparents got too sick to share them. What Katherine would give to have a piece of Grandma Mame's fresh apple cake. Maybe she'd try to make one herself one day.

With the groceries put away, Katherine treated herself to a peanut butter and banana sandwich. It wasn't her favorite meal, but her Grandpa Clint had loved the salty and sweet combination. Somehow eating it made her feel less lonely.

Katherine tidied up her mess and went outside. At almost seven o'clock the nighttime noises were starting to creep out of the darkness. The pond across the road was habitat to some mighty large bull frogs by the sound of their croaking. The sweet tune of the insects serenaded her while she sat on the rock that served as a porch step. Before she knew it, dusk had overpowered the light and lightning bugs flew around everywhere. Nothing new since there were an abundance of the fireflies in West Virginia, but had Katherine ever really taken the time to watch them? No, Katherine never took time off from her duties as caretaker to do much of anything for herself.

Katherine pulled her knees up and wrapped her arms around them, realizing how thin she'd become. Maybe she'd have another bowl of popcorn before bedtime. As darkness filtered out the light, an overwhelming feeling of homesickness made Katherine have to swallow back the tears. She knew there was nothing to be homesick for back in West Virginia, but she couldn't help herself as tears flowed down her cheeks.

How silly to be acting like a small child crying for her grandma. Katherine wiped her face with her shirttail, stood up, and went inside. She wasn't really scared, but she turned every light on in the small house anyway. When she went to the front and side doors, she found that there was not only a key lock but also a security chain that could be fastened. This made Katherine feel much better knowing Tracy wouldn't be able to get in using the key as long as she had the chains secured. Again, Katherine chided herself for mistrusting her sweet neighbor.

The next few days went by in a blur. Katherine cleaned her little house from top to bottom, bed linens and bedspreads, curtains and towels. She even took the bed pillows and couch and chair cushions out and spread them on a clean sheet on the ground to air out.

When Sunday morning rolled around, Katherine wasn't one bit homesick anymore. She had rearranged the furniture, making the home feel more like hers than Grandpa Clint's. She'd found some handmade doilies that dressed the place up to look more like a lady's home than a man's.

As she sipped her morning coffee, Katherine couldn't help but smile as she looked around. Home. Yes, that's what it was, not just a house but a home. *Her* home.

When she heard a soft tap on the porch door, she knew it was Tracy. He'd stopped by a least twice a day since Wednesday to check on her. Today he was carrying what looked like a pie.

"Morning, Miss Katherine. Mama, Mama, Mama, she made you this here chocolate pie. She makes them really good, homemade from cocoa, sugar, flour, and vanilla flavoring. Rolls out the crust homemade, too."

While listening to Tracy, a thought formed in Katherine's head. When Tracy stopped talking for a few seconds, Katherine jumped in with her question.

"What are your plans for the afternoon?"

"I reckon not much of anything. Might dig me a few red worms and head down to the creek to see if I can catch me a red eye."

"I was hoping you would say that. Do you think I could go with you? I'd love to see Carter Falls."

Katherine had been in Elkin five days now. She'd been too busy to think about the falls, but since today was Sunday, Katherine thought she needed a break, especially with school starting tomorrow.

"Why, Miss Katherine, I'd be happier than a hog eating slop to give you a tour of the falls, and I'll tell you the history of it being a hydroelectric power plant. But first, I hate to ask, but could we, maybe cut Ma's pie? I been smelling it cooking and it shore has made me right hungry."

Katherine couldn't help but smile at Tracy's candid honesty. "Of course. How rude of me not to have already asked."

The pie was indeed delicious. Tracy didn't miss a beat asking for a second slice. When they were finished, Katherine sat the small plates and milk glasses in the sink.

"Well, are you ready?"

Tracy eyed Miss Katherine for a few minutes before saying anything. "I don't reckon I've ever been to the creek with a gal wearing a dress. You might just want to put on some britches. They'll help keep the ticks and chiggers off your legs."

Katherine had dressed first thing that morning in her best thrift store jumper. She thought she might ride around and find a church, but that was before Tracy arrived and her notions had turned to an outdoor adventure to see her Grandpa Clint's beloved falls. Grandma Mame always did say there was more God in nature than you'd ever find inside a church with all them gossiping hypocrites.

Katherine realized her grandma was awfully hard on people, and rightly so, for she'd heard the snickering and whispering from the townsfolk during her and Grandma Mame's occasional trips to town.

Katherine was determined to forget all that and learn to trust people until they proved themselves otherwise.

"I suppose pants would make more sense."

"Or, if you want to wade around you can put you on some short britches, or just roll up the legs of your long ones."

"No, I think looking around will be fine for today. Besides, the air has a slight feel of fall in it this morning. Too cold for swimming."

"Can I take Little Bit outside to play while you trade clothes?"

"Sure, I won't be but a few minutes."

Katherine quickly changed into a faded pair of jeans and old sneakers. The white shirt she already wore under her jumper would do just fine.

Before heading out the door, she grabbed her keys and called for Little Bit to come back in the house before she locked up.

"Here, Little Bit. Come here, girl. Get back in the house."

It took a while to coax the playful kitten back inside, then Katherine shut the door behind her and locked it.

"Do I need to drive to your house, Tracy?"

"Shucks no, Miss Katherine, ain't but a half mile to the pasture, then just down the hill is the head waters of Carter Falls. 'Sides, you can't see the country in a moving car. The world passes by too fast."

Again, Katherine smiled at Tracy's simple logic. He was a plain boy with plenty of head smarts.

Tracy led the way down the dirt road, approaching the bridge that crossed the Big Elkin Creek. Katherine stopped right in the middle of it.

"What are these carvings?"

"Oh, these whittled-out letters and hearts?"

Tracy stopped beside Katherine and ran his fingers over some of the letters.

"You see, the thing to do around here is to carve you and your sweetheart's names or initials in the wooden rail of this here old plank bridge. There's been many a couple who have scribed their names here. Right over there is my mama and pops, Dori and Matt. Reckon that would have been carved around twenty-five years ago. My sister, Phyllis, just turned twenty-three and Mama told me Pop carved this when they were courting. This here's history, that's what it is. Your grandpa carved his name right over here, and put some woman's name with it. Told me she was the love of his life. Always did wonder why they lived apart if they were all that in love?"

Katherine followed Tracy over to the other side of the bridge and ran her fingers across the carved names, Clint and Mame. She didn't understand all the reasons they stayed apart all those years either. She did know enough to decipher that theirs was a complicated love, nothing pure and simple about it.

For the next two hours, Katherine got the grand tour of the sixty-foot waterfall and the smaller falls down below that encompassed one of the most beautiful spots Katherine had ever seen. Tracy showed her where the dam was before it was blown out in 1967 when the hydroelectric power plant was dismantled because a part of the flume line had busted out a few years before in 1963.

The spot where the blowout occurred looked as if a large machine had ripped a hole in the side of the cliff. Lots of remnants were strewn here and there, steel cables, cement, and rock foundations that held the flume line, a few fallen power poles, and then the spot where the powerhouse sat. Two smaller waterfalls graced the area. Carter Falls, once a gathering place for picnics, dates, and socializing, now grown over by bushes with thorns and small trees. Would the beauty someday be shared with the world again? Or would it remain one of the area's best-kept secrets, especially since you had to walk in to see it across private property. No worries for Tracy though, since his grandparents owned the property on the West side of the falls.

Katherine was in no hurry to leave, but Tracy insisted it was well past his lunch time. "I'll bring you back to the falls anytime you want to come Miss Katherine, but right now I know my mama's got fried chicken waiting on me. You want to come eat with us?"

"Oh no, I couldn't intrude. I'll just head back home."

"Are you sure? Mama would be happy to have you. She always cooks extra, just in case somebody stops by, and besides, Phyllis has the weekend shift down at the hospital so she won't be home to eat. Mama's been talking about wanting to meet up with you, but she don't drive herself, and it's too far for her to walk since she got the gout in her left big toe last month. Hurts like needles prickling her upper lip, except it's her toe, she says."

"No, I'll meet your family another time. I need to go on back home and get ready for class in the morning."

"You're going to love it at the community college. Everybody was real nice to me when I took that welding class this summer. Might go back and enroll in another trade class or two. That one on diesel motors sounds right interesting to me."

"So, you're not going to school this fall?"

"No, ma'am. Graduated from high school this spring and I don't reckon I need any more book learning. I just need to know how to work on equipment and fix stuff. I'm pretty good with my hands but, well, my brain can't keep up with my thinking, or my thinking can't keep up with my brain, one or the other."

Katherine couldn't help but laugh. Tracy had such a gentle spirit it was hard not to love him.

Katherine started walking in the direction toward home while Tracy kept talking. When she could finally get a word in, she told Tracy she was fine and that he didn't need to walk her home.

"Oh yes, I do. My mama would tan my hide good if I didn't see to it that you got home all right."

Tracy talked the entire fifteen minutes that it took to get back to Katherine's house. "Did your grandpa ever tell you that you might be kin to them folks the Carters that the falls was named after? He said his mama was a Carter before she married. He told me all about the Carter mark behind your ear, and that part of your clan left Virginia and West Virginia and settled right here on the banks of the Big Elkin Creek. Seems like one was named Barney, and another one Samuel."

"Wait a minute. So, you're telling me I may have relatives here close by?"

"Well yes, ma'am. There are Carters all over these parts. Some may be your clan; others may be part of another spoke in the wheel."

"Grandpa Clint told me all about his mama's Carter heritage and the birthmark on us, but I never associated our Carter roots being the same as the people who the falls were named for. Interesting, very interesting. I'll have to do some research and see what I can find out, but it won't be easy since Grandpa Clint was an only child and there is no other family that I know of in Beckley."

Back at the house, Tracy escorted Katherine to the side porch door and waited until the door was unlocked, then turned to leave. "You have a good afternoon now, Miss Katherine. You come on down to see my mama one day. She'd know more about the Carter clan that lives around here than I do. Good luck at school tomorrow."

Katherine watched Tracy as he walked and half trotted back down the road toward the bridge that would take him across the creek to his house. He looked like a full-grown man, but Katherine knew a part of him would always remain an innocent young boy.

Innocent child? That was someone she'd never been able to be.

But none of that mattered now, she felt as if she could mount up on the wings of an eagle and go anywhere she wanted, and do anything she felt like doing.

CHAPTER 28

Ye are of your father the devil, and the lusts of your father ye will do.
He was a murderer from the beginning, and abode not in the truth,
because there is no truth in him. When he speaketh a lie, he speaketh
of his own: for he is a liar, and the father of it.

~ John 8:44

ABOUT TWENTY MILES NORTH OF Beckley, Benny Bauguess sat in a sleazy motel room in a small town called Shady Springs. He rubbed the spot on the back of his head that still sported a pretty good-sized knot. A week had passed since he'd walked up to cousin Katherine's back door to ask for his daddy's whistle and note. He was still piecing together what might have happened that night. Right before he knocked on the door he had peeked through the window. He could hear the noise of either a radio or television playing and he'd seen what he'd come after, the whistle and the piece of folded paper that was lying on the table was probably the note his daddy had given to his mama.

How could such a sweet boy turn out to be so horrible? Part of him still didn't believe all the awful things Hank had told him about his daddy. This cousin Katherine had probably made most of the stories up, or, Hank was lying. One or the other, things didn't add up.

Benny had wondered if the door was unlocked. If it was, he could have his daddy's belongings and not even have to talk to the girl. Unlucky thing was, Benny never got a chance to turn the knob. Quick and sharp, Benny felt a blow to the back of his head that took him to his knees. Right before he blacked out, he smelled something sweet like a wisteria vine. He thrashed around and tried to fight off the effects of the unusual aroma, but the pain overcame him.

The next thing Benny knew, he was sitting in the passenger seat of his pickup truck in the driveway of the company house where he had been staying. It took him a few minutes to clear his head enough to remember what had happened.

He didn't have to recall the blow, because he could feel the knot on the back of his head pound in pain with every heartbeat. When his fingers touched the spot, it was the size of an egg. At least he didn't feel any blood.

It took him a few minutes before he could regain his complete memory. He'd been at Cousin Katherine's house, and right before he opened her house door to get what was rightly his, everything went black. All he could remember was the pain, then a sweet smell.

Had Katherine been outside watching for him? No, she couldn't have known he would be coming by. Who was it then? Who had pounded him on the head?

When he opened the truck door the overhead light came on and he saw the piece of paper lying in his lap.

He picked it up, but it was still too dark to make out exactly what it said. Slowly, Benny slid down from the seat, pushed the door shut, and made his way to the front door of the company house. He soon found out he'd left the keys in his truck, or at least he hoped they were there. Back at the truck he could see the keys still dangling in the ignition. He opened the driver side door and reached in to get them. He must have bent and moved a little too quickly because his head started to spin and he felt sick to his stomach. Swallowing the bile that rose in his throat, he made his way back to the house, inserted the key in the lock, and opened the door.

Benny sat down on the edge of the couch and closed his eyes for a few minutes to try and clear his vision and regain his balance. Finally, when he could focus, he saw the wall mounted clock tick 11:30. It had been over an hour since he'd been peeking in Cousin Katherine's window. Still holding the note, he flipped the switch on the lamp beside him and opened the folded sheet of paper from a notepad of some kind. He began to read the words.

Do not come near Katherine ever again.
If you do, I'll slit your throat, just like your pedophile daddy got his slit.

Benny sat in the hotel room and read the note again. He memorized the twenty-two words. He knew the note had to have been written by one of the uncles. Who else would have known his daddy's throat was slit?

It made sense that they would try and get rid of him so they could keep his inheritance all to themselves. They were probably worth millions. All Benny wanted was a small portion. How could anyone be so greedy?

Benny still couldn't decide what to do. Should he tuck his tail between his legs and run away from these crazy people, or figure out a way to get his money and get even for what they'd put him through?

The night he got hit on the head he knew he had to run. To get away from Beckley. So, he'd took a handful of aspirin and gathered his belongings. Before he left, he'd tidied up the place and left the key to the house on the table. Whoever had hit him would see that he was gone for good. But, was he? Would he be able to give up so easy?

Over the next several days, Benny went back to Beckley a couple of times. Wondering how he'd get inside the homeplace to get the whistle and note, he'd hid behind the barn on Wednesday and watched Cousin Katherine pack up her car with her belongings and a cat. He wasn't sure where she'd gone but he knew she wasn't back yet. Yesterday he'd watched the house all day and saw no sign of her. How could he find out where she was and when she'd be back?

A couple of days before, he'd gotten his nerve up and snuck up to the house and looked in the window. Where his whistle had once laid on the table, now was empty. Wherever Cousin Katherine went she must have taken his things, or did she leave them here at the house hidden away?

Right at the edge of dark last night, he'd seen an old man get in a truck that had the Blackwell name on the side. Benny's intention was to break into the house as soon as the old man was out of sight. Just before he started toward the house, another vehicle pulled up the drive. This time a younger man stepped out of a car. He didn't even go to the door to knock and see if anyone was home. He went straight to the barn and stayed in there at least five minutes. It was almost dark when the man got back in his car and left.

Benny knew neither of the men were the uncles because he'd met each of them a couple of times. Probably another relative or someone the uncles had watching the place. It wouldn't be a good idea to search the house with so many people coming and going. Best thing Benny could do was find Katherine and make her tell him where his things were. He was also pondering trying to find himself a good lawyer, one who could stand up to the Blackwell clan. It was his right to have his part of his daddy's inheritance and he meant to have it.

How could he find Katherine? If he started snooping around and asking questions in town it would get back to the uncles and then he'd be dead as a four-day corpse. He had to get inside the homeplace. Maybe there was a clue as to her whereabouts.

Tonight he'd head back to Beckley and see what he could find out.

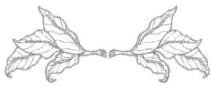

The night was cool. The heavy smell of autumn and rain wafted up Benny's nose. The air was wet, not really raining, but damp from a heavy fog. Benny was thankful for the darkness. He'd hid his truck up an overgrown saw mill road just a little way up the road.

In the darkness Benny made his way to the house. He cautiously tried both doors. Of course, they were locked. He probably could have rammed his hip against the porch door, but then ever who was checking on the house would know someone had broken in. Benny wanted to keep everything as it was if possible. He didn't want the uncles to come looking for him. Next time they might leave him with more than a bump on the head.

Of course, all the windows were secured with a couple of nails. With a hammer Benny was sure he could turn the nail, or pull it out. He didn't want to go all the way back to his truck, so he snuck through the shadows to the barn.

It looked like a regular old barn inside. Maybe a little messy, but of course it had not been used in decades. Cousin Katherine probably hadn't stepped foot in there in years. After a bit of pilfering, Benny found the hammer he was looking for.

Light-footed as a doe, Benny took the hammer and made his way to the backside of the house so if anyone came by, they wouldn't see him.

After just a couple of tugs, the one nail that held the window shut popped right out. Unfortunately, there was another nail on the inside bent over to lock the window.

Another trip to the barn and Benny found a file. He stuck the end of it through a crack between the window casing and house and tapped the end of the file, driving it through the crack and into the nail, edging it up and out of the way.

Since the window was low, Benny easily hoisted himself up and through the now opened window. Landing on his feet, he started his search in the kitchen. Every drawer and cabinet held the usual stuff: eating utensils, pencils, can opener . . . but no whistle.

Benny moved on into the living room, he flashed the small handheld light around the room. Nowhere to hide anything in there. He then went into what had probably been his Grandma Mame's bedroom. A strange sense that he wasn't alone overwhelmed him and he quickly switched off the flashlight. For five minutes Benny stood motionless, hearing nothing and seeing nothing. He flipped his light back on and started going through each drawer in the room. Again, nothing turned up of any value. Still, he couldn't shake the feeling of being watched, so he moved on to the other bedroom, Cousin Katherine's. Benny still felt eyes following him so he kept looking over his shoulder.

This room was painted a light color of purple. He could tell it hadn't had a fresh coat of paint in many years, as well as the other rooms in the house. Benny had been careful to not mess up the contents of the drawers in Grandma Mame's room so no one would know he'd been there, but he didn't have to worry about it in Katherine's room because the drawers were empty. Sure sign Katherine was on a long vacation, or gone for good. But to where?

A quick look inside the bathroom showed no evidence of a woman's toiletries. The house was empty of life—and the whistle.

Realizing his breaking and entering had turned up nothing, he started back toward the open window. In the darkness he hadn't noticed the corner secretary. Lying right there on top was a large brown envelope addressed to Miss Katherine Paddington and the return address sticker that said, "Surry Community College, Dobson North Carolina." Opening the envelope, he saw information about nursing school classes. One sheet was a copy of an application. Katherine had applied for nursing school and her address on the form read, "Katherine Paddington, Route 2 Box 242 Elkin, NC 28621."

Of course, the house her grandpa had left her. Another inheritance he was being robbed of. Not rightfully his, or maybe so. He didn't know who or what to believe. Twins having two different daddies? No way.

BACK AT THE SLEAZY HOTEL, Benny looked at the address he'd jotted down. Then he took out his map, the one he and his mama had picked up at a service station before getting on I-77 heading for the penitentiary in West Virginia. Best Benny could tell, it would take him around two hours to get to Elkin. He'd start out first thing in the morning. He'd find Cousin Katherine and get his whistle and note. Then what? Benny didn't really know what his next step would be, but he did know one thing. He was tired of being jerked around by the Blackwells and Paddingtons, the ones who were dead and the ones who are still alive.

CHAPTER 29

But the meek shall inherit the earth;
and shall delight themselves in the abundance of peace.

~ Psalms 37:11

KATHERINE TOSSED AND TURNED ALL night looking at the alarm clock at least every hour. She was so excited about her first day of college. Katherine Paddington, registered nurse. It sounded good rolling off her tongue.

At five o'clock she went ahead and got up even though the alarm clock was not set until six o'clock. After oversleeping a couple of weeks back Katherine wanted to be sure she wasn't late for her first class that began at eight o'clock. Just three short hours and she'd start the next chapter of her life.

Thoughts of Grandma Mame and Grandpa Clint circled through her mind. The past year had been filled with every emotion imaginable. Sadness, fear, laughter, and pain. If she could blink and bring them back, she wouldn't do it. That is, unless she could turn back time and fix all the lies that had kept them apart for so long. So many changes in just a few short weeks.

She also couldn't help but think of Stan. She'd spent a few hours almost every day with him for the past two years. She knew she must have really hurt him, because he'd not called her once, and it had been nine days. She couldn't blame him. If only he'd not proposed they could have remained friends, but Katherine knew a friend was not what Stan Matthews wanted. He needed a wife. Who knew what would happen these next two years while she is in school? Stan may marry someone else and have a couple of kids. Part of that made her sad, but she knew deep down inside she could never be the wife that he wanted and deserved.

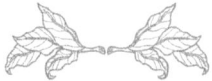

Stan rode by Katherine's house, just like he had every day since she turned down his proposal. Her car had been gone since Wednesday, so he was sure she was in North Carolina at Grandpa Clint's house. He'd give her another few days before he called to check on her, or better yet, he might just take him a scenic drive down to the foothills of North Carolina and surprise her.

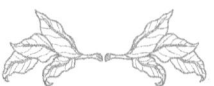

Katherine took the country roads through the communities of Poplar Springs and Jot-Um-Down to Dobson that Tracy had told her about. He said he hated the busy interstate and always went the country roads when he'd taken his welding class at Surry Community College. He also told Katherine she could go up Pleasant Ridge Road and turn right on Old Highway 21, then left across Highway 21 and onto Mountain Park Road.

The drive had been lovely. The sun cast shadows as it rose east of the Blue Ridge. Katherine had left early just in case she lost her way. When she pulled into the parking lot of school her watch said 7:32. Maybe the room would be open and she could get organized for her first class.

Indeed, the door was open with three people already inside sitting at oversized desks, not the small ones Katherine remembered from grammar and high school. When Katherine entered the room the other three occupants looked at her. Two were girls, maybe a little older than herself, and the other was a guy.

Katherine had never really thought about a man being a nurse, but then she remembered Stan. He had received his training in the army as a field medic. There was no shame in being a male nurse, Katherine thought. Why not?

The three sat apart from one another, leading Katherine to believe they must not know each other. She stepped out of her shell and waved at them, then sat down right next to a girl with long brown hair that was pulled back in a ponytail.

"Hey, I'm Katherine. Nice to meet you all."

"Hi, I'm Emily."

"I'm Tina, and this is Garrett."

So Tina and Garrett did know each other. Katherine guessed her nerves were getting the best of her because her tongue started rattling like a baby toy.

"Do you guys live close by?"

Garrett spoke first. "Yes, I live in Elkin, right off North Bridge Street on Gwyn Avenue."

"I live here in Dobson," Emily said.

"I'm just up the road in Mount Airy," Tina said.

"Are you all first-year nursing students?" Katherine asked, feeling more relaxed knowing these young people knew nothing of her past.

"Yes, I finally got into the program," Emily said. "My grades were not that great in high school, so I had to take some general classes to raise my GPA. So really this is my second year of college."

"This is my first day of my first year," Tina said, "and I am more than a little bit scared. Not sure if I can do all the stuff nurses do. Shucks, I pass out when I try to pull a splinter out of someone's finger."

Katherine couldn't help but laugh at Tina's sarcasm. Especially with her words dragging out in a long southern drawl.

Waiting for Garrett to speak, Katherine looked his way. He was a average looking young man, not too heavy, and not gangly like a young boy either. He looked like he might be a few years older than she was. While she was still looking him over, Tina spoke up. "I wish I was like Garrett and had all his experience. He's a trained EMT. Been working for, what, a year now?"

"Eleven months. I love what I do, I just want to take it to the next level, and since I can't afford medical school right now, I've joined the nursing program while I work weekends as an EMT. What about you? Katherine, was it?"

"Yes, Katherine Paddington. I have always wanted to help people and when this opportunity opened up for me, I jumped at the chance."

"You don't sound like a local. Where you from?"

Oh no, here they come, the questions. She'd have to be honest but give them the least amount of information she could.

"No, I'm not local, but my grandpa was. Sort of, anyway. He lived in Elkin for twenty years before he passed away."

"Who was he? I've lived in Elkin all my life. I might have known him," Garrett said.

"Clint Paddington."

"Made furniture, right? We've got a desk in our family room that he built. Fine piece of craftsmanship. What happened to him? Seems like he just fell off the radar one day," Garrett said.

"He got cancer, so he came to live with me so I could take care of him. I live in his house now down in the Pleasant Ridge Community."

"Yep, I went with my dad to the shop behind his house to pick up the desk. So where did you come from before moving here? That accent of yours puts you a little more up north, doesn't it?"

Katherine was thankful the class had filled up and the teacher now entered the room. No more small talk. She'd already shared too much.

From the minute Ms. O'Toole wrote her name on the board, Katherine was spellbound. The day passed like a summer thunderstorm; here one minute, gone the next. Before Katherine knew it, she was in Grandpa Clint's car driving toward home.

She wasn't surprised to find Tracy sitting on her back porch step.

"I thought it might be time for you to get home from school. Mama said you'd want someone around to talk to when you got here, so here I am, ready to listen."

Katherine couldn't help but smile. She sat down on the step beside Tracy and laid the four books she was carrying on her lap.

"Your mama is pretty smart; I've got to go visit her soon. It was a busy day. See all these books? I have reading to do in each of them tonight. I loved it, though. My day was perfect. Busy but perfect."

Katherine felt renewed. She felt perfectly at peace, and she was tickled to death that her new friend, Tracy was here for her to share her day with. Life was finally shifting. Luck was beginning to be on her side, that is, if there was such a thing as luck.

All those years of being afraid of Uncle Ben, then the past several years of watching her grandparents fade away. All that was in the past. Right now she was so happy she turned and hugged Tracy's neck.

Blushing, Tracy looked away from Katherine and hung his head.

"What's that for?"

"I'm just so happy. Please tell your mama thank you for sending you my way. Now let me tell you more about my day."

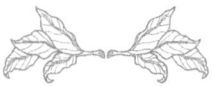

Benny was backed into the driveway where a tent of Kudzu vine covered the entrance of an old, deserted house. He watched Katherine as she passed by. Her house was not more than a quarter of a mile down the road.

Confident his truck was hidden from the road, he made his way through the woods on foot and stopped when he was in view of the small frame house. He'd already rode by and found the address on the mailbox. He saw Katherine sitting on the step, with a young man sitting beside her. Then he watched as she reached out and hugged him.

Who could that be? No one had lived with Cousin Katherine in Beckley since her grandma and grandpa died. He'd have to be careful until he found out exactly what the situation was. For now, he could hide out in the deserted house. It was so old and run down no one had even bothered to lock the door. It would be a great hideaway for him.

CHAPTER 30

And another also said, Lord, I will follow thee; but let me first go bid
them farewell, which are at home at my house.

~ Luke 9:61

THE WEEK PASSED QUICKLY. BEFORE Katherine knew it, she
was heading home from school on Friday afternoon. She had the
car window rolled down and she was singing the lyrics to a new
Rod Stewart song.

Katherine had never felt so carefree in her life. Yes, she had hours
of reading and homework to do over the weekend, but she didn't
care. What else was there to do? Of course, Tracy would stop by, but
he didn't wear out his welcome when he saw she was working on
school stuff, and the only other distraction she had was when the
phone rang. Every day one of her uncles called. She was sure they had
assigned days to call just so one of them would talk to her every day,
just like they'd checked in on her in Beckley, and of course Little Bit
needed attention, too.

Every day when she talked to the uncles, each one had asked if
she was ready to come home. It was hard for them to believe she
wasn't homesick.

Yes, there were moments when she would close her eyes and see the West Virginia mountains and the Blackwell Cemetery up on the hill behind the homeplace, she even yearned for the sight of her kinfolk at times. But she had bid her loved ones at home farewell. She missed Grandma Mame and Grandpa Clint but they were gone, just like the mama and daddy she couldn't remember, ghosts, spirits, or whatever we become when we die. There had been too many past regrets and heart breaks. The future was hers; the phantoms of her past were just that, her past. Or were they?

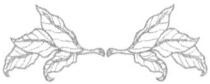

All week Benny had been staked out watching Katherine's house. He knew it was creepy stalking his cousin, but he had to figure out a way to get the rest of his daddy's belongings. Even if he had to break in and steal them when Katherine wasn't home. Why was she keeping the note and whistle anyway, was she just a vengeful person? Did she hate him just because his daddy was her Uncle Ben? Either way, he would get what was rightfully his.

He knew she left around seven o'clock every morning and got back home by four o'clock in the afternoon.

The only other person he'd seen was that boy who'd been beside her on the step. He'd been waiting for her every afternoon. Benny would see him coming up the road about 3:30, walk to the step, and sit down. When Katherine got home, she'd sit with him for ten or fifteen minutes and talk. Most days there was laughter, but he never saw them hug again. They could have been cousins, or best friends, but he didn't see any romantic connection between the two.

Early that morning Benny had snuck to the house. Using a hammer and screwdriver, much like he'd done to break into the homeplace, he climbed in through a back window. His feet hit the floor of what looked to be a spare bedroom. As neatly as possible he went through every drawer and closet looking for his whistle. It was nowhere to be found.

Easing back out the window, he used the screwdriver to turn the nail back, securing the window. Then he made his way to the shed and ransacked it, searching, but not finding the slightest clue as to where the whistle might be. All he found was a shed full of half-finished furniture.

The time had come. He was tired of sneaking around like a hungry raccoon looking for scraps. He'd always got stuck with the leftovers. No more. After that boy left, he would pay Cousin Katherine a visit. The uncles were too far away to hurt him this time.

Benny sat on a fallen log waiting patiently for the boy to leave, until finally he stood. Benny watched as the young man made his way down the dirt road and out of sight.

Benny waited and watched the house. What was he going to say to Katherine? He'd never really thought about it, but she was one of his closest kin. His stomach fluttered with a bad case of nerves. Slowly, he rose from the log. Should he walk over to the house or go get his truck? Deciding on the truck, Benny walked back through the woods toward the hidden shack.

By the time Benny drove back to Katherine's it was almost 6 p.m. He turned into the driveway and parked behind Katherine's car. He let the truck idle a few minutes while he collected himself. Was the whistle and note all he wanted? Would he be satisfied, or did he want revenge? But, revenge for what? Maybe revenge on the uncles for hitting him in the head, but Cousin Katherine hadn't done anything to him. Yes, he'd just collect his belongings and be on his way.

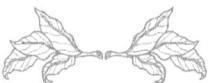

Katherine heard an engine running and looked out the kitchen window. There it was, the black truck, the same one that had delivered that boy named Benny, Ben's son, to her door in Beckley. That day she hid from him. Knowing he'd soon be knocking on her door, she made a quick decision. Opening the silverware drawer, she took the butcher knife in her hand and waited.

Katherine watched out the window as Benny turned off the engine and opened the truck door. She saw him slide off the seat, shut the door, and face the house. The sight of him brought back a bushel basket of memories, none of them good. Maybe she would hide from him after all. Katherine didn't know that Benny was just as nervous as she was.

Benny slowly made his way to the side door, opened the screen, and walked up on the porch. Four steps and he was at the door. He knocked. No answer. He knocked again.

Katherine's hand was sweating so much she feared she would lose her grip of the knife. After the third round of knocking, Katherine made her decision to face her fears head on.

"Who is it?" Katherine felt silly asking him that because there was no way she wouldn't recognize this young man who looked just like her uncle.

Benny heard Katherine. Should he lie and say he was someone else? No, lying didn't suit him.

"Name's Benny. Benny Bauguess. My ma told me my daddy was your uncle, his name was Ben Marsh or Paddington, depending on who you talk to. I heard you got my pa's whistle and a note he wrote to his mama. I want his things then I'll be on my way. I don't want no trouble; I just want what's mine."

Katherine heard every word Benny said. Should she believe him? Was he a dirty rotten killer like his daddy? Could the blood that runs through this boy's veins make him mean like his daddy and his grandpa, Jack Marsh? Or did one have to be raised to become a monster? Katherine didn't know one thing about this boy, but she knew she had to face her fears.

Slowly, she took a few steps toward the door. She turned the metal button that unlocked it. When she opened it, she made sure Benny saw the knife in her hand.

"Whoa, lady. Put that thing down, all I want is the whistle and note, then I'm out of here. Don't want no trouble, sure don't want another knot on my head like your uncles gave me the other night."

Katherine lowered her guard just a bit. The young man seemed harmless, all except he reminded her way too much of Uncle Ben.

"What are you talking about? None of my uncles would lay a hand on anyone unless they were provoked. What did you do?"

Benny knew she wouldn't like his answer but told her the truth anyway.

"The other night while you were still in Beckley, I came to your door to get my whistle and the note. The next thing I know I woke up in my truck with a knot on my head the size of an egg, and a headache the size of a house. Took me a week to get to feeling normal again. There was a note in my lap that warned me to stay away from you."

"Oh, no. That couldn't have been my uncles. They would have told me about that and warned me about you."

"Well, I didn't see who it was, but who else could it have been?"

Katherine didn't have an answer. "I don't know."

"Don't reckon it matters, I just want my daddy's things and I'll be on my way."

Katherine's mind started racing. Had it been the same night she'd fallen asleep on the couch and the rat had eaten the leftover popcorn and stolen the whistle and note? Had it really been vermin, or a human pest?

Katherine relaxed her grip on the knife. How could she tell this young man a rat had made off with his daddy's stuff? She needed to explain as best she could. On a leap of faith, Katherine opened the silverware drawer and put the knife back inside.

"Listen, I don't know you, or anything about you, but I need to explain what happened to your whistle and note. Come, let's sit at the table."

Benny was shocked that Cousin Katherine was inviting him in. As he pulled a chair out from under the table, he couldn't help but admire the craftsmanship. "This table is beautiful, a work of art."

Katherine was surprised he'd noticed. "My Grandpa Clint built it."

"You mean my Grandma Mame's husband, who would have been my Uncle Walt's daddy but not my daddy's daddy?"

Katherine could not believe what she was hearing. "How do you know all that?"

"Your Uncle Hank filled my head with hours of words. Some I believe, some I don't. Whoever heard of twin babies having different daddies? Some of the things Uncle Hank told me made me sort of happy I didn't grow up in this family, or with a daddy who would kill his own brother, and a grandma who would help him hide the body, plus all the cruel things Uncle Hank said my daddy did to you. I must be crazy to want any part of a man like that, but for some reason I need my daddy's belongings. From what I've heard, the whistle and note were the only good parts of him."

Katherine couldn't believe how much Benny knew about her family. It saddened her to think she didn't have the whistle or note to give him.

"Benny, I am so sorry, but I don't have your daddy's things. The night you met with Uncle Hank he called me and said you wanted the whistle and note and that he'd stop by the next morning and get them to give to you. So I took the items out of Grandma Mame's memory box and laid them on the table. That was the same night you said someone hit you in the head, right?"

"Yes, it was the night I'd talked to Hank. I decided I didn't want to wait till the next day, that I wanted my stuff and to get out of there."

Katherine was trying to make all the pieces fit. "That night I had fallen asleep on the couch. When I woke up it was midnight and I felt so sleepy I just sat the leftover popcorn on the kitchen table and went straight to bed. The next morning I overslept, something I never do. I woke to Uncle Hank knocking on my door. He'd come for the whistle and note, but they were gone. I turned the homeplace upside down that day and there was no sign of the items. We came to the conclusion that a pesky old rat that I'd seen several days before had carried your things off and ate the leftover popcorn. I know that is pretty far-fetched but it was the only explanation we could come up with. Now you're telling me that someone else was at my house that night, someone who hit you in the head and left a threatening note? Do you still have the note? Maybe I can recognize the handwriting. I can't imagine anyone I know doing such a thing."

"To tell you the truth, I don't know where the note is. I could have thrown it out the window for all I know. My head hurt so bad I didn't have good sense for a few days."

"If someone besides you came to my house that night and came in, why did they only steal the note and whistle? Nothing else was missing except a half-eaten bowl of popcorn. None of this makes sense."

"So, you're telling me a rat, or a phantom person, has the note and whistle?"

Katherine stood and started pacing. "I know this doesn't sound logical. Who would want a whistle and note? Right?" Katherine was confused, then a thought came to her.

"Are you lying to me? Did you come into my house that night and get your daddy's things? Are you just using the whistle and note as an excuse to get into my house? What do you really want?"

Benny stood and faced Katherine, but she didn't feel threatened. "Now, just wait a minute. I told you someone hit me in the head before I could knock on your door. I never went into your house."

Benny couldn't help but feel guilty for going through her house earlier that day without her knowledge. Part of him wanted to confess, but for some reason he wanted to gain Cousin Katherine's trust. So, if he told her, she'd never believe a word out of his mouth. If she didn't ask, then it wouldn't be lying.

"To be honest with you, I don't know what I want. My daddy is dead, my mama passed away just a few months back, and that leaves me with a whole lot of nothing."

Katherine couldn't help but feel Benny's pain, for she too had lost a daddy and mama that she didn't remember because she was so young when they died. A part of Katherine's heart tugged toward Benny. Looking at him, she didn't feel threatened.

Even though he was Ben's son, that didn't make him an evil person. If that was the case, then Katherine also shared her uncle's blood, and they were cousins, actually first cousins. Katherine had a sudden desire to know more about Ben's son. Who was he? What did he want from life? Was he a thief and crook, or just a young man who had had a hard life, like herself?

"How would you like to stay for supper? I was going to fix myself a can of soup and a grilled cheese. We can talk more and get to know each other better."

Benny was shocked at the invitation and started to decline, but then his stomach rumbled. "I guess that would be all right. Ain't none of them uncles coming to see you, are they? I sure don't want another knot on my head."

"We'll have to talk about that more. I know none of my uncles would hit someone on the head. There has to be a logical explanation."

Katherine and Benny ate their supper, which Benny thought was delicious. It reminded him of suppers with his mama. They'd shared many a can of soup together.

Katherine and Benny talked more and asked questions about each other, how old the other one was and such. Katherine shared her dream of becoming a nurse and Benny told her about his life in

Folly Beach and how he and his mama had looked for his daddy all his life, just to find him inside the dungeon of a prison with a severed jugular vein.

"Maybe it's for the best. If my daddy was as mean as Uncle Hank said he was, then I'm just as well off, better to have never known him. All my life, I've searched for the man who deserted my mama, who made her cry herself to sleep at night. I often wonder if he'd known about me would he have wanted me? A question I'll never have an answer to."

"So, now what? Will you go back to Folly Beach?"

"I honestly don't know. There's really nothing there for me. Before I talked to Hank and you, I wanted my daddy's inheritance. I thought I deserved Ben's part of the Blackwell empire, but it appears Grandma Mame was only left the homeplace and a few acres of land. I saw the homeplace and it don't look like much. What will you do with it? Will you go back to Beckley when you finish school?"

Katherine stood at the sink finishing up the dishes. She listened as Benny opened up his heart to her. She didn't really like the way he downed the homeplace. It had been her home her entire life, but she did realize it wouldn't look like much to someone who held no sentiment toward it.

"I don't know what I'll do after school. I haven't really thought that far ahead. I'm still in shock that I got into the nursing program so quickly."

Suddenly a thought came to Katherine. "Where are you staying?"

"A little place not far from here." He thought it best to avoid telling her he'd been holding up just up the road in a run-down shack. "It's getting late. I probably should go."

"Wait. This may be completely crazy, but would you like to stay in Beckley? I could talk to my uncles and they could give you a job at the warehouse and you could live at the homeplace. I know it's not much but it's comfortable, clean and warm. You could stay there until you get your feet on the ground, or until I need to come home."

"Why in the world would I go to the homeplace? The uncles will probably hunt me down and kill me when they find out I've come to see you."

"I can assure you, I know my uncles had nothing to do with someone hitting you on the head. Here, let me call Uncle Hank. That is, if you want a job and a place to stay?"

Benny was suspicious of all this kindness. What did he want? Go back to Folly Beach, or to Beckley and get to know his family? On a leap of faith, he answered, "Are you sure they won't kill me?"

"Yes, I'm sure, and maybe they can help you figure out who did hit you on the head and possibly took the whistle and note."

"Okay then, if you're sure. I ain't never had nobody except my mama be nice to me. I reckon I just never let anybody close enough to me to give them a chance."

Katherine knew how Benny felt. She'd never let people close to her either. "I'll call right now."

Benny stepped outside while Katherine spoke to Hank.

"Are you sure, Katherine? We really don't know this boy. I guess I could give him a job and see how he does, but to let him live at the homeplace? I'm not so sure about that. Where will you stay when you come home to visit? The holidays are just around the corner."

Katherine hadn't really thought that far ahead. She only knew that if Grandma Mame were still alive she'd welcome him into her home.

"I'm only doing what I think Grandma Mame would have wanted. After all, Benny is her grandson, just the same as I'm her granddaughter."

Hank hadn't thought about it that way. "If you're sure, Katherine, I'll have a job waiting for him on Monday morning. Tell him to come to the office by 7 a.m. Don't you think it would be better if he found his own place to stay? Or I could let him use the company house where he stayed before?"

"No, I think Cousin Benny needs to come home."

"Okay. It's your house and your decision, but I'm still not sure about the boy, and I'm certainly not sure about someone hitting him on the head, but I'll keep my eyes and ears open."

"Benny, come on back inside, it's all settled. Uncle Hank said for you to meet him at the office Monday morning a little before 7. I would give you my key to the homeplace but I only have the one, and I might need it sometime. When you get to the homeplace there is a key hidden in the barn. In the first stall there is a loose board about halfway down on the right wall. The key is there hanging behind the board. You can have a spare made down at the hardware store and put the hidden one back in the barn in case you ever lock yourself out."

"Yes, I'll do that, and I'll be at the office bright and early Monday morning to see Hank. Is it okay if I drive back to Beckley and stay at the homeplace tonight?"

Katherine looked at the clock. "I suppose it will be okay, but it's already eight o'clock. It will be close to midnight before you get there."

"That's true. On second thought, I don't think I want to show up there again after dark. I'll just head up the road first thing in the morning."

Katherine and Benny may have been cousins, but they still didn't know each other well enough to hug, so Katherine stuck out her hand for a shake.

Benny didn't know what to say. "Thank you, Katherine. I appreciate your kindness. I wish my mama was here to meet you. She would have liked you."

"Thank you, Benny. I'm just doing what Grandma Mame would have done. When I first saw you, I was frightened because you look so much like your daddy, but the more I'm around you the more I can see Grandma Mame in you. The way you think about things before you speak, and your eyes . . . well, every time I look at them it feels like I'm looking into Grandma Mame's. Do you believe in second chances, Benny?"

Again, Benny hesitated before he spoke. "I didn't, not before today, but maybe so. Maybe I can right some of the wrongs my daddy did. Maybe that will be his second chance, since he will never be able to apologize for his mistakes."

"I don't think you should worry about fixing your daddy's faults. I believe you should just concentrate on building your own life and not live in the shadow of your father. I think we both should look to the future. The past belongs to our memories, the future belongs to our dreams."

Benny didn't say another word, he just backed himself out the door and threw a hand up, waving goodbye.

"Hey, one more thing. I never said I was giving you a free ride. I left the power on at the homeplace so when the bill arrives, I'll be forwarding it to you. Wait just a minute and I'll give you my phone number just in case you have questions about anything, or if you need me."

Katherine stepped over to the table and jotted her phone number on a sheet of paper. "Call me if you need to and keep in touch. I know we'll be talking often, and give the uncles a chance. They are all fine, decent men. It won't take them long to see Grandma Mame in you."

Benny nodded his head, stuck the folded piece of paper in his jean pocket, and turned and left.

On his way back up the road to the shack, his head was full. Things had turned out way better than he could ever have imagined. Suppose just telling the truth was the best thing to do. Sure did pay off this time. He had a job and a place to stay, and family. Now *that* was going to take some getting used to. This little turn of events would buy him some time.

CHAPTER 31

*His mouth is full of cursing and deceit and fraud: under his tongue
is mischief and vanity.*

~ Psalms 10:7

BRIGHT AND EARLY BEFORE DAWN Saturday morning, Stan drove to the homeplace. He didn't want anyone to see him there. He pulled into the driveway and parked. Getting out of his car, he walked to the barn and slid the door open, letting himself inside. He went directly to the first stall, turned the loose board sideways, and saw the house key hanging on the nail.

Almost two years ago, when he was coming to the homeplace to check on Miss Mame, Katherine had shown him the key's hiding place. It had come in handy more than once. He then reached inside his pocket and took out the whistle and note and laid them inside the hiding place. He wasn't sure how he might need the two items, but one never knew.

Living in a small town, he'd heard about Ben Marsh's son Benny being in town, but since the night he'd hit him in the head, there had been no sign of the boy. Good riddance. One less person to worry about, and he would protect Katherine no matter what. He had to get her back home to Beckley where she belonged.

Could he really persuade her that she may already be showing signs of dementia, just like her Grandma Mame? When he'd taken the whistle and note he wasn't sure what he'd do with it, but a plan was falling into place. He just had to get her back home. Then he'd somehow lock them out of the house so Katherine would have to go to the barn and get the spare key and then she'd find the whistle and note. Katherine would then think that no one but herself would have hidden the items in the barn.

The chloroform that he'd knocked her out with could always be used again if he needed it. Hopefully she'd spent enough time alone and would be homesick and ready to come home. Then when she found the whistle and note she'd really think she was losing her mind. She'd realize that she needed him to take care of her.

He saw the blood again. It was everywhere. This time it didn't come from his own doing, but he'd use it to his advantage. He had to—he must get to Katherine.

CHAPTER 32

Yet man is born unto trouble, as the sparks fly upward.

~ Job 5:7

KATHERINE WOKE A LITTLE PAST seven. She'd slept in because she had had a restless night. She couldn't help but think about Benny. Had she done the right thing? Should she have trusted him? Should she live her life like Grandma Mame had and trust no one? Or should she bury the past and go forward, relying on her gut instincts?

Katherine remembered the lonely, tormented life her grandma lived. As much as she loved Grandma Mame she didn't want to turn out like her. She wanted a life full of love and laughter, and she wanted people around her.

Stan? Again, she questioned herself. Had she made the right decision breaking it off with him? Could she have him and a career? Did she really want that?

No. She was just tired and not thinking straight.

The phone rang just as she was stepping into her slippers. Looking at the clock, it was 7:25. Probably one of her uncles.

"Hello?"

"Katherine, it's me, Benny."

"Hey Benny. You okay? You sound a little out of breath."

"And you, Katherine, sound sleepy."

"Well, I did sleep in this morning. Couldn't rest last night after our talk. Where are you? Getting ready to hit the road to Beckley?"

"No, I'm here already. I left before five this morning."

"So, what's wrong?" Suddenly the hair rose on Katherine's arms.

"I don't know, maybe nothing. I'm in the barn. I found the house key, but there is something else. When was the last time you used the key?"

Katherine thought back. "Not since before Grandma Mame passed. I went to the mailbox one day and locked myself out. I had to use the spare key that day."

"Well, we may have a problem then, and it's not a rat."

"What do you mean?"

"Behind the board I found the key, but also a whistle and note that says, *I wuv you mommy. Ben.*"

Katherine sat down on the edge of the bed. Her legs were shaking. What was happening?

"Are you jerking me around, Katherine? Why didn't you just give them to me?"

"I don't know what you're talking about. I didn't put those things in the barn. I told you I laid them on the kitchen table, that was the last time I saw the whistle and note."

"Well, something is not right. I need to know what happened that night. Someone hit me in the head. Obviously, someone came into your house. If you didn't hide the whistle and note, somebody else did. Who knows about the key's hiding place?"

Katherine couldn't imagine who could have been in her house with her sleeping right there on the couch.

"Maybe it was the rat? It could have crawled between the boards and stuffed his loot."

"No rat has had a hold of this note. It's not chewed up and there are no spit stains on it. Someone had to put it there. So, who knows about the key?"

Katherine thought for a minute. "Of course all my uncles and aunts know, and my older cousins, but none of them would hit you or steal and hide a whistle or note."

"Well, somebody did. I'm going to do some snooping around for myself. I'll let you know what I find out."

Benny hung up the phone before Katherine could answer. She'd just remembered that Stan knew about the key, but she decided not to call Benny back. She would bet her life that Stan would never do anything to hurt another person. Benny didn't need to know about Stan because he was harmless.

Katherine dressed and decided she'd give her Uncle Hank a call and tell him about Benny and what he'd found before she ate her breakfast.

"I don't know, Katherine. Benny's story sounds too far-fetched to me. Maybe he was the one who came into your house that night and took the whistle and note, and this is just his way of getting the stuff out in the open. He saw a way out of breaking into your house that night and now he's using lies to get himself off the hook. I bet you ten to one that he didn't even get hit on the head."

"Uncle Hank, no one broke into my house that night. They would have had to have a key, or knew where the key was hidden. No windows were broken and nothing else was out of place except for the popcorn being eaten. It had to be someone I know."

That thought scared her. Who would be playing these tricks on her?

"I don't know, Uncle Hank. Benny is there at the homeplace. Hopefully this has all been a joke of some kind and it will blow over. It wouldn't hurt for you to talk to Benny, but there is no way he could have known where the key was hidden."

Katherine and Uncle Hank hung up. Both had an uneasy feeling about more than just Benny. Something was off. Once again, the universe was tilting in the wrong direction and there was not a thing she could do about it. Would Katherine's newfound happiness only last for a fleeting moment?

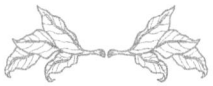

At 9:05, Katherine heard the sound of tires in her driveway. She was washing the bowl she'd made oatmeal in, so she dried her hands and went to the side porch door just in time to see Stan getting out of his car. What was he doing at her house? It had been two weeks since they'd said goodbye.

Katherine opened the screen door and stepped outside. "Stan, what are you doing here?"

Stan made his way to Katherine and took her hands in his. "Oh Katherine, I had to come check on you. I haven't heard a word from you for two weeks. You can't expect me to forget a person I've seen almost every day for the past two years, and I wanted to see your new home."

Katherine felt uncomfortable standing with Stan holding her hands. She pulled away from him and spoke. "I tried to call you a few times but you didn't answer. I guess it was just bad timing."

"Well, I am here now and I have the whole day. You can show me around, then maybe I can take you out for a nice dinner before I head back home."

Katherine's bottom lip fell. Stan was acting as if nothing had happened. It was like he'd never proposed, and she'd never said no. But maybe this way they could be just friends.

"Yes, Stan. I'd be happy to show you my new home, and then we can take a walk to Carter Falls, but then I have to do a lot of reading for school so maybe we can make it a late lunch, early dinner?"

"Sounds perfect. Now show me this place that has stolen you away from me."

Katherine led the way inside the house and showed Stan every room, which didn't take very long since there were only five rooms.

Back in the kitchen, Katherine offered Stan something to drink. Can I get you a glass of tea or a cup of coffee?"

"Coffee would be excellent. I was so anxious to get here I didn't even have a cup before I left home."

Katherine poured coffee into two cups stained from years of use. She set Stan's down in front of him, then lowered her cup to the table and sat down.

"Tell me, Katherine, what have you been up to these past two weeks? Are you bored and lonely yet?"

Katherine didn't really like Stan's tone of voice. He was addressing her as a parent would a wayward child.

"No, as a matter of fact, I am far from bored, and I have a neighbor who stops by every day to chat. He also does my lawnmowing and uses his tractor's bushhog to cut the bottomland."

For some reason, Katherine didn't want to tell Stan about Benny. He would flip out if he knew Ben had a son, and that she had offered to let him stay at the homeplace. There was no reason she should have to tell Stan all her business.

Stan, on the other hand, wanted to know everything about Katherine and what she was doing with every second of her day. He especially wanted to know about this neighbor who had been paying her visits.

"So, you've already made friends with the neighbors?"

"Just Tracy. He and Grandpa Clint were close friends. Tracy was the caretaker here while Grandpa Clint was at the homeplace with me and Grandma Mame. They'd known each other all Tracy's life. I've enjoyed hearing stories about Grandpa Clint from him. They went fishing together, and built furniture.

"Look at this very table. Grandpa Clint carved it himself. Tracy said he built custom furniture for people for miles around, all the while working at the cotton mill here in town. I guess he just needed to keep busy so his mind wouldn't wonder back to Beckley and Grandma Mame. He may have never sought her out if he didn't have cancer. Knowing you're dying has a way of fixing a lot of wrongs. If cancer is good for nothing else, I guess it's good for forgiveness. I know Grandpa Clint wanted to make things right before he died. He had always loved Grandma Mame, even after she broke his heart."

Stan sat and listened as Katherine went on and on about her dead grandpa and Miss Mame. Sure, he'd thought a lot of them, but what he really wanted to know was who this Tracy man was?

"When does your friend Tracy usually stop by? I'd like to meet him."

"During the week, he waits on me when I get home from school, but today he may show up anytime. This is only the second Saturday I've been here, so I'm not sure."

As if on cue, there was a knock at the side screen door.

"Miss Katherine, it's me. You all right? Looks like you got company."

Katherine stood and went out on the porch and motioned for Tracy to come inside.

"Hey Tracy, this is my friend, Stan, from back home in Beckley. Stan, this is my new friend, Tracy, the neighbor I've been telling you about from down the road."

Like the gentleman he was, Stan rose and shook Tracy's hand. He no longer felt threatened when he noticed how young the boy was, and he seemed to be a bit slow and spoke with hesitation. No, this boy was harmless. Stan watched the young man kneel down and pick up Little Bit. He seemed more interested in the cat than in Katherine.

"Looks like Little Bit has made a new friend, too," Stan said.

"Yes, she loves the attention Tracy gives her."

Katherine couldn't help but smile at Stan. She had to admit she'd missed his easy-going nature and their friendship. Yes, maybe they could stay friends.

When the phone rang, Katherine jumped. Before answering it, Katherine suggested Tracy take Stan out to the shed and show him the furniture he and Grandpa Clint had been working on.

"Sure, Miss Katherine. Come on Stan, I'll take you there right now."

Tracy grabbed Stan by the elbow and out the door they went.

Who could that be calling? "Hello?"

"Katherine, it's me. I found something."

Katherine recognized Benny's voice right away and was glad she'd had the good sense to send Stan outside.

"What did you find? I didn't know anything else was missing."

"You remember the note I told you about that someone had left for me the night I got my head bashed in?"

"Yes, the one that told you to stay away from me."

"That's right. Well, I didn't throw it away after all. I found it laying in the floor board of my truck along with some trash. You said you might recognize the writing."

"I might, but you're two hours away. I'm not sure if I'd be able to tell anything from the writing anyway."

"It wasn't written. It's plain, printed letters. One thing I didn't remember about it though was at the top of the paper from a print company it says:

Bayer-Pharmaceutical Lab for Phenobarbital
Treatment of Epilepsy

"What do you think that means? Do you think it's a clue to who wrote the note?"

Katherine didn't even want to think it, but who else did she know in the medical field? Was it just a coincidence? It had to be. Stan Matthews would never strike another person. He healed people, not hurt them.

"I don't know if it is a clue or not. Sounds like the paper came from a note pad advertising that drug for epilepsy. Anyone could have had a pad like that to use as scratch paper."

Did Katherine believe her own words? She couldn't tell Benny about Stan. She wouldn't accuse a person for something that most likely didn't happen. Was her Uncle Hank right? Had Benny made the whole thing up about getting hit in the head and hiding the whistle and note himself?

Maybe she would have believed that could have been the case, but not now. Benny may have made up the story about the note, but could his imagination have dreamed up an endorsement for medication?

"Katherine are you there?"

"Yes, I'm here. I don't know what to think. Just save the note and I'll look at it the next time I'm home. It may be Christmas, so don't lose it."

Katherine hung up the phone and collected her thoughts before joining Stan and Tracy in the shed.

Stan was admiring an unfinished serving table. "Your grandpa was a talented craftsman. Tracy was just telling me about carving the 'M' on every piece in honor of Miss Mame. So sad that they couldn't have been together all those years. So much wasted time and missed dreams."

Katherine watched as a glazed look came over Stan's eyes. What she didn't know was Stan was not thinking of Clint and Mame, but of himself and Katherine.

She realized Stan knew the story of Clint and Mame. He'd been around the family so much he knew most of their past secrets and struggles.

Stan didn't want Katherine to ever have to go through hard times again. He wanted to shield and protect her. That's why he'd hit that son of Ben's in the head when he caught him peeking in her window. He hadn't wanted to kill him, he just wanted to keep him away from Katherine. If he really was blood of Ben Marsh, then anything that came out of that man was soiled, unclean to the core. That boy was shackled to his father's sins whether he liked it or not.

That's why he'd made a quick decision to come and get Katherine. He couldn't wait for her to come pining back to him. That boy might find her, he might hurt her, and if he did, Stan would have to break the vow that he'd made to God and himself to never kill again. The day he left Vietnam was the day of his freedom from death.

"Stan, are you okay?" Katherine asked.

"Yes, yes, I'm fine. Just remembering the days with your Grandma Mame and Grandpa Clint. Sad and hard times, but I'm blessed to have known them."

A warm spot in her heart opened up a tidal wave of emotion. Who else would ever know her the way Stan did? All the ugly things that Ben tried to do to her. All the days and nights of caring for her grandparents. Nights without sleep and a heart that would break every time a moan escaped her grandpa's lips because of the incurable cancer that was gnawing its way through him. Yes, Stan Matthews had seen her at her worst, at her lowest. Did that bond them together forever?

Katherine was feeling very confused until the phone conversation with Benny came to mind and the note wrote on the pharmaceutical pad. Was Stan the person she'd always known him to be or someone else?

"What about that trip to the falls? I can't wait to see them," Stan said.

Katherine turned to Tracy. Realizing how quiet he was, she was now concerned about him. Was he feeling left out?

"Hey Tracy, do you want to be our tour guide? You know so much about the falls and its history. I'll probably leave something out if I'm left to do it."

"I'm sure you'll do just fine, Miss Katherine. I need to head on back to the house. I told mama I'd be back by lunch time."

"Are you sure? I'd love for you to come."

"No ma'am, got to go home. I'll check back on you later today, and that's a promise."

Katherine watched Tracy leave the shed and head for the road that would take him home. She saw him stop and look back toward the shed. How very strange he was acting. Was he jealous of Stan? He didn't even say goodbye.

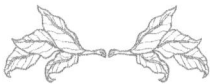

No. Tracy was not jealous, he was confused. He had an uneasy feeling about Stan. A feeling like when you're walking in the woods and your sixth sense tells you there's danger near, that you need to be on the lookout, because there might be a snake nearby, or worse, a bear. Nine times out of ten, the predator will be close by, just off the beaten path ready to defend his turf any way he has to. Yes, that's how he felt about Stan Matthews. He acted like he was the boss over Miss Katherine.

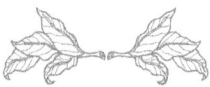

The afternoon went by in a flash. Katherine had made peanut butter and honey sandwiches and they'd taken them to the falls along with a quart jar of sweet tea. The afternoon autumn sun reflected off the granite rocks and warmed them despite the cool breeze that blew across the rapids.

Katherine was content. The day had been relaxing. There was no pressure from Stan. He'd been just like an older brother, but it was getting late and she had tons of reading to do.

"Stan, I really need to get back. I have a couple hundred pages to read before Monday morning."

Until then Katherine hadn't really thought about it, but Stan had not asked her one thing about her first week of school. You'd think he'd be interested since he was in the medical field, too.

"Oh yes, of course. We should get back so you can get your work done."

They packed up the handmade quilt and sandwich wrappers and headed up the hill back toward Katherine's house.

"Thank you for sharing the falls with me, especially the history. Why, to think your very own ancestors all the way from England settled here. What a coincidence that your Grandpa Clint found this place."

"I think it was fate. I know God knew I'd end up here one day, so He placed me on the same ground my ancestors came from so I'd feel more at ease. Honestly Stan, I haven't felt one bit homesick. It's as if I have lived here forever."

Those words were not what Stan wanted to hear. He'd been hoping she'd cry when it was time for him to leave and beg him to take her home to Beckley. His plan to be patient was not working. Should he give her a couple more weeks to see if she changed her mind, or should he just go ahead and do what he knew was best for Katherine?

The conversation was casual during the thirty-minute walk home. No pressure, no promises.

"Katherine, may I use your restroom before I head back to Beckley?"

"Of course, come on inside."

"I'll be there in just a second, I want to roll down the windows in my car so it will cool off. It got much hotter today than I thought it would."

Katherine thought it odd that Stan would think it was hot inside the car since the air was so cool, but she went on into the house anyway and watched Stan roll all his windows down. She didn't notice that he had paused over his medical bag and slipped something in his pants pocket.

After a gentle knock, Katherine told Stan to come back inside.

"The bathroom is right there."

While Stan made his way to the bathroom, Katherine went to the kitchen sink to wash up the few dishes she'd dirtied that day. Shortly, she heard the bathroom door open and heard the old floorboards squeak. Right before she turned to face him, her world went black.

Stan caught Katherine as she withered to the floor. He removed the handkerchief from her nose and picked her up and laid her on the couch. He had to hurry before that boy showed up again.

Katherine would need some clothes, so he went into the bedroom and grabbed handfuls of clothing, stashing them inside a pillowcase he'd taken off a pillow from the bed. He wouldn't worry about toiletries; he'd already bought her a new toothbrush, toothpaste, and hair brush.

Stan took Katherine's belongings to his car and threw them in the trunk. Back inside, he went into Katherine's bedroom and took the other pillow off the bed and carried them out to the car. Katherine would have to ride shotgun. The chloroform would wear off so he'd have to dose her up several times before he got her home. He could have given her a shot of something much stronger but he would never do anything to harm her. The chloroform was the safest way to sedate her.

Back inside, he glanced around the small living room and saw that silly kitten Katherine called Little Bit crouched in the corner. There was no way he was going to haul that cat all the way home to his house. He didn't want a pet, or anything to take up Katherine's time. He wanted her all to himself. They were going to be so happy.

Quickly, he took the notepad out of his back pocket and the pen from his shirt pocket and wrote:

Tracy, I had to leave. Please take care of things, especially Little Bit.
Thank you, Katherine

When Stan was sure the coast was clear, he lifted Katherine off the couch and made his way back out to his car with Katherine in his arms. Sitting her in the front seat, he tried to make her as comfortable as he could using the pillow from her bed to prop her head up.

Then he went back to the house, shut the main door into the kitchen, and stuck the note he'd written to the boy in the screen door where he'd be sure to find it.

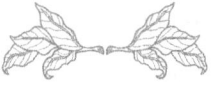

Katherine couldn't move. She wanted to but couldn't. Her eyelids, arms, and legs weighed too much. She was helpless and knew beyond a shadow of a doubt that something was very wrong. But this time it wasn't Ben who was trying to hurt her, it was Stan. It appeared to Katherine that she was just born unto trouble.

CHAPTER 33

But if a man walk in the night, he stumbleth,
because there is no light in him.

~ John 11:10

WHEN TRACY CAME AROUND THE bend in the road, he saw that man Stan's car driving away. Soon it was out of sight. Good, Tracy thought. There was just something about that fellow that made Tracy nervous. He was nice and all, but he seemed phony. There was a dark shadow hanging over that man. Tracy was glad he wouldn't have to see him again.

When Tracy got to the door of Katherine's house, he saw the piece of paper sticking out from the closed screen. He opened the door and the note fluttered to the ground.

"Miss Katherine, somebody left you a note. Can I come in?"

When Katherine didn't answer him, he started knocking on the door inside the porch. When she didn't answer he went back to the screen door and kneeled down to pick up the note. She was probably in the shed or out for a walk. Tracy tried to think where she might be. Then he picked up the note and read it:

Tracy, had to leave. Please take care of things, especially Little Bit.
Thank you, Katherine

What in the world was going on? Where could Katherine have gone? Her car was still in the driveway. How long would she be away? All kinds of thoughts raced through Tracy's mind.

Of course, she probably needed to get back home to Beckley for some reason or another and her friend Stan was taking her there. In a couple of hours, he'd call her house in Beckley. Clint had given him the number when he'd moved there just in case Tracy had needed him. Tracy still had the number memorized.

Tracy folded the note and put it in his back pocket. Then he turned the knob on the side door and opened it. He couldn't believe Miss Katherine had left her door unlocked. She knew he still had a key to get in to take care of Little Bit, so why didn't she lock her door? Something just didn't seem right. Miss Katherine wouldn't just leave without explaining why. Something really bad must have happened.

"Here kitty. Come here, Little Bit."

Tracy saw the white half-grown kitten come out from under Miss Katherine's couch. He walked across the room to pick the cat up and noticed the drawers of Miss Katherine's dresser in her bedroom were open, and looked empty.

"Looks like Miss Katherine shore did leave in a hurry."

Tracy knew in his heart that something was not right. What could have made Miss Katherine leave in such a rush?

Tracy sat on the floor petting Little Bit for a long time, just thinking. Then he stood and checked to make sure the cat had food and water. When he was sure Little Bit would be okay for the night, he turned the button to lock the door and headed home. Surly Miss Katherine would call to let him know what was going on. If he didn't hear from her in a few hours then he'd call her.

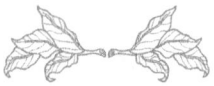

The ride back to Beckley was short. Just having Katherine in the car with him made Stan happy, even if he'd had to give her four more whiffs of the chloroform to keep her asleep. She was knocked out, but it was much more pleasant pretending she was only sleeping.

During the two-and-a-half-hour drive to Stan's house, he formed all kinds of plans in his head. No need in taking Katherine to the homeplace, he'd move her right in with him. Of course, she'd have one of his sisters' bedrooms. He'd never compromise her integrity. He would wait until the honeymoon just like a gentleman should.

Just when Stan switched the engine off, Katherine opened her eyes. She blinked a few times and swallowed the foreign taste of something in her mouth. What was she doing in Stan's car, and at his house?

"What's going on? Why am I at your house, and how did you get me here?"

"Why, what are you talking about Katherine? You begged me to bring you home. You said you had changed your mind and that you wanted to marry me. I didn't see the need of you staying at the homeplace, especially since you were sleeping so much, I thought you might not be feeling well. Monday we'll go to the justice of the peace just like you suggested, then our life together will begin. Until then I'll take your things up stairs to Annie's room."

"No, this is not right. I didn't want to come here, and I still don't want to marry you. Why are you telling me all these lies? Take me home—now. I want to go to the homeplace until I can figure out how to get back to Elkin."

"Oh, my dear Katherine, what has come over you? I only did what you asked me to do. You're acting very strange; you must be running a fever."

"No, I don't have a fever, but I'm not okay. How dare you take me from my home against my will? What did you do, drug me?"

"I didn't take you, or drug you. You willingly walked to my car, got in, and laid your head over on the pillow that you took from your own bed and you slept the entire trip here. Don't you remember?"

When Stan reached over to feel of her forehead, she slapped his hand away. She was beginning to get scared. What was happening to her? Was this all a dream?

"Come into the house and I'll fix you some tea. You're still half asleep. Have you not slept since you left Beckley? Things will be clearer when you're rested."

When Katherine opened her door and tried to stand, her knees buckled and she hit the ground. Was she sick? Had she been hallucinating with fever and said all those things to Stan? Did she deep down really want to come home, to be Stan's wife?

In a flash, Stan was at her side scooping her up off the cold earth and into his arms, then into the house.

"Here, let me sit you on the couch for now. I'll get you that tea and you'll feel better. Good thing I came to see you today. As sick as you got, you'd never have been able to tend to yourself at your grandpa's house."

What was Stan talking about? She hadn't been sick. The last thing she remembered was standing at the sink washing dishes.

"I guess I'm just your guardian angel. I'll be right back. Just lay your head back and rest."

Rest. How in God's name could she rest? In a matter of hours her perfect life had come unglued. She put her hand to her forehead. It was cool as a morning dew on bare feet. She tried to stand again but her legs still wouldn't hold her upright.

"Here you are, chamomile tea. It will soothe you. I'll just go out and get your things. Be right back."

Katherine took a sip of the sweet tea mixture. It helped to cover up the strange taste that clung to her tongue. What had Stan said? He was going to get her things? What things? She didn't remember packing anything.

When Stan walked in with a pillowcase stuffed full of her clothes, she knew she hadn't put them in there.

"Why are my clothes in a pillowcase?"

"I was trying to look out after you. You didn't take anything with you when you went to my car. You said you couldn't wait to get out of there. So, I went into your bedroom and took the pillow out of its case and crammed all the clothes I could get into it. Sorry they're such a mess. You can hang them upstairs when you feel like it."

"Where is Little Bit? Where is my kitten?"

Katherine became hysterical when she remembered her cat. She tried to stand and fell back onto the couch.

She couldn't help herself and started screaming, "Where is my cat? Where's Little Bit?"

Stan sat down beside Katherine and started rubbing her back to calm her. "Here, here now. Little Bit is fine. You gave her to that neighbor of yours . . . that boy, what is his name?"

"Do you mean Tracy?"

"Yes, him. You said he loved to pet her and you didn't want to separate them. I tried to talk you into bringing her with us, but you wouldn't hear of it."

"No, that can't be right. Tracy does like Little Bit, but she is my cat. I'd never give her away."

Now Katherine was in tears. What was happening to her? She had to get out of Stan's house and away from him. Her mind flashed back a few years to Ben, to the horrible life she'd had when he lived with her and Grandma Mame. She had to get away.

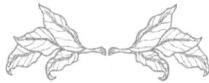

At six o'clock, Tracy made his way back to Katherine's house. He hadn't heard a word from her and it had been over three hours since he'd figured out she was missing.

Just in case she'd come back, he knocked on the door and called out her name before going in. He found no sign of her inside, and Little Bit was hiding under the couch again. If that kitten could talk, she'd tell him where Miss Katherine was, and what had made her leave so quickly.

Tracy had told his mama about Miss Katherine being gone and he'd shown her the note. Dori told her son to check the shed and around the house just to make sure she wasn't there before he called her.

Like always, Tracy did as his mama told him to do. By the time he'd checked the shed and walked the property it was close to seven o'clock. It'd be getting dark soon. It was time to call.

Tracy let himself back into the house using the key Clint had given him many years ago. He went to the phone that hung on the wall and slowly dialed the number to the homeplace.

Benny stood outside. He'd searched the property, but all he could find was three different sets of footprints around the barn. He climbed the steps up to the hayloft. He wasn't sure, but it looked to him like there was an impression of a person's body in the dried-out hay. Could someone be sleeping up there? Was that someone the person who'd hit him on the head?

When Benny heard a vehicle pull up in front of the house, he climbed down the steps and went to see who it was. He recognized Hank's truck immediately.

"Hey, Benny. Katherine called me earlier today and told me I'd find you here. I wanted to tell you face to face that neither I nor one of my brothers hit you on the head. I don't know what's going on here, but if you're trying to play us for a bunch of old fools, well, then you're going to have your hands full because the Blackwells will come after you. We're not a violent bunch, but we do take care of our own. Now, you come on down to the warehouse Monday morning and I'll give you a chance to prove yourself. Is that fair enough? Time will tell the truth. I don't know if it's a good idea for you to stay here at the homeplace, but if that's what Katherine wants, so be it."

Benny stood and listened to Hank without moving a muscle. When Hank was done talking it was Benny's turn.

"I know you have your doubts about me. Can't say I blame you. You really don't know me, and I don't know you either. I am telling you someone hit me on the head two weeks ago. If you come with me, I'll show you something."

Hank followed Benny into the barn and up the ladder to the loft.

"What do you think? Don't it look like somebody has been laying there in the hay?" Benny asked.

Hank glanced around the loft. Nothing seemed out of place, just the smell of old hay and mouse droppings.

"I don't know, Benny. Could be where somebody slept?"

"Maybe that someone was the person who hit me?"

"I reckon that's possible, but not likely. Who would be stupid enough to try and live here in the barn when it's this close to the house?"

"Well, you know the house has been empty for almost two weeks now. Someone could have been watching the place and saw Katherine pack up and leave."

"I don't know, seems too far-fetched to me."

Hank and Benny climbed back down the ladder and Hank went inside the first stall where the spare key was hidden.

"I've already got the key."

"I know. Katherine told me, and about the whistle and note also being behind the board. Something very strange is going on here. If you didn't put the whistle and note there, then who did? I just don't know what to believe," Hank said.

When the phone rang inside the house, both men jumped.

Benny ran into the house, Hank following at a slower pace. "Hello?"

Tracy knew right away it wasn't Miss Katherine who'd answered the phone, and it didn't sound like that Stan person either.

"Is Miss Katherine there? I need to speak to her."

Benny held the receiver out so both he and Hank could hear the person on the other end. "No, Katherine isn't here. Who is this?"

"My name is Tracy. Tracy Gentry. Miss Katherine is my neighbor. She left me a note in her door asking me to take care of her cat, but she didn't tell me for how long."

Upon hearing this, Hank took the phone receiver from Benny. "Hello, this is Hank Blackwell, Katherine's uncle. Remember me? I met you the other day when Olivia and I came to see Clint's house with Katherine. Tell me exactly what the note said."

"I sure will, sir. I remember you. I'll read it to you right now. 'Tracy, had to leave. Please take care of things, especially Little Bit. Thank you, Katherine.'"

"Is that it? Is that all it says?"

"That's all that's hand-printed, but there are words at the top of the paper that I can't say."

"Well try. Spell them out if you have to," Hank said.

"Bayer P-h-a-r-m-a-c-i-t-i-c-a-l. Lab for P-h-e-n-o-b-a-r-b-i-t-a-l. Treatment of E-p-i-l-e-p-s-y. That's all the words on the page," Tracy said.

"Whoa, wait a minute." Benny pulled out the note he found from his pocket.

"Look, the labeling at the top says the same thing as this note that was left for me the night I got hit. It has to be the same person."

Hank took the note and read it. Nothing about the handprinted words was familiar to him.

"What the heck is going on? Is there anything else you can tell us Tracy?" Hank asked.

"I don't know of nothing, Mr. Hank. I just figured Miss Katherine wanted to go home. I'll call her again tomorrow. Maybe she and that man are just taking their time getting there. Bye, now. It's getting dark, Mama will be worried."

Before Hank could stop him, the boy had hung up.

"Shucks. He didn't give me his phone number. Do you think Katherine is on her way back here? I feel certain she would have called and let me know. What on earth is going on, and did Tracy say she was with a man? Lord help us, what's going to happen to that girl next?" Hank asked.

Benny could see how worried Hank was. The creases in his forehead looked more like valleys than wrinkles.

"Surely all is well. Maybe Katherine decided to go for a drive, or shopping. Maybe she's met a friend and they went out for supper? I'm sure she's okay. She is a grown woman. She don't need to check in with you, or that neighbor, every time she makes a move."

Hank listened. Benny's words calmed him a little.

"Guess you might be right. I'm going on back home now, but I'll keep trying to call her. If you see any sign of her, or hear from that neighbor again, get his phone number and call me."

"Sure will, if I don't see you before, I'll see you Monday morning. In the meantime, I'm going to try to find out who writes notes on drug advertisement note pads besides Katherine."

Hank didn't think much about the two notes being written on the same kind of pad. The notes were written over one hundred miles apart, and one came from Katherine. If someone had hit Benny on the head and written him a warning note to stay clear of Katherine, then he felt sure it was a coincidence.

Hank pulled out of the driveway and steered his truck down the hill toward home. It was past suppertime.

Supper was the last thing on Benny's mind. He reached into his pocket and took out the house key he'd retrieved from the barn. He went through the living room and into the kitchen. Again, he reached into his pocket, this time taking out the whistle and note. He wasn't sure how many times he'd read the note, but the words were etched in his mind forever. *I wuv you mommy.*

These words were written by his very own daddy. This was the closest to him he'd ever be. Darkness had overcome the light in more ways than one. Just as the night sky envelopes the sun, the darkness from the depths of the earth took a sweet little boy who wrote his mommy love notes and turned his soul over to the evils of the darkness.

Benny didn't want to think about his daddy spending eternity in hell. But dead is dead, and there was nothing he could do to bring his daddy back. He needed to focus on who hit him, and if that person was still snooping around, sleeping in the barn loft. It was going to be a long night.

CHAPTER 34

Trust ye not in a friend, put ye not confidence in a guide: keep the
doors of thy mouth from her that lieth in thy bosom. For the son
dishonoureth the father, the daughter riseth up against her mother,
the daughter in law against her mother in law; a man's enemies are
the men of his own house.

~ Micah 7:5-6

AT HALF PAST MIDNIGHT BENNY watched the shadow move toward the barn. He'd turned all the lights off at eleven and made sure both doors were locked. Benny was sure a person had snuck into the barn. He hadn't really thought about what he'd do if he actually caught someone in the barn. Was it a drifter or his assailant, or both?

The man climbed the ladder up into the barn loft. He'd not planned to sleep there again tonight but he hadn't found what he'd been looking for, so he needed another day to look around. He could have gotten a room in town, but he didn't want to chance someone recognizing him. Odds were, no one would, but better safe than sorry. He also wanted to know who that young man was he'd seen earlier walking around the homeplace property.

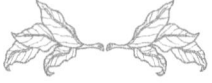

Benny watched the barn door for another thirty minutes trying to decide what to do. He could rush in and surprise whoever it was, but what if they had a knife, or worse, a gun. If he waited until morning, he'd have the advantage. Maybe he'd try to sleep a couple of hours and start watch again before daylight. Hopefully he'd catch the trespasser on his way out of the barn.

Benny woke up at 4:55. The couch springs squeaked as he lifted himself off the cushions. He went back to the window and stared out into the early morning shadows. Nothing moved. He could hear a hoot owl in the distance.

He turned and made his way to the back door. As quiet as possible he snuck outside and crouched down behind a fifty-gallon water barrel at the corner of the barn.

Benny listened and watched as the day started to wake up. The first thing he noticed were birds singing, then he jumped when a squirrel scampered across the yard and climbed a tree. As the eastern sky began to lighten, a silhouette appeared in the arch of the barn door.

Benny didn't have time to be scared. He pounced at the shadow.

The man, not been expecting the force thrown against him, fell backward onto the ground. He lay still while Benny positioned himself above him with his fist drawn back. Strangely enough, the person lying prone did not attempt to fight back.

"Who are you, and what are you doing here?" Benny asked.

The man didn't answer, or resist. Benny stood and pulled the fellow upright by his shirt collar. The stranger hung his head so Benny couldn't see his face in the dawning morning light.

"I asked you a question, mister. What are you doing here?"

Benny watched as the man lifted his head and spoke. "I've come to see Katherine."

Benny didn't know what shocked him more, the man's answer or the horrible scars that covered every angle of his face. He let go of the stranger's collar and took a step back away from the horror of this man's mangled flesh.

Benny was at a loss for words. The scars of the stranger were like nothing he had ever seen. More horrible than one could imagine. His right eyelid was sewn together halfway, leaving the appearance of only having half an eye. His upper lip had tucks on each side where it had been stitched together and the eyebrow over his left eye was missing all together. The man's cheeks looked raw, like pink hamburger. Benny took another step backward, turning his head before he threw up.

The stranger felt sorry for the boy. He knew how sickening he looked; he made his own self sick. There was only one reason God had let him live and that was to find Katherine Paddington. He had to settle things with her.

Finally, Benny stopped gagging. He wiped his mouth with the back of his hand and spoke. "Who are you? What do you want with Katherine?"

"I only want to talk to her for a few minutes. Is she here? I haven't seen her since I arrived day before yesterday."

"Why have you been snooping around here, and why are you sleeping in the barn? Why didn't you just knock on the door?" Benny asked.

"Look at me. Do you think anyone would open the door to their home and let someone with a face like this in? If you'll tell me where Katherine is, I'll be on my way. Who are you, her boyfriend?"

Benny thought it best not to tell the stranger any more than he had to, so he avoided his question. "It don't matter who I am, but I can tell you Katherine isn't here."

"What do you mean she's not here? Katherine is always at the homeplace."

"Not anymore. She moved down to North Carolina a couple of weeks ago. Her grandpa left her his farm so she's moved there to attend college to become a nurse."

Benny didn't know why he was telling this stranger these private things. For some odd reason Benny wanted to trust the man. But then he remembered the blow on his head.

"Did you hit me over the head several nights ago while you were spying on the place?"

"Hit you on the head? No. Why would I hit you in the head? I only want to talk to Katherine and I'll be on my way."

Benny still wasn't convinced this man wasn't his assailant. He reached into his back pocket and took out the note. "Did you write this?"

The stranger took the note and read it out loud. "Do not come near Katherine ever again. If you do, I'll slit your throat, just like your pedophile daddy got his slit."

The stranger stared at the note for a long time. He didn't understand its meaning, but that wasn't what got his attention. There was something familiar about the short letter.

"Well, did you? Did you hit me over the head and write this?" Benny asked.

"No to both, but I think I know who might have written it. I've seen notes on pads like this before."

Benny turned back toward the house when he heard the phone ring. He knew he probably shouldn't, but he asked the man in. "Let me get that phone. You can come inside."

Benny rushed up the back step and into the kitchen, the stranger following him.

"Hello?"

"Benny, it's Hank. Have you seen or heard from Katherine? I've tried calling her every hour all night. I'm really getting worried."

"What do you think we should do? Katherine wouldn't have taken off without letting someone know where she is, would she?" Benny asked.

"I don't think so. Something's not right here. Let me talk to my brothers and I'll call you back when we decide what to do. In the meantime, let me know if you hear from her."

Hank hung up before Benny could answer him or tell him about the strange man he'd found in the barn.

The man stood just inside the kitchen door. "Were you talking about Katherine? Has something happened to her?"

"We're not sure. She left a note yesterday on the same kind of notepad my assailant used asking her neighbor to take care of her cat. No one has heard from her since yesterday morning."

The unknown man crossed his arms as if he were thinking, then the phone rang again.

"Hello?"

"Is Miss Katherine there now? I came to feed Little Bit and she's still not home."

"No, she's not here either. You're her neighbor, right?"

"Yes, I'm Tracy. Who is this? I know you're not that Stan guy who came to see Katherine yesterday. You don't sound like him, or her Uncle Hank either."

Benny didn't answer Tracy's question. He had too many of his own for the boy. "First, please give me your phone number so we can stay in touch."

Benny wrote the number down on the back of the note the assailant had left.

"Who did you say came to see Katherine yesterday? Is he another neighbor?"

"No, that Stan guy don't live around here. He said him and Katherine were friends from back where she came from in West Virginia."

"Did Katherine leave with him?"

"I can't say for sure. I saw his car driving away, but it was too far away to tell if anyone was with him. I just know I ain't seen Miss Katherine since that Stan fellow left."

"Okay, thank you, Tracy. You've been a big help. I'll call you if I find out anything and please call me if Katherine comes home."

"I sure will. Bye now." And with that, Tracy hung up.

Benny turned toward the stranger, who had not moved from the kitchen doorway.

"I couldn't help but hear your conversation. I think I may know where Katherine is. Do you trust me to take you to her?"

Benny had no clue why, but he did trust the man. He didn't even know his name but the stranger acted like he sincerely wanted to help.

"I ain't sure what to believe, or who to trust. My mama always told me not to trust anyone, but I reckon if you can help me find out where Katherine might be, I'm going to have to believe you. What's your name, anyway? And how do you know Katherine?"

"Name's Fred. Does that truck of yours run?"

"Course it does."

"Then let's go find Katherine."

CHAPTER 35

And that they may recover themselves out of the snare of the devil,
who are taken captive by him at his will.

~ 2 Timothy 2:26

IT WAS ALMOST MIDNIGHT BEFORE Katherine had enough strength in her legs to climb the stairs up to Annie's bedroom. She was exhausted and knew she wasn't strong enough to go home by herself right now. How could she have gotten so sick so quickly?

Katherine knew she must have been out of her mind with fever. Sick or not sick, she knew she wouldn't have agreed to marry Stan. He had to have misunderstood, she was just talking out of her head.

After helping her upstairs, Stan hung all her clothes up in the closet and laid out a pair of Annie's pajamas, since he'd not brought any from Katherine's own house.

"Really Stan, there is no need in hanging my clothes up. I'll be going home just as soon as I'm feeling better. I do appreciate you taking care of me, but I must get back to Elkin. I have school on Monday."

"Now don't you worry about anything. I'll take care of everything. You'll feel better soon and all will be back to normal, the way it was before you left me."

Katherine didn't have the strength to argue. She knew Stan meant well. She'd just have to call and get one of her uncles to take her home tomorrow.

"If you need me, I'll be right next door. I'll sleep in Rebecca's room so I'll be closer to you. Just call out if you need anything."

"Thank you, Stan. I'm sure I'll be fine in the morning. Good night."

Stan left the room and Katherine stood on trembling legs and slowly made her way to the door and closed it. There was no lock, but that was okay. She trusted Stan. But should she?

Katherine changed into Annie's pajamas and slid between the sheets. The next thing she remembered was waking to the smell of coffee brewing. She uncovered and sat up in bed. Her head seemed clear this morning and when she stood her legs were strong. She quickly dressed. The light was on in the upstairs bathroom. When she walked in, she saw a hair brush lying on the vanity, and what appeared to be a new toothbrush still in its packaging. Stan really had thought of everything. Quickly, she went through her morning routine and headed toward the steps and the smell of coffee.

Out of nowhere, Stan appeared at the bottom of the staircase, "Wait, let me help you. You're not strong enough to come down these steps by yourself."

"I'm fine this morning. I must have had a twenty-four hour flu of some kind."

"No. Stop. I'll help you. You can't be strong enough to take the steps alone. You need me."

A tingle ran up Katherine's spine. Stan had always been the type person to take charge, but Katherine took offense this time. She didn't need him. She had to set him straight.

Before she could object further, Stan was at the top of the steps taking her by the arm, escorting her down the stairs.

"Really, I'm fine. Can you take me back to Elkin, or do I need to call one of my uncles? I really wish you hadn't brought me all the way back here to Beckley."

"This is where you belong, Katherine. I know you must be a little confused from the fever, but you'll be fine once we're married and you're settled in as Mrs. Stan Matthews. First thing in the morning, we'll go into town and find the justice of the peace and we'll make our future a reality. I knew you'd have a change of heart once you spent a little time away from your real home. I knew you'd miss me."

Katherine let Stan lead her into the kitchen and she sat when he pulled a chair out for her. He poured coffee into a mug that was already sitting on the table, then lifted the cream pitcher and added a few drops.

"A touch of cream, just the way you like it. Now, do you prefer your eggs boiled or scrambled this morning?"

Katherine was speechless. What in the name of God was wrong with him? Was he really saying all this crazy stuff, or was she still sick and imagining it?

"Stan, I need to call my Uncle Hank and let him know where I am. I talk to one of my uncles every day. They'll be worried if they can't find me."

"Oh, there's plenty of time for that. You can call him later."

Katherine watched as Stan stood at the stove and broke four eggs into a skillet. He scrambled them, then dished them out into two bowls.

"I know you're not a big eater in the mornings, but you need your strength, so gobble it up."

Katherine ate about half her eggs and sipped her coffee.

"You've barely touched your food. Come on now, eat," Stan insisted.

"I'm full. Remember, I don't eat much in the mornings. Now. I'm going to call Uncle Hank."

Katherine stood and started toward the phone that hung on the wall beside the back door. Before Katherine could lift the receiver, Stan took hold of her wrist.

"Now Katherine, I told you there would be plenty of time for calling your uncle later. Since today is Sunday and I don't have to work I thought we could fix a nice lunch together and take it down by the stream to eat. Just like we did before when we first met. It will be like old times."

Yes, Katherine remembered. She also recalled the heated kiss that had scared her to death. Had that been a premonition of things to come? Stan had frightened her then and he was frightening her now. What was she going to do?

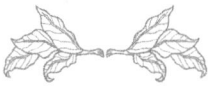

The sun filtered its way through the fog when a sweet little cottage came into view.

"Stop. Let me out here. If Katherine is there, I don't want her to see me until she is warned about my face. Stan has been sweet on Katherine since the first day he laid eyes on her. Guess they decided to become a couple. If you can persuade her to come back to the homeplace I'll hitch a ride back there to talk to her. I'm going to creep a little closer so I can see if she gets in the truck with you. If you need to tell her something to get her to go, tell her some of her kin wants to see her at the homeplace."

"Okay, I'll see what I can do."

Fred opened the truck door, got out, and slipped into the woods.

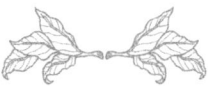

"Stan, I'm sorry, but I must get back to Elkin today."

Again, Katherine tried to lift the phone receiver and once more Stan stopped her. When he let her wrist go, she made her way out the back door.

"Katherine, wait. Where are you going? Come back here."

"No, I'm going to the homeplace to call Uncle Hank. He'll take me back to Grandpa Clint's farm."

Before Katherine could take another step, Stan grabbed her around the waist. With her kicking and screaming, he hauled her back toward the house.

Benny saw what looked like a struggle between Katherine and a man. Were they just fooling around or was Katherine in trouble?

Stan heard an engine rev up and looked down the road. Who could that be? He shoved Katherine into the house.

"Don't you make a sound. I mean it, Katherine. We've come this far together and I won't let anyone ruin it for us. Do you hear?"

Stan was hollering and shaking Katherine's shoulders while he issued his warning. She'd never seen him like this. He had a glazed expression in his eyes and he had taken on a wholly different personality.

As soon as Stan closed the back door, Katherine made her way to the front door.

BENNY WAS OUT OF THE truck before the wheels stopped rolling.

"Where's Katherine? I need to see her."

Benny had watched Stan push her in the door, then close it. He knew something was wrong.

Stan's nostrils flared in rage. Why did this boy need to see Katherine? Were they secret lovers?

Before Stan answered, Benny saw it. The familiar header of a notepad stuck out of the man's shirt pocket. The same pad that both notes were written on. This wasn't a coincidence.

"Get off my property," Stan said.

Stan was only a couple of inches taller than Benny, but he outweighed him by forty pounds. Benny realized Stan could whip him, but at this point he didn't have a choice but to confront him.

"Listen, man, I just need to talk to Katherine. I don't want any trouble. Just go get her."

"I'll give you two seconds to get back in your truck and get out of here."

Benny stood his ground and started calling for Katherine. "Katherine! It's me, Benny. Come out, I need to talk to you. Katherine?"

Benny knew he was writing his own death sentence, but he couldn't help himself.

"You're the one who hit me in the head the other night, aren't you?"

"Could have been. Now you're about to get a lot worse than a tap on the noggin. You were snooping around, peeping in Katherine's windows, and now here you are again plying for her attention. I'll give you one more chance to get out of here before I cram your teeth through the back of your skull. Katherine don't need a snotty-nosed boyfriend. She has me."

"I'm not her boyfriend, I'm her cousin, Benny Bauguess. Mame Blackwell Paddington was my grandma."

"That's a lie. I helped tend to Miss Mame the last two years of her life. I know all her kin and you are not one of them."

"Oh, yes I am. My daddy was Ben Marsh . . . Ben Paddington. No one in the family knew I even existed until a few weeks ago."

Stan stood face to face with the boy. He remembered Ben well, and all the times he had been mean to his mother, Mame, and the awful things he tried to do to Katherine. If this was Ben's boy, then the gates of hell had opened up and released another one of the devil's angels. He did see the resemblance. Maybe this was Ben's son. Another good reason to keep Katherine away from him. Danger was all around. The boy had to go.

The stranger with the mangled face had eased his way closer to the cottage and heard almost every word the boy spoke. Then he saw Stan swiftly raise his arm and backhand the boy.

The stranger took off running toward the two, who were now on the ground punching each other.

Suddenly, Fred caught movement in the corner of his good eye, and before he could stop her, Katherine ran right smack dab into him. He caught her before she fell to the ground.

Looking up, she stared into his mutilated face. Katherine gasped, then let out a bloodcurdling scream.

Stan and Benny heard Katherine and stopped fighting, both scrambling to their feet and running toward the woods and Katherine's screams.

Katherine pulled herself away from the monster and turned back toward the house. On weak knees, she half ran, half walked to the edge of the yard where she met Stan and Benny. Both had bloody noses and Benny's right eye was already turning black.

Katherine didn't know what to do. Who would protect her from that grotesque monster? She couldn't trust Stan, not after the way he had been acting the past two days, she didn't even know who he really was. Had he been playacting all this time, pretending to be someone he wasn't? Grandma Mame was right—no one could be trusted.

Not knowing which way to turn, she ran into Benny's arms and held on tight. "Please take me away from here. Away from these two."

"Katherine, calm down." Pointing to Fred, Benny peeled Katherine off him and turned her toward the stranger. "He won't hurt you. I sort of know him. He's okay."

"Okay? Are you insane? He looks like a monster."

Katherine was sorry the moment the words left her mouth. Had Katherine really looked at the stranger? Should she judge a man by the way he looked? Of course not. Grandma Mame would be rolling over in her grave if she could hear the way Katherine was being mean to this man just because of the way he looked. That's how people had always treated them. Guilty, Katherine started to apologize.

"Mister, I'm sorry. I didn't mean . . . I don't even know you."

Katherine couldn't look at the man's face. Just the quick glance she'd had earlier would be etched in her mind forever. What was it about him that seemed familiar?

Then the man spoke. "Yes Katherine, you do know me."

A lifetime of dread and hate washed over her. She made herself look into what once were the eyes of her worst enemy. They were different now. Not just the scars, but the depth, the part that mirrored the soul.

Katherine stepped closer to the stranger. "Uncle Ben? Is that you? No, it can't be, you're dead."

Katherine didn't need for the man to answer, she knew it was true. This was her Uncle Ben back from the cold, dark grave.

Benny couldn't believe what they were saying. She had to be confused.

"Katherine, what did you call him?"

Katherine was so shocked, she shook her head and blinked her eyes, wondering if she was still under the effects of the drug Stan had given her. Looking at the man again she was sure. "This is Uncle Ben, my father's twin brother, and your daddy."

"No. This can't be possible. I saw my daddy dead. I stood witness that his throat was sliced wide open. He is dead!"

Ben was as shocked as Benny. He'd just heard Katherine say he had a son.

Ben turned toward the boy. "No, I'm not dead. I'm very much alive."

Ben searched the boy's face. Did he resemble him? How could a man not know he had a son?

"Where you from, boy?"

Ben was running every affair he could remember over in his head. Which mistress did he most look like? As soon as the boy answered his question, he knew.

"I'm from Folly Beach, down in North Carolina."

"Trudy Bauguess, that's your mama's name."

Benny stepped closer to Ben, so close he could see every detail of his horrible scars. "You bastard. My poor mama pined for you until the day she died. You deserve to be dead. What did you do—sell your soul to the devil to get to come back to life? No, from what I've heard you've been in the devil's army all your life. How did you bargain your way out of hell?"

Ben had been keeping an eye on Stan as he listened to the boy.

Stan took Katherine's hand and started leading her back toward the cottage. She was still so shocked she didn't resist him.

"Stop. Katherine needs to stay. I have something to say to her. But first I want to explain a few things to this boy. Benny, I don't know if you are my son or not, but if you are, I know I don't deserve you."

"You're right, you don't. Even if I am your son, you are no more to me than a stranger off the street."

"You are absolutely right. I don't deserve to be anybody's father. I'd like to tell you that had I known about you I'd have been a daddy to you, but that would be a lie. I wouldn't have cared about you. Not then. I've lived with bitterness all my life. That resentment turned me into a selfish, evil person. A man I am now ashamed of."

Katherine shook her hand loose from Stan's and took a few steps toward her uncle. She faced him squarely, searching for the evil she'd always seen there. It was gone.

"Katherine, I have to make things right with you. I once lived to torture you. Every time I looked at you, I saw your daddy, my brother Walt and his sweet wife, Emily. Oh, how I hated my brother for being the chosen son. For being Clint Paddington's offspring. And I was the spawn of Lucifer. I've had so much hate in me I've took it out on everyone in my path, including my own mother." He touched him on the shoulder. "And your mother, too, Benny."

"Well, at least you remember her."

"Yes, I remember her, and every single thing I've done to everyone I've mistreated. I changed while locked up in that penitentiary. Yes Benny, I used your mama then tossed her aside. You have every right to hate me for what I did, and didn't do. I'm not worthy enough to have a fine-looking son like you. I don't even deserve to know you."

Benny listened to the man who claimed to be Ben Marsh. This man didn't fit the terrible things he'd heard about his so-called daddy.

"How can I know you are Ben Marsh? Your talking don't fit what I've heard about you, and I know Ben Marsh is dead. I saw him myself. He's six feet under dead."

Ben took his cap off and scratched his head. "How can I explain in a few words? You see, in a prison like the West Virginia State Penitentiary, if you have money, you can buy almost anything you want. I made so-called friends with one of the guards. He kept me informed about everything that happened and was going to happen in the pen. I had drug money that my associates on the outside filtered in to me. That's how I made 'friends' with the guard. I paid him. There is no real friend in a prison unless you've got something they want. You have to watch your back at all times. The guard told me that there was a plot to kill me. Most of the inmates had it out for me, because up until a few months ago, I had it out for everyone else. So, me and another inmate were on the hit list. We knew exactly the time and place where we'd get jumped; we just weren't sure how it would all come down.

"The other prisoner, Fred, was due for release soon. We were all jealous of him. That's why the other inmates wanted to kill him. I knew that if I could just stay alive and then switch my name tag with Fred I could get out of that place. Fred and I looked enough alike to get by with it, especially with the help of the guard. What I hadn't counted on was four men against Fred and me, and one of them had a makeshift knife. If it hadn't been for the guard, I'd have been dead just like Fred. As you can see, those four men sliced me up really bad, and well, you saw Fred. Our faces were so mangled no one questioned the switched name tags that identifies every prisoner.

"The guard pulled the four men off of us but it was too late to help Fred. He bled to death. I didn't want him to die, I just wanted his name tag. The guard hurried me to the infirmary. The doc patched me up as best he could, but there are no plastic surgeons in prison. I was released a week ago, with everyone believing I was Fred. It's took me this long to hitchhike here."

Benny couldn't take his eyes off the man. Could this really be his daddy? If only his mama was alive to see him.

Katherine felt Stan tugging at her hand, trying to move her closer to the cottage.

Stan had listened to this stranger, but didn't believe a word he'd said. He had to get Katherine away from these lunatics.

"Come on, Katherine. This has nothing to do with us. Let's go back to the cottage while they figure things out."

"No, I'm not going anywhere with you."

Katherine jerked her hand from Stan's grasp and walked toward Ben, stopping only a few feet from him.

"What do you want, Ben? Why are you here? Have you come back to ruin the rest of my life? Are you and Stan working together to make me think I've lost my mind?"

"Katherine, I don't know what you're talking about. I've not seen Stan in years. What's going on? Has he hurt you?"

"Not exactly, but he somehow brought me here without me knowing it. He said I was sick, but I really don't think so. He wants me to marry him, but he won't take no for an answer."

Then she turned to Benny. "Will you take me to the homeplace? I need to call Uncle Hank to take me back to Elkin and away from here."

"Please Katherine, before you leave, I need to say something to you," Ben said.

"What could you possibly have to say to me? Go back to your drug money and leave me alone. I never want to see you, or Stan, ever again. Benny, can we go now?"

"Katherine, I don't want you to go," Stan said, "but if you must I'll go gather your things. All I've ever wanted was for you to be happy."

With a sad look on his face, he turned and made his way to the cottage, but he didn't go to Annie's bedroom for Katherine's clothes. He went to his bedroom. Reaching under the mattress, he took out the Colt 1911 pistol. The same one he'd used in the Vietnam war. The one he'd killed with.

Kill them, wound them, patch them up. Blood everywhere, a foot here, an arm there, guts, brains, bone. He'd seen it all.

What type of person could ever come back from that godforsaken place with any sense of peace about him? Stan knew he suffered from PTSD. He faithfully took his antidepressants, but when Katherine left him, he stopped thinking straight. He didn't take his meds on schedule, or he just didn't take them at all. He didn't know why. He didn't really care. He'd just gone into combat mode when Katherine left him and that's where he still was. Ben, and Benny, were the enemy. They were out to capture Katherine; he must stop them.

Katherine watched Stan walk to the front door of his cottage and go inside. She then looked from Ben to Benny. Even with the scars she could see the resemblance between the two. When she'd gotten the news that Ben was dead, a weight had been lifted, and now here it was again, about to smother her into the ground. Would she ever feel safe with Uncle Ben on the prowl again?

Then she remembered. "Oh no. That man who is really Fred is buried in the family cemetery." Pointing at Uncle Ben she said, "That was supposed to be you. Grandma Mame insisted that you be buried there beside my daddy."

The tears flowed down her cheeks. Too much had happened. Stan had gone crazy and Uncle Ben had come back from the dead. Maybe she would go stay with Uncle Hank and Aunt Olivia after all. Surely Ben wouldn't stick around here. The authorities would be after him as soon as they learned he'd switched the name tags, and they would learn. Katherine would make sure of that.

Katherine stared through blurry eyes as Uncle Ben closed the gap between them. She flinched when he touched her cheek, wiping away her tears.

"Don't touch me. Will you never leave me alone and be out of my life?"

"Oh, Katherine. I promise that after I tell you what needs to be said you'll never see me again. There are some things I can't do, like talk to my mama, but I can try to make things right with you. Mama didn't do right by me and we all know it. There's nothing on this side of heaven that I can do about that, but I can try to mend some of the wrongs I've done to you. Katherine, do you believe in forgiveness?"

Ben didn't wait for her to answer. "Up until six months ago, I didn't believe in much of anything except revenge. I especially didn't believe in forgiveness. Then I met a man named Pastor Glenn. He is the chaplain at the penitentiary. That man wouldn't leave me alone. Every day he'd stand outside my cell and read me chapter after chapter of the Bible. Those words that he read were not just for me, they were for every ear that was close enough to hear. Pastor Glenn was a man after God's own heart, and he had a mission. He knew most of us inmates were on death row, or had life sentences. That chaplain said he wanted to change our hearts. He wanted to help us close the chambers of sin and open up new doors to what could be an eternity spent with God.

"Can you believe that, Katherine? Change someone like me? In my own strength, that would be impossible, but then one day something happened. I not only heard Pastor Glenn's words with my ears, I started feeling them in my heart. He kept reading me verses about God's forgiveness. He said that God would forgive anyone for anything if they'd only call on His name and ask. He said the first thing a person had to do was forgive themselves, then others. He said that when we stand praying if we hold anything against anyone, we should forgive them, so that our Father in heaven will forgive us our sins. If we don't forgive others the Father will not forgive us, plain and simple.

"One day, Pastor Glenn's words starting making sense, but I still didn't know how a pure and holy God could ever forgive me, the worst sinner of all time. After a few weeks, the hard shell around my heart started to crumble and peel away. I struggled to forgive, and still do, but I believe in it, Katherine. I know beyond a shadow of a doubt that God has forgiven me. My favorite verse is Hebrews 8:12. *For I will forgive their wickedness and will remember their sins no more.* I've been forgiven. I've been redeemed by the shed blood of my Lord and Savior, Jesus Christ. My sins have been cast as far as the east is from the west. I don't know much at all about those words in the Bible, but I do know in my heart I've been miraculously saved from the pits of a burning hell.

"I'm here to see you, Katherine, because I need to plead for your forgiveness. I don't deserve it, and I never will. I can't ask Mama for forgiveness, or Walt, or all the other people I've hurt, including your mama, Benny. But I can try to make it right with you, Katherine. I'm only asking for your forgiveness, nothing more. Please Katherine, will you forgive me? Can you?"

Katherine stood staring at this man she'd hated all her life. Tears streamed down his scared cheeks and dripped off his chin. Who was this man? Was he really Fred come here to play some awful joke on her? No, the man in front of her was certainly Ben Paddington, and he was standing not two feet from her, crying like an innocent baby.

When Benny reached out to his daddy and hugged him, Katherine stood frozen. What was happening here? A miracle or a trick from the master of wickedness, the devil?

"Benny, I didn't know about you, but I need your forgiveness, too. Please forgive me for the disrespectful way I treated your mother. I'm so very sorry."

"I do forgive you. I am saddened that I've wasted all these years being bitter. Mama and I should have made a better life for ourselves instead of blaming you for all our bad luck and hard times."

Katherine listened to the exchange between father and son. Yes, she was touched, but how could she ever forgive a man for all the terrible things he'd done to her? Katherine thought she'd already forgiven him all those months ago at the grave, but she knew in her heart that she really hadn't. Because of him she'd never known her mother or daddy, and she honestly believed Ben was the cause of Grandma Mame losing her mind.

"Look Daddy, I've got your whistle and the note you wrote to your mama when you were a little boy."

Ben took the whistle and ran his fingers over the engraved "B." Then he opened the note and read the words out loud. *"I wuv you mommy."* Looking up to the sky, Ben spoke to the heavens, "I do mommy, I love you. I am so sorry for being jealous of Walt. I am so sorry for all the hell I put you through. If you are listening up there, I'm begging you to please forgive this wayward son of yours."

Katherine watched the scene unfold in front of her. Could this be for real? Then an avalanche of memories flooded her memory. Grandma Mame did desert Ben. She left him with that evil man, Jack Marsh. How many times through the years did she find Grandma Mame sitting at the kitchen table with her head bowed, asking God to forgive her, and asking Ben to forgive her, too.

Did Katherine believe in forgiveness?

The sound of the front porch door slamming brought their attention back to Stan. He was walking toward them, but he didn't have Katherine's clothes with him.

"Stan, where are my clothes? I'm ready to go. I'll just go inside and get them myself."

"No, you can't."

"What do you mean I can't?"

"I've been thinking about us and we are meant to be together. You're young, Katherine. You don't know what's best for you, but I do. Come on inside now and let Ben and Benny be on their way. They've got a lot of catching up to do."

Benny stepped between Stan and Katherine. "Come on, Katherine, get in the truck. That fellow is the one who hit me in the head. You can't trust him. He's crazy."

Ben stepped forward and faced Stan. "We go back a long way. I didn't like the way you were always hanging around Mama and Katherine, but you seemed like a decent person. What's happened to you? Go on back inside now and get Katherine's clothes. We don't want any trouble."

Stan stared at the distorted face that was talking to him. He remembered when he was deep in the jungles of 'Nam. A young Vietnamese boy crawled up to him for help, pulling himself along with his arms because his legs were gone. His face had been mostly blown away. He only had one eye and it was pleading for a miracle. He did the most humane thing he could possibly do. He stuck the Colt 1911 to the boy's temple and pulled the trigger. The boy's suffering was over; Stan had been his savior.

That's what he needed to do now, put Ben Marsh out of his misery. It would be a sympathy kill, just like in 'Nam. If Ben didn't leave him and Katherine alone, that's what Stan knew he was going to have to do.

"Katherine, come inside with me. We still have time for our picnic down by the stream."

Katherine took a step closer to Benny.

"I'm not going anywhere with you. What is wrong? You've never acted like this before. Who are you?"

"You boys need to get on out of here. This is between Katherine and me. Come on, Katherine, let's go home . . . *now*."

Katherine listened as Stan's voice rose higher and higher and his eyes took on that glazed look again.

"No. I'm going to my Uncle Hank's, and I'm going to tell him how you've treated me."

"How have I treated you, Katherine? Like a princess, that's how. Because that's what you are to me. You'll stay with me even if I have to keep you drugged."

As soon as the words were out of Stan's mouth, he knew he'd slipped up.

"Drugged? What do you mean drugged? That's it, that's why I couldn't remember the drive here, and why my legs wouldn't work. You kidnapped me and brought me here against my will. I wasn't sick, I was *drugged*."

Katherine turned and ran toward Benny's truck. Ben and Benny backed away from Stan, making their way to the truck, too. That's when Ben saw it. The gun had been behind Stan's back, but now it was pointed at Katherine.

"If I can't have you, then no one else will. I'll give you one more chance to come with me. It's your choice, Katherine. Trust me. I know what's best for you."

Katherine froze. What should she do? Surely Stan wouldn't shoot her. Would he? He went as far as to drug her, who knows what he might be capable of? A stone wall of determination built up inside Katherine. She was so tired of being used and manipulated; the decision was made. She had to play this game carefully, though, or someone was going to get hurt.

"Okay, Stan, put the gun down. I'll go with you."

Stan lowered the pistol and smiled. "That's my little princess. Come with me." Stan walked past Ben and Benny and took Katherine's hand.

In a low, growling voice, Ben spoke, "Let her go, now."

"Stay out of this. Katherine has made her decision."

"No, you made the decision for her. What kind of man would force a lady to stay with him while hiding behind a gun? I'll tell you what kind of man—a coward," Ben said.

Stan saw red; blazing hot blood red. Who was this freak to talk to him that way?

"Shut your mouth or you'll regret it," Stan said.

Stan grabbed Katherine by the arm and jerked her to him. "Let's go. Now."

Ben looked at Benny, and Benny looked at Ben. When Ben nodded his head, they both lunged. Benny grabbed Katherine while Ben tackled Stan.

The sound of gunfire ricocheted through Katherine's head. One, two, three shots. She was afraid to look, but she had to. Both Ben and Stan lay motionless on the ash-colored West Virginia soil.

Benny let go of Katherine and rushed to his father. "Daddy, are you hurt?"

The answer to that question was obvious when a crimson stain appeared on Ben's shirt near his abdomen.

When Stan moaned, Katherine looked his way. A deep gash in his head was oozing blood. Katherine bent over and picked up the pistol that had been dropped during the struggle.

"Katherine, give me the gun and go call an ambulance," Benny said, "and bring me some towels . . . hurry."

Katherine passed the Colt off to Benny, then ran into the house and quickly made the call for an ambulance. Then she grabbed some towels and Stan's medical bag.

Benny took the towels and applied pressure to the growing stain on his daddy's shirt. Stan tried to sit up, but fell back to the ground holding his head.

Katherine opened the medical bag to see if there was anything in it that they might use to help keep Ben alive. She spotted the bottle of chloroform. She was familiar with this drug. Stan had often given her Grandpa Clint the drug to keep him sedated in his last days because of the pain. This is what he'd given her to knock her out. It felt good when she opened the bottle and poured a bit of the liquid on a rag and held it to Stan's nose. "That should keep him knocked out for a while," she said.

Benny heard Katherine but paid no attention to what she'd said. He was too busy trying to keep his daddy alive.

The devil's snare had worked. If he couldn't have Ben's soul, then he'd take his life, or would the evil one be overruled?

CHAPTER 36

To open their eyes, and to turn them from darkness to light, and
from the power of Satan unto God, that they may receive forgiveness
of sins, and inheritance among them which are sanctified by faith
that is in me.

~ Acts 26:18

KATHERINE SAT ON A BENCH outside the door of the intensive care unit at Beckley Regional Hospital. Her hands still shook. Benny was on the other side of the door with his daddy.

The wound was nasty, going through Ben's abdomen. The surgery had lasted five hours and the doctors said it would still be touch and go for Ben because he had lost a lot of blood, and the open bowel could cause an infection.

As soon as they'd gotten to the hospital, Katherine had called her Uncle Hank to let him know she was all right. She'd given no details. She just told him that she'd been with Stan and he'd had some kind of breakdown and that he was at Beckley VA Medical Center.

Uncle Hank had offered to come pick her up, but she told him Benny was with her and she'd talk to him a little later and give him all the details. How could she tell him over the phone that Ben was alive? After what Benny had proposed while they'd sat waiting for Ben to get out of surgery, would she ever tell her uncle the truth?

When Katherine had called the VA Hospital to check on Stan, they'd asked her how he had hurt his head. She told them the truth that he had fallen. She also told them about his strange behavior and that he had drugged her and kidnapped her. A sheriff came to the hospital and took her and Benny's statements.

The VA Hospital told her that Stan had been in and out of the hospital for the past ten years. He suffered from PTSD. When he took his meds, he was fine, but when he didn't, he was irrational.

The sheriff told them Stan would likely be in a facility the rest of his life. Even if it had been an accident, he had shot a man and kidnapped and drugged Katherine.

Katherine sat rubbing her hands together. She needed to get home, back to Elkin, to her safe place. There was no way she would be able to make it to school tomorrow. With all that had happened she was way too rattled to even think about school.

Benny's proposal weighed heavy on her mind. Could she live with herself if she agreed to what he'd asked her to do? Could she live with herself if she didn't?

Katherine closed her eyes to the long day. Would Ben live? Did she care? Exhaustion overcame her and she fell into a restless sleep. She woke to someone shaking her shoulder.

"Katherine, the police want to talk to us again. Have you thought about what I want us to do? Will you help me? Please."

Benny looked like a small child begging for ice cream. Before she answered him, the memory of the dream she'd had just before Benny woke her up flashed through her mind. It was her Grandma Mame, and she had been looking at her with the same pleading eyes that Benny now was, the same eyes as Uncle Ben when he'd begged her for forgiveness.

Katherine still couldn't believe Ben had saved her from Stan, taking a bullet that originally had been intended for her. Had Ben Marsh really changed? Was there a God powerful enough to fix the heart and soul of such a sinful, corrupt man?

Yes, she knew God could save anyone if that person was willing to repent and turn from their wicked ways. Was Ben just playacting like Stan had been the past two years? Or was he sincere?

Then she remembered Ben's eyes as he was asking her for forgiveness. They were no longer full of hate; they were at perfect peace.

"Katherine, are you okay?"

"Yes Benny, I was just thinking about Grandma Mame."

"We better go. The sheriff is waiting on us in Daddy's room. I'm begging you again, Katherine, please do this one thing for me. Do it for us. I've only had a daddy for a few hours, please don't take him away from me."

Katherine didn't answer. Her mind was still twisted and troubled by all the uncertainties. This decision was probably the most important one of her life.

THE SHERIFF STOOD WHEN KATHERINE and Benny entered the room. "Ma'am, state you name again please."

"Katherine Paddington."

"In your statement to the other officer you stated that a Stan Matthews was trying to accost you against your will, and that this man,"—the officer pointed to Ben lying in the bed—"struggled with Mr. Matthews and the gun went off while he was trying to save you from Mr. Matthews. Is that right?"

"Yes, sir." The gun had actually fired three times but only one bullet had found its mark. Katherine saw no use in divulging this information, the less she said the better.

"How do you two know this man? What's his name?"

Katherine paused, so Benny spoke first.

"Sir, I don't know where he came from. He's just a drifter, I guess."

"Ma'am, do you know this man and how he might have gotten those scars on his face?"

Katherine's mouth went dry. She had never been able to lie. Could she do what her heart was telling her to do? Was that the right thing? What would God and Grandma Mame have her to do?

Katherine closed her eyes. She could see Grandma Mame sitting at her kitchen table reading the Word out loud and praying for God to forgive her for the way she'd treated Ben. Katherine held the gift of forgiveness in her hands. How had it all came down to this? Why was this burden of forgiveness hers after all Ben had done to her? Then Grandma Mame's favorite scripture, Hebrews 8:12, came to mind, the one she'd heard her recite a hundred times. *For I will be merciful to their unrighteousness, and their sins and their iniquities will I remember no more.*

The officer was growing impatient. "Ma'am, do you know this man or not?"

Katherine knew she had to make her mind up and quick, then she realized Grandma Mame's memory verse held the answer she needed. She knew what she had to do.

"He walked out of the woods and helped me. He said his name was Fred."

Benny didn't realize it but he'd been holding his breath. Relief flooded over him. Katherine's words meant the world to him. He didn't know if all the horrible stories he'd heard about his daddy were true or not, but he was sure of one thing and that was forgiveness. God had given Katherine the mercy she'd needed to forgive.

Benny had forgotten all the years he'd hated his daddy the second Ben asked for his forgiveness, and he could tell his daddy was especially sorry for wronging his mama. Benny knew Trudy was truly at rest now, because he himself was at peace.

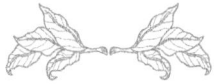

Ben was lying in bed, presumably asleep, but he'd heard every word Katherine had spoken. With his short knowledge of Bible verses, his favorite Scripture so far was the same as his mama's. The words ran through his mind like a cleansing rain washing away the sins of the world . . . *For I will be merciful to their unrighteousness, and their sins and their iniquities will I remember no more . . .*

On the hill behind the homeplace where Mary Margaret Blackwell, "Mame," lay six feet under the cold black coal, there were no angry rumblings under the earth, no headstones shaking. Finally there was true peace. The dark-haired son had forgiven his mama, a mother that had never hugged or cuddled him. A mother who never spoke the words "I love you."

For the first time in his life, Ben Paddington felt a peace he'd never experienced. God had pardoned him. Katherine had forgiven him, and now he had a son. He knew he didn't deserve these blessings, but he would thank God every day for them, and pray that someday he'd see his mama again, a mama who lived a tormented life because of her sins. Regardless if Ben's last name was Marsh or Paddington, he now knew that deep down his mama had loved him, she wouldn't have wanted him to be buried in the family cemetery if she hadn't.

Most importantly, Ben knew he didn't have to be shackled to his father's sins anymore.

The tormented soul of Jack Marsh may be burning in hell, but Ben Paddington was forgiven.

EPILOGUE

THREE DAYS AFTER SURGERY, BEN signed himself out of the hospital. Ben had told the police he was a vagrant, living as a nomad for years. He had just happened to be at the wrong place at the wrong time when he'd got shot and when his face was mangled.

Ben's name from that day forward was Fred Carter. He didn't have the Carter birthmark, but he now had the Carter name. The closest thing to Clint Paddington's son he'd ever be.

Four people knew what happened that day at Stan's house: Katherine, Benny, Ben, and Stan, and no one would believe him even if he tried to tell what happened that day. Since his breakdown, he'd drifted off into another world. A world of silence. No one but these four would ever know. If the truth came out, Ben would spend the rest of his life in prison, or be executed.

Benny took his daddy back to the coast, to the place of his childhood, the spot he felt closest to his mama, Folly Beach.

BEN TOOK THE REST OF the drug money he had stashed and donated it to a local homeless ministry. He and Benny decided the illegal money was tainted; they could never use it for their own personal gain, a far cry from what the former Ben would have done.

Benny introduced Ben as his friend, Fred Carter. All Benny's life he had lived chasing his father's shadow, shackled to the past. Now he knew that he and his father were bonded together forever, because they were family. All was forgiven, no more living in the coal mine shadows of the past. Benny had his inheritance; it was his father.

KATHERINE STAYED WITH HER UNCLE Hank and Aunt Olivia until Wednesday when they took her back to Elkin. She never shared the truth with them or anyone else. Uncle Hank thought Benny had just disappeared with no explanation. All for the best.

As time passed, Katherine thought about her cousin Benny and Uncle Ben less and less. She didn't hear from them ever again, and she never visited Stan at the sanitarium, but she would never completely forget any of them or what happened that day.

She is at peace with her decision, and she knows in her heart that Grandma Mame is finally okay, resting up there high on the hill above the homeplace. For somehow Mame knows her dark-haired son and the grandson she'd never met are together, and one day they will all be reunited.

Katherine is now a registered nurse, and is enrolled to start back to school to become a nurse practitioner. She still lives in Grandpa Clint's house in Elkin. Little Bit has grown up and sleeps most of the time, and her neighbor Tracy often stops by. Then there's that boy named Garrett that Katherine met four years before on her first day of college. You might say they are an item, but that's another story.

Katherine sometimes questions her decision to let Uncle Ben go free, then she remembers the story of a little boy and his whistle and a scribbled *"I wuv you mommy"* note.

And forgive us our debts, as we forgive our debtors. And lead us not into temptation, but deliver us from evil: For thine is the kingdom, and the power, and the glory, forever. Amen. For if ye forgive men their trespasses, your heavenly Father will also forgive you: But if ye forgive not men their trespasses, neither will your Father forgive your trespasses.

~ Matthew 6:12-15

For more information about

Sarah Martin Byrd
and
Shackled to My Father's Sins
please visit:

www.sarahmartinbyrd.com
www.facebook.com/SarahMartinByrd
www.twitter.com/SarahMartinByrd
www.SarahMartinByrd.com/blog

For more information about
AMBASSADOR INTERNATIONAL
please visit:

www.ambassador-international.com
@AmbassadorIntl
www.facebook.com/AmbassadorIntl

If you enjoyed this book, please consider leaving us a review on Amazon, Goodreads, or our website.